YOU MADE ME KILL YOU

By
ED DANKO

This is a work of fiction. Unless other indicated, all the names, characters, business, places, events and incidents in this book are either the product of the authors imagination or used in a fictitious manner. Any resemblance to actual persons, living or dead, or actual events is purely coincidental.

CHAPTERS

Chapter One 1

Chapter Two 6

Chapter Three 12

Chapter Four 20

Chapter Five 27

Chapter Six 40

Chapter Seven 49

Chapter Eight 56

Chapter Nine 61

Chapter Ten 70

Chapter Eleven 79

Chapter Twelve 88

Chapter Thirteen 96

Chapter Fourteen 104

Chapter Fifteen 115

Chapter Sixteen 121

Chapter Seventeen 135

Chapter Eighteen 139

Chapter Nineteen. 149

Chapter Twenty 158

Chapter Twenty-One 167

Chapter Twenty-Two 175

Chapter Twenty-Three. 188

Chapter Twenty-Four 213

Chapter Twenty-Five. 224

Chapter Twenty-Six 238

Chapter Twenty-Seven 246

Chapter Twenty-Eight. 256

Chapter Twenty-Nine 271

Chapter Thirty 278

Chapter Thirty-One. 285

CHAPTER ONE

The rope snaked its way around Paul's arms and legs constricting him to the heavy oak chair. His eyelids fluttered, blinking repeatedly to clear the blur from his eyes. Glancing up his gaze met a malevolent stare looking down at him.

"Untie me you sick bastard for the love of God don't do this," Paul begged as he tried to shake his head free from the effects of the sedative.

"What's that Paul? You're looking for mercy? You want me to show some thread of human decency, some compassion for your life?"

"Where am I and how do you know my name?"

"Where was that decency and compassion when I needed it, Paul?" Paul recognises a hint of familiarity in that face. His mind whirls and searches until the trickle of familiarity washes up the connection from his past to his present.

"Wait, I remember you, you're Danny, Phil Rosen's kid brother."

"Where was the respect for life when you threw that string of firecrackers into my minnow bucket twenty-five years ago?"

"For Christ sakes I was only thirteen years old. It was just some stupid frogs."

"Those frogs were my pets, Paul; I was taking care of them. I was going to let them go, give them their freedom. I was only seven years old. I begged you not to do it. You laughed and pushed me down on the ground, I was in tears. You lit the wick and closed the lid. Who was the sick bastard then Paul?"

"Come on, kids do stupid shit like that all the time and forget about it, Danny. Back when I hung out with your brother, we did all kinds of stupid things."

"I didn't do things like that. I didn't forget about it either. You opened the lid and what was left of my pets was stuck to it. A leg an eyeball, you laughed your head off while I cried."

"Come on Danny, this is crazy, you can't do this. I'm sorry, okay? Just let me go and I'll never breathe a word of this, honest."

"It's too late for that Paul. I hated you for what you did. I was devastated, I had nightmares. You just went on your merry way causing grief in other kids lives for fun. Have you ever wondered what it felt like to be blown apart? Have your limbs ripped from your body? No, I didn't think so, but you saw the aftermath and thought it was funny. You saw my anguish and thought that was funny too."

"Danny I'm sorry it fucked you up, you gotta let that go, you gotta let me go."

"That's two powerful firecrackers you feel taped to the sides of your legs below your knees, devil blasters they call them, quite dangerous actually. Not big enough to dismember you but powerful enough that the pain from the explosion and resulting burn will be quite nasty I imagine. The long wicks will allow me to step out and give you time to anticipate the pain and think about what you did."

"For the love of God HELP, somebody HELP me," Paul screamed out.

"It's pointless to scream, nobody can hear you in here."

Paul scans the room but can't get a sense of where he is or what time of day it is. The room is well insulated but has no windows. The concrete floor is smooth and painted a light grey. A solid door provides only one way in and one way out of the room. He could be underground in a basement, or a garage or God knows where you can end up when you're abducted.

Danny sparks a lighter and touches it to the first wick, instantly sizzling it to life. He sparks the lighter again, igniting the second wick as Paul watches in desperation. Danny walks out, closing the door. Paul struggles frantically against the grip of the ropes, sweat beading across his brow as the lit wicks hiss across the floor and chase up his pant legs. There is a slight delay, and then the first of the fireworks explodes followed by the second one eight seconds later. The pain stabs into his legs as Paul screams out in agony.

"You bastard, you sick demented bastard," Paul yells out as Danny opens the door and enters the room.

"Those were my thoughts exactly. Now you know how a helpless animal feels when it's suffering."

Paul can feel the burn razoring into his skin as the blood trickles down his legs absorbing into his socks.

"You got me back, you got me back good. I don't know what happened to you, but enough. Enough okay."

"It's not what happened to me Paul that has already happened, it's what is going to happen to you. You see, I don't enjoy this, it's just something that has to be done, unfinished business to make things right," Danny said, taking two smaller firecrackers from a package.

Paul lets out a terrified "NO, NO, FUCK NO."

Danny holds Paul's head and inserts one red firecracker up each of his nostrils. He lights the long wick again making his retreat, closing the door. He can hear the muffled screams of terror but has no sympathy for him. Paul struggles in vain as he watches the sizzling wick dance up his chest. He pitches his head violently from side to side in a futile effort to dislodge the explosives from his nostrils. The wick crackles against his chin and momentarily sputters as it divides into the second wick, and then it regains its furious spark. He tries in vain to spit the fuse out, but his mouth is dry from screaming. He can smell the burning gunpowder as he tightly shuts his eyes.

Paul is barely conscious as he opens his eyes. His vision is blurred, and he can hear Danny faintly talking to him through the ringing in his ears. He can taste the blood on his tongue as he breathes mostly through his mouth and partially through what is left of his torn open nose. He tried to focus on what he thought were pieces of his nostrils on the floor. He thought back to his adolescence. Sure, he had been callous at times and a bit of a bully. Whatever happened to this kid Danny growing up wasn't all on Paul, but he was paying for his part of it now. Whatever kind of a rough ride this guy had as a kid has twisted him right over the edge.

"Goodbye Paul, we're going on a little ride now. I won't be there when you wake up," Danny says as he puts an injection into Paul's arm.

"Where are you taking me? I need a hospital. I need a...." Paul's head slumps as he loses consciousness.

The slim light of the end of the day slips quietly out of the alleyway allowing the evening shadows to start drifting in. Paul regains consciousness in the dimming light of his car. He opens his eyes to a device on his lap, the countdown timer just passing under five minutes. He struggles against his seatbelt holding him securely to the passenger seat. His heart is racing as a timer passes under four minutes. His hands and legs remain firmly bound, immovable. The timer passes under three minutes. There is a hole cut in the blood-soaked bandage that wraps around his face allowing him to breathe through his mouth. His breathing is rapid and shallow as the timer flashes under two minutes. He desperately calls out against the closed windows as he peers out into the alleyway, but nobody is there. The timer flashes into double digits as it counts below sixty seconds. He frantically twists in the seat and lurches back and forth, but the seatbelt only cinches him in tighter. The last of the day's light steals away from the interior of the car. The only light remaining flashes out from the countdown timer as it counts below ten seconds. The changing shapes of the red digits pulse their glow off the small round frog face staring back at him from the dashboard. Paul clenches his teeth and slams his eyes closed. He is in the minnow bucket now.

CHAPTER TWO

Danny sat about halfway back in the outside row beside the windows in Mrs. Adam's grade three class. He was a polite, quiet student who didn't bother anyone and happily did what was asked of him. He sat at his desk listening to the drone of Mrs. Adam's voice. His gaze turned to the window as boredom began to set in. There was a whole big world out there full of wonder and excitement and Danny began to daydream how he was going to discover it all. The sun poured over his desk warming his skin and pulling at him like a magnet. His mind drifted from the classroom and out through the warm glass of the window. There were mysterious places to explore, higher hills to climb and new adventures just waiting for him out there. The sun was shining, and it was the kind of day that beckoned you to venture out in a wanderlust far removed from the schoolyard, past the meandering path of the trickling creek, along the never-ending blue shoreline of the lake. He could travel through the mysterious shadows of the forest, up to where the foothills met the sky where he could look out forever into the horizon deciding which direction the wind would take him—the possibilities were endless. The wind flexed the tall trees back and forth, waving like giant fingers urging him forward as if saying "come this way Danny, come and explore, you've never seen this before." The slap of the wooden ruler across his desk yanked him back from his escape, recoiling him back through the window and into the hard reality of the classroom. The loud crack of the wood spiked into Danny's eardrums and made him jump.

"What did I just say, Danny Rosen?" Mrs. Adams demanded.

Danny stared up speechless into the glare of her piercing eyes seemingly set in stone, edged by the stark black frame of her glasses. Her dark hair was pulled straight back, disappearing into a ball behind her head. Fine lines creased across her brow and spoked out from the corners of her eyes, accentuating with her anger. The classroom sat frozen into silence watching as she stood scowling over Danny. He could feel her contempt raining down, pelting against him in an unleashed torrent.

"Repeat what I just said to the class."

"I don't know," Danny quietly offered. He wanted to say he had been distracted trying to figure out how to conquer the world, but he never got the chance. He was being marched up to the front of the class by one arm, the heat of embarrassment radiating off of his troubled face.

"I want you to write on the blackboard 'I will pay attention in class twenty-five times."

Danny began writing as his teacher continued with her lesson. Ten lines into his task the recess bell rings, and his classmates excitedly funnel through the door to their outside escape. He looks at Mrs. Adams and she sternly points back to the blackboard without saying a word. The white chalk clicks and squeaks as he ripples the words down the board. His hand is cramped and sweaty as he finishes writing his sentences and quickly puts the chalk down into the powdery ledge.

"May I go outside now?" Danny meekly asks.

"No, you may not. You may go stand in the corner until recess is over."

He sulks to the corner and stares at the paint faded wall as Mrs. Adams places the pointed dunce hat on his head completing her process of humiliation. Danny feels an anger and resentment swelling up in him that he hadn't felt since the previous summer when his brother's friend Paul so cruelly annihilated his pet frogs. The recess bell rings, and his classmates file back in past him again. He remains fixed in the corner, a statuesque figure hearing the passing whispers and snickers of his peers. He is past embarrassment now.

"You may take your seat now, Danny."

Danny breathes in and exhales a small sigh of relief without opening his mouth. He pulls off the hat of shame and places it on his teachers' desk without looking at her. He doesn't want to see the 'did you learn your lesson' expression on her face. He won't give her that satisfaction after what he has endured. He walks back to his desk defiantly looking out the row of windows, his face turned away from the classroom. He has been made an example of and taken his punishment for the crime of looking out into the world. A punishment that will linger with him like an indelible stain on his heart.

Future recesses became a game of watch your back. Some of the kids taunted him with name calling, "Danny the dunce, Danny the dunce." He wasn't interested in engaging anyone. He would simply walk away, which made him an easy target for someone to jump on him from behind, back pick-ing they called it. It was against his nature, but Danny learned he had to fight back if he didn't want to spend his recesses in continual headlocks. The fifteen minutes of carefree play he had once so much looked forward to had become anxious minutes of avoid and defend. One particularly tall for his age bully named John who wasn't even in his class took Danny for a pushover and continually came after him. One day Danny quit running and turned around to face John. He had to jump up to hit him in the face. After that, John didn't bother him anymore. Danny didn't like who he was becoming; this wasn't the person he wanted to be. Circumstances made him the person he had to be.

Curiosity would get Danny in more trouble than he could imagine. One afternoon after riding the bus home from school, another kid on the bus named Ian suggested they put their leftover apples from lunch under the back bus tires. They were excited to see how badly the huge bus would squash the apples, an entertaining experience for an eight-year-old. They got off the bus and placed their apples firmly under the dual wheels, and then they stood back to watch the crush. The bus driver spotted them in the mirrors and hastily put an end to their experiment. The next day Danny's parents got a phone call from the school telling them that he was to be suspended for three days because of the incident. It had seemed like such an innocent idea at the time. A self-taught experiment in physics at best, an impulsive act of childhood foolery at worst.

Upon returning to school Danny didn't expect any repercussions from his actions. Mrs. Adams didn't make him disclose his actions on the blackboard or stand in the corner wearing the dunce's hat. He had learned from the other kids that while he was absent someone from the fire department had come in to talk about fire safety. Everyone in the class had received their own shiny red plastic fireman's hat to take home. Danny noticed one of the hats sitting high up on a corner shelf.

"That's your hat Danny; the fireman left one for you as well," Mrs. Adams smiled. Danny's eyes immediately lit up.

"We are going to leave it on display for the class though for now – we don't reward bad behaviour." Danny's heart sank. He wanted that hat badly and Mrs. Adams knew it. She was going to make him sit in class every day and long for it. Two weeks went by, and he got the courage up to ask for it. He waited until the other kids had left the classroom. He thought she may have forgotten about it and would be ready to give it to him now.

"Mrs. Adams, may I have the fireman's hat now?"

"No, I think we will leave it there until the end of the school year." Danny swallowed hard and walked out of the room to catch his bus. For two more months he would watch his shiny red hat slowly collect dust on that shelf every day. For two more months he would be punished for having the curiosity of an eight-year-old child. For two more months he would resent Mrs. Adams every day.

The remaining days of the school year passed routinely by. Danny had formed a friendship with Steve and Ian, an alliance of sorts. It provided a greater sense of security at recess from random acts of aggression. There was a sense of safety in numbers but not always guaranteed. The last day of school had arrived, and so had the anticipation of summer. His long wait would finally be over. The prize of that red hat he had longed for every day would finally be his. Danny collected his things and presented himself at the front of Mrs. Adam's desk.

"Yes Danny, what can I help you with?"

"May I have my fireman's hat to take home now?"

Mrs. Adams looked up at the hat, then back at Danny. "No, you may not." She looked down continuing her paperwork ignoring him as if he were invisible.

"But you said I could now," Danny protested.

"Have a nice summer," she said without looking back up. Danny stood motionless, glaring at her. How could she sit there in the class watching his anticipation grow every day when her only intention was to deny him in the end. How could she be so heartless as to simply dismiss him, brush him off as if he were a piece of worthless fluff that had descended on her sleeve. How dare she.

"Liar." The word leaped out of his mouth and tumbled recklessly out of control across the paper-strewn desk.

"Danny Rosen, wait! Come back here." There was no waiting; he had waited long enough. He was out the door and there was no turning back now. A trust had been broken. Danny stomped up into the bus, swung into his seat and pressed his forehead against the window. He stared out, his heart pumping rage through his veins. There was no sign of Mrs. Adams. There was no one pursuing him or trying to confront him; after all, he had learned how to fight back now.

CHAPTER THREE

Detective Casey cautiously shines his flashlight grimly observing what is left of Paul and the shattered interior of the car. The windows are blown out, but the outside of the car remains surprisingly intact. Sergeant Kent is a seasoned officer, but she involuntarily gags and momentarily looks away from the gruesome scene.

"I'm sorry detective, I just needed a moment to catch my breath. Whoever did this certainly had a score to settle with this person, they didn't leave much of him intact. I'm assuming it's a him by the shoes that are left on his feet. That's the only thing that remains normal, they haven't left much else to go by." She turns her head as she steps back, retching again.

"They've left us nothing and everything to work with at the same time. You going to be alright?"

"Yes, thanks," Kent says after taking a deep breath. "I've already run the plate. They are registered to a Paul Brown if that's him. I'm sure though when we check his house, he won't be coming home any time soon."

"Whoever did this wanted to make a statement. They wanted to blow this guy apart, not burn the car out with him in it. They could of sunk him in the lake, made him disappear. It's like they wanted him to be found with his parts all over the car, closed in, in the alleyway.

Sergeant Kent puts the back of her hand up touching her lips.

"Sorry about that," Casey says.

"No, it's just, I just noticed there are parts of him stuck to the roof liner."

"It's not a pretty sight. We'll tarp the car, get it on a flatbed, and get it into forensics to go over it. Here come the floodlights. Let's get this alleyway cleaned up," Casey says, flashing his light across the glass pebbled pavement and up the tired brick wall. "Hopefully, most of him stayed inside the car."

Sergeant Kent walks over to her car, opens the trunk, and takes out the evidence bags.

*   *   *   *   *   *   *

Danny's report card described him as a capable student who was sometimes prone to daydreaming. He performed well in reading, writing, and math and, although quiet by nature, interacted well with his classmates.

"This is a very good report card," Danny's mom complimented him. "I'm very proud of you."

Danny was somewhat relieved that there was no note from his teacher but was apprehensive whenever the phone rang over the next few days. It took a week before he would let down his guard for fear of Mrs. Adams calling his parents. He never mentioned the fireman's hat to them. He just kept quiet about the whole thing even though it stayed with him, rotting away inside him like a forgotten lunch pail banana.

Ian lived relatively close to Danny in the neighbourhood, which made for easy get togethers over the summer and allowed the cultivation of a stronger friendship between them. Steve lived out of town, so he joined them occasionally for an overnight campout in Ian's back yard when his mom could drive him in. Danny and Ian would spend many lazy afternoons exploring the shoreline of the nearby pond and trying to catch frogs or poking sticks into a newly found dead fish. They would occasionally run into this mean-spirited kid Vince who lived close to Ian's place. Vince was four or five years older and seemed to take great pleasure in tormenting the both of them anytime they crossed paths. Vince was a full-time bully who enjoyed making life miserable by picking on kids younger than him. He would stop Danny and Ian on the street, grab the handlebars of their bikes, and push them backwards until they fell off onto the pavement. Whenever he caught them down by the pond, the abuse continued. Both of them on several occasions had been held down with a knee in their back, their faces pushed into the dirt.

"Eat dirt you little faggot," Vince would yell out. Then he'd slap the back of their heads before getting up and walking off.

Danny was experiencing the same torment he went through in the school yard and worse, but they weren't fighting back against kids their own age now. In fact, they were afraid to fight back at all. It wasn't just that Vince was bigger; he had a deliberate meanness to him and seemed void of any emotion or sense of accountability. Danny and Ian had spent weeks building a play fort in the woods up behind Danny's house. They had tirelessly fastened together an array of small logs, branches, and all other material that they could get their hands on. They enjoyed their little hideout only to find it one day kicked in, smashed apart, wrecked beyond repair. They knew this was Vince's handiwork and just felt fortunate not to be there when he had discovered it. They thought he had even been watching them struggle to build it and waited for them to complete it, only allowing them a small taste of enjoyment before destroying it. His mean spirit had no bounds. Danny and Ian spent most of the summer just trying to avoid him; looking over their shoulder just became part of their daily vigilance.

Ian had started a small paper route, and Danny would sometimes go along with him to help him deliver. Two of the customers lived in a small apartment building not far from Ian's house. This was the same apartment building that Vince lived in, and up to now they had been lucky enough to get in and get out quickly without running into him. One customer lived on the second floor, and the other was on the third. Danny and Ian scampered up the stairwell, each with a newspaper in hand. Ian headed down the second-floor hallway as Danny continued up the stairs to the third floor. He pulled open the fire door and sprinted down the hallway, dropping the paper in front of door 308. He spun on his heel and headed back to the fire door, pushing through and stepping down the stairs. As Danny rounded the stairs to the second floor, there was Ian with his back against the railing. Vince had the front of his shirt bunched up in his hand. Danny froze to a stop on the stairs.

"What are you two little maggots doing in my building?"

"We are just doing the papers Vince," Danny replied.

"You never asked my permission to come in here."

"Didn't know we had to," Ian responded.

"What are you stupid or something?

"No," Ian replied.

"Do you think I'm stupid?"

"No," Ian replied again.

Suddenly, Vince pulls a pocketknife out and holds the blade against Ian's face. His eyes are vacant and cold.

"Maybe you need a lesson."

"Let my friend go," Danny blurts out, his voice shaking.

Vince turns to Danny, his knife still on Ian's cheek. "What are you going to do about it you little shit. Maybe you would like to watch me carve him a new face."

Danny's gaze shifts to Ian. There is a darkening patch shadowing down the front leg of his pants.

"Let him go," Danny says louder as Vince presses the knife blade firmly against Ian's skin.

Suddenly, there's the sound of the bottom stairwell door opening and footsteps shuffling in. Vince folds the knife back into his pocket. "Get the fuck out of here," he says.

Danny and Ian scramble down the stairs, racing by the older couple heading up. They burst through the apartment doors and slow their frantic exit to a walk once they have distanced themselves from the building.

"I've got to go home," Ian quietly mumbles, the wet clamminess of his pants weighing against his leg.

Danny looks down into the paper bag and takes the remaining four papers out. "I'll deliver these on my way home." They walk silently down the street and Ian turns into his driveway.

"Thanks Danny."

Danny gave a short wave and continued on his way, checking over his shoulder after every paper he delivered. He hadn't seen Ian for several days and decided to go call on him. Upon arriving at his house, Danny was surprised to find a 'for sale' sign planted on the front lawn. Ian had had to explain the wet patch on his pants and had related his frightening experience to his parents. For the rest of the summer, they managed to enjoy their days mostly conflict free, avoiding any major confrontations with Vince. On the last day of August, Danny stood and watched Ian and his family pack up and move out of the neighbourhood. His friend waved at him through the open car window as they rolled down the street. Danny waved back and slowly shuffled home. The street felt empty and hollow now. He felt empty and hollow now as if a great lifeless canyon had opened up inside of him. This loss of his best friend was all Vince's fault. Vince was guilty of creating this aching void within him, and he would never forget that.

* * * * * * *

Detective Casey reads over the forensic report and throws it down on his desk. Sergeant Kent pokes her head inside the office door.

"Are you coming down to the garage with me? It may be worth another look at the car."

"They couldn't come up with any clues on the driver's side, nothing. The damn car didn't drive itself there," Casey grum-bles as he leans out of his chair and walks into the hallway.

"The blast damage was pretty extensive throughout the interior," Kent says. "Anything they found in Brown's car, well, let's just say it was all him. A meticulous killer, a blasted interior, there's no freebies there."

"They did establish that the time and cause of death was the explosion. He was still alive when the device went off, the killer didn't do him any favours there, made him sweat." Casey opens the door to the stairwell and motions to Kent.

"They roughed him up a bit, maybe tortured him somewhat before blowing him up. The dried blood on his socks was older than the rest. There was gunpowder residue in his nasal cavities, wasn't from the explosion. Pieces of bandage were all over the car, somebody patched him up to take him to the alleyway."

"There wasn't anything out of place at his house, no sign of a struggle, they sure didn't rough him up there," Kent says. "Do you think he was tortured for information?"

"I don't know for sure, it's hard to tell what dead men know—sometimes."

Casey and Kent's footsteps echoed off the smooth floor of the garage and went silent as they stood beside Paul's death car. Broken bits of glass stubbornly clung to the window frames daring gravity to pull them free.

"What does your gut tell you about what we're dealing with here, Detective? Killers or a lone wolf?"

"I'm not sure yet. What does your gut tell you, Sergeant?"
"I'm still on the fence but leaning a little towards lone wolf. "Why's that?"

"Brown didn't seem to be involved with any schemes or illicit group activity. No drugs. Everything looked orderly at his house, didn't seem like anyone was looking for anything. This seems personal to me. But still."

Casey quietly studies the car as if waiting for it to talk to him. He peers through the driver's door and then circles the car and eyeballs the inside through the passenger door. He curiously notices a small sticker stuck to the dashboard in front of the passenger seat. "This sticker looks worn, but it's mainly just damaged from the blast." He studies it closer. "This looks like a frog sticker. Did Brown have any kids?"

"No, he didn't."

Casey takes his pocketknife and lifts the edge of the sticker. "This hasn't been on there baking in the sun. It's not dried out; the adhesive is still sticky. I'm thinking this was put here for our victim Paul to reflect on in his last minutes."

"Why in the world?"

"Why is always the big question," Casey says. "I'm pretty sure it's a lone wolf now. Someone was making a point; what a frog has to do with it, that's a head scratcher."

"So, we have a bombed-out car, a victim blown up for no apparent reason, and a frog sticker," Kent says.

"And a killer with a strange motive," Casey adds.

CHAPTER FOUR

It was a good size turnout of family and friends that filled the special occasion room at the motor inn. The table in the corner was filled with cards from well-wishers and, although the invitation said best wishes only, several gifts had found their way to the table. A white banner with blue lettering stretched its way above the cake. The message on both read 'Happy Retirement, Nora.' Everyone raised their glass for the toast.

"Congratulations to Nora, or, as she has been used to hearing for so many years, Mrs. Adams, on her retirement from teaching."

After dinner the speeches and celebrating lingered on into the evening. Nora thanked everyone for coming and appreciated the guests' help carrying the gifts to her car. A twenty-minute drive brought her happily home. One push on the opener and she was in the garage, parked for the night. Weary from her celebration, it felt good to be home. She set the bag full of cards on the kitchen table; there would be plenty of time to open and read them tomorrow. Nora walked back into the garage and opens the car door to collect her gifts off the back seat. Bending over she feels a sudden jab of pain from behind and steadies herself on the seat. The strength fades from her arms and she helplessly falls forward, blacking out onto her gifts on the seat.

She wakes up in the front passenger seat of the car. A wide belt circles her neck and is fastened around the headrest. The rope secures her arms to her legs and binds her ankles. She feels lightheaded, confused; this really can't be happening. She must be dreaming.

"Hello Mrs. Adams."

The voice startles her and as she starts to scream, the belt quickly tightens to choke off her voice.

"Now now, we can't have you waking the neighbours. I can loosen this off and let you breathe again, but no screaming, promise?"

She nods her head and gasps to breathe again as the belt loosens.

"Don't make me have to cut off your air again. Believe me, I know what it's like to be deprived of something you want badly."

"What do you want from me? There's money in my purse you can take."

"I'm not here to rob you, Mrs. Adams, I'm here to teach you a lesson; you can appreciate that."

"How do you know me? Who are you?"

"You're not paying attention. Repeat after me. I was a vindictive teacher."

"I will not say that." Nora gasps for air as the belt tightens around her neck.

"Not just once; I need you to repeat it twenty-five times, understand?" Nora nods her head and repeats the statement after catching her breath.

"Do you feel humiliated saying that? Believe me, I know the feeling."

"I don't know you, why are you doing this to me?"

"Oh, I believe you do. Perhaps I can jog your memory. Let's get one of these pointy party hats on you. Boy that brings back classroom memories. Now let's put one of your retirement cards on the dashboard. Here's a nice one I picked. It's got bright flowers on it, blue skies, sunny days ahead to retire it says. There's something that was promised to you, something you desire that you're looking forward to, something you waited a long time to enjoy. What if someone lied to you and suddenly told you that you couldn't have it. I think you would feel crushed, like a kid cheated out of his shiny red fireman's hat."

Nora slowly turned her gaze from the card. "You're Danny—Danny Rosen."

"You were a vindictive teacher, you enjoyed doling out the punishment, making an example of me, embarrassing me in front of the class. Then I had to endure the name calling and bullying, the ostracism. You had no idea what you had done, or maybe you did."

"There had to be discipline."

"Not like that, there didn't. What about the fireman's hat? Was that your own special touch of discipline?"

"Danny, you can get help."

"Now you want to be the good teacher; it's too late for that now; you're retired. How many other kids did you traumatize with your brand of discipline in your career of misery?"

"Danny I'm...."

"Sorry? You want to tell me you're sorry? I've heard people tell me they're sorry all my life for things they shouldn't have done. Tell me you regret what you've done. Tell me you regret smashing a little kid's hope so callously. That I could believe."

"If I could go back and change things I would."

"That's the thing now, we can't go back and change things; we can only make things right. Take care of unfinished business is how I see it. This is my therapy, how I can diminish the rage in my mind, bring a sense of balance and justice back into my world. "

"By hurting people?"

"By making them finally face and experience the misery they caused in someone else's life. You gave me false hope for over two months and then snatched it away from me. You never really did intend on giving me that hat, did you? I won't be that cold hearted. You will only have about forty-five minutes, maybe less, to think about being deprived of your retirement. I won't make you wait two months. That should be long enough to reflect on what you did and what you'll miss. I still miss not having that hat."

"You'll regret this; you're going too far."

"Those were my thoughts at the time," Danny says as he sticks the duct tape over her mouth. He turns the key and starts the engine. Nora's muffled screams of terror merely vibrate through her taped lips. At best she can only squirm in the seat.

"That's the nice thing about carbon monoxide: it's painless, you'll just go to sleep. We'll both sleep better tonight." Danny closes the passenger door and looks at the retirement card. "Sunny days ahead; that's all any of us really wanted, isn't it, Mrs. Adams? It's a shame that you won't have longer to enjoy your retirement, but then again, that would be rewarding bad behaviour, wouldn't it?" Danny closed the drivers door and walks up the garage steps.

* * * * * * *

Detective Casey takes a drink of lukewarm coffee and sets his cup down on the desk beside the Paul Brown file. The pages are dog-eared and note-scribbled; question marks punctuate most of the notation.

"It's been eight months and we are no further ahead; that's frustrating."

"It certainly seems like the case has gone cold," Sergeant Kent says. "We couldn't come up with any clues at his house. The blasted car didn't leave us much to go on, and nothing came up in his history to establish a motive. We are at the end of the road unless someone gets careless or comes forward out of the blue, but we've questioned everyone he knew."

"There's always something in the history," Casey says. "We just haven't been able to go back far enough for it to rear its ugly head. Or maybe we missed it, something so subtle that it slipped right past us."

"Everything else considered, it's pretty tough building a case around a frog sticker; maybe that was just a red herring."

"I don't think so. That sticker was put there to get Brown's attention, not distract ours. There is some sort of a connection to it, Brown and the killer from the past."
Casey answers his phone and attentively listens to the one sided conversation without interrupting.

"Thanks, we'll be right over."

"Something else is up?" Kent asked.

"They just found a retired schoolteacher in her garage with the car running, dead from carbon monoxide poisoning."

"Suicide?"

"Only if she started the car then tied herself up. Let's go."

Casey surveyed the scene before him inside the garage. Adam's lifeless body gagged, tied, seat belted in with a leather belt strapping her to the headrest; unopened gifts waiting in the backseat of the green sedan, heat still cracking off the tired engine. Kent walks in from checking the house to join Casey.

"No sign of a struggle inside the house," Kent says. "She just returned home from her retirement party; cards are still on the table in a bag unopened. "

"Except for this one," Casey says, pointing to the dashboard. "The gifts are still on the back seat."

"No sign of a struggle in here either," Kent says, looking around the garage.

"Aside from being tied up, it doesn't appear that she was roughed up. She has been in here all night though. The party apparently broke up around 9:00 pm. She left there alone. Looks like her killer was waiting for her to get home. Hell of a way for your party to end," Casey says, taking the pointed hat off Adams. "Who found her?"

"A neighbour dropped by with some flowers and heard the car running. When nobody answered the unlocked door, she went in, peeked in the garage, saw her tied up, and called 911," Kent said.

"Good thing she didn't come in here. She would have dropped like a stone."

"So, no assault or robbery. Who would have it in for a retired schoolteacher?" Casey said.

"A disgruntled student or co-worker are the most likely suspects," Kent says.

"Maybe even Brown's killer. Brown wasn't a teacher but both he and Adams here were left with something on the dashboard to think about in their final moments."

"Could be the same killer."

"I'm almost positive it is. Both victims are left with a reminder for some past transgression in their lives and the lack of evidence from both crime scenes makes me think we have the same operator here," Casey determined.

"Yeah, there's not exactly a trail of breadcrumbs left," Kent says.

"No, and I bet we don't get a hair or a fingerprint out of the house or this car, probably didn't even sit in it." Casey takes a picture of the card on the dashboard.

"Probably the same when they do the autopsy," Kent said. "I don't imagine poor Mrs. Adams here will be able to tell us much."

"Well, at least the killer didn't blow her up," Casey said. "I imagine she was just as terrified going this way."

"If this killer would only slip up and leave us one good clue in the right direction," Kent said.

"I'd be all over it like stink on a wet dog," Casey vowed.

CHAPTER FIVE

Danny felt lost without his buddy Ian around to call on. He felt abandoned, vulnerable and alone. The neighbourhood felt empty without a comrade to explore and play with. Ian had told him that he had overheard his parents planning the move because of their altercation with Vince that day. They knew that Vince was trouble, and, after the knife threat to their son, they weren't taking any chances staying there. They also knew reporting it to the police would only get Vince a slap on the hand but would surely endanger the boys further and bring reprisals to their own personal property. How Danny hated Vince for the loss of his friend.

When Danny returned to school that fall, he had looked for Ian's familiar smile, but it wasn't to be found in the classroom or on the playground. Danny assumed he was attending a different school now, but, as far as he knew, Ian could even be living in a different town now. He still hung out with Steve at school but the close bond he had developed with Ian just wasn't there. It was more of a buddy at school friendship of convenience that served to ward off some of the bullying from a few of the older aggressive kids. If Danny happened to see Mrs. Adams in the hallway he hurried by her, looking down at the floor to avoid eye, contact. She never made any attempt to confront him or get his attention. She acted as if he didn't even exist; perhaps she chose to forget the whole ordeal that had stayed burning inside of him. One day at recess Danny peered through the window of his old classroom. He saw the figure of a student standing in the corner staring at the same faded paint with the same pointed hat on his head. He could feel the old outrage festering up again. He glanced over to the corner shelf expecting the red fireman's hat to still be perched there, but the shelf lay empty. Gone. Mrs. Adams looked up from her desk as Danny spun away from the window, his back flattened against the coarse brick wall.

"Come on Danny, let's shoot some hoops," Steve called out, bouncing a basketball with one hand.

"Yeah, sure," he replied. It would be a good distraction from that nagging memory.

The rest of the school year would pass by easier than the last. Danny would not have to contend with Mrs. Adams, which in itself was a huge relief. Danny and Steve still had to be vigilant on the playground, but taunts from their previous year of embarrassment did not come back to haunt them. Danny went out of his way to avoid run-ins with Vince but was a target for Vince's mean spirit on the days he unwittingly crossed his path. There had been occasional petty thefts in the neighbourhood, mostly from automobiles. Danny saw the police cruiser parked outside of the apartments Vince lived in, and there was no doubt in his mind who they were there to talk to. Vince had gained a reputation now and had also become a person of interest to the police. No surprise to Danny.

* * * * * * *

Harvey sat on the park bench gazing out in a fixed stare through his black plastic framed sunglasses. He sat motionless except for the constant movement of rubbing his thumb and forefinger together as his hand rested on his right leg. Although the temperature was comfortable and a slight breeze danced the leaves on their branches, fine beads of sweat dotted his brow and made the plastic arms of his glasses stick to his temple. He frequented the small park with its mature trees and well-equipped children's playground. He sat on the same bench every visit, not because it afforded him any shade, but because it was the closest to the playground. Occasionally a parent of the playing children would rest on the same bench and eventually strike up a polite conversation with him. Harvey would ask them which one of the children was theirs, and, upon answering, the parent would return the question. When he replied he didn't have any children, there was an awkward moment of silence. The parent became uncomfortable that they had just identified their children to someone not there as a parent. They got up from the bench, collected their kids, and hastily left the park.

Behind the dark glasses, Harvey's eyes followed every motion of the playing children for several more minutes before he got up from the bench and walked home. Opening the closet door, he slipped off his sunglasses to place them and his hat on the shelf. Just as his eyes were adjusting to the interior light, he felt the sharp pinch, and everything started to go dark as he turned his body towards the direction of his pain. The pain didn't register anymore as he lost consciousness and his legs folded towards the floor.

Harvey slowly opens his eyes and is able to focus on his lap, his chin resting on his chest. He tries to bring his arms forward into view then realizes they are bound behind him around the back of a kitchen chair. He tries to shift his feet, but they are also bound, secured tightly to the legs of the chair. He gasps in a breath, realizing he has momentarily forgotten to breathe as he lifts his head. He recognizes the familiar flowery patterned wallpaper on his kitchen walls and becomes aware of where he is and of someone moving behind him.

"Oh, good, Harvey, you're finally awake," came an unfamiliar voice passing beside him.

"Why are you in my house? Why am I tied up?"

"Why, why, why. I've asked myself that question all my life, Harvey. Sometimes damn near impossible to get the answer. Wouldn't you agree?"

"You know my name; I don't know you."

"I'm sure you do, but then you may have forgotten, because it's been quite a long time and there has probably been so many others. There have been so many others haven't there Harvey."

"I don't know what you are talking about."

"Oh, but I think you do. I think you very well know what I'm talking about." Harvey shifts uncomfortably in the chair, but the ropes allow him little movement. "Perhaps I can refresh your memory. You don't know my name, but you may recall me and my friend Ian."

"I don't know any Ian."

"Ian used to deliver your paper many years ago, and I used to tag along to help him sometimes. One day we came to do collections to get you to pay up on the bill." Danny pulls up a kitchen chair and sits on it backwards resting his arms on the chair back.

"I don't know what you are talking about."

"You told us to come in and said you would get the money for him. It still makes me shudder to come in here now after all these years." Danny looks around at the same old curtains on the window, the same old clock on the wall, the same old feeling of terror hanging in the musty air.

"I don't remember you."

"Maybe you remember what you did to two eight-year-old boys, you perverted son of a bitch. You reached down and groped both of us. We were young and naive and weren't sure what was happening, but we knew it was wrong. We broke free and Ian grabbed for the door. I fell against the table and knocked a folder onto the floor. Pictures of children that I didn't understand spilled out, pictures that never should have been taken, pictures that nobody should ever have. You started grabbing up the pictures, grabbing for me. I pulled a chair over and it caught the corner of your eye. You released your grip on my leg and I jumped to my feet. Ian and I ran out the door and ran until our lungs were burning in our chests. That was the day we learned that monsters are real and are nothing like the ones in the fairy tale books. We were too scared to tell anyone, afraid no one would believe us, so we buried the trauma deep inside us where no one would find it. The monster did come back, though, to chase us in our nightmares. I've had to live with that monster chasing me ever since."

"What do you want from me," Harvey said dejectedly.

"I'm here to collect once again, Harvey. Here to collect my and Ian's due in hopes it will put the monster to rest. Your time to pay. Pay for all the kids you've molested. Pay for all the lives you've ruined. It's time to pay the piper, Harvey, to make things right."

"No, you got me all wrong, I'm a changed man now, that's not me."

Danny stands, shoving his chair away, and walks over to the counter. "I've got a folder full of pictures here, Harvey, that tells me different, you lying piece of shit." Danny swings the folder, smacking it across Harvey's face. "And don't tell me you don't remember me. You remembered me every time you looked in the mirror and saw that scar in the corner of your eye. You continued on, though, devoid of any guilt or shame. I'm the one living with the guilt now, in trying to suppress the memory for all this time of how I failed to act. I failed to act sooner. How many other children could I have saved from the same fate if I had only acted sooner? I have to live with that guilt, but I will get some satisfaction knowing how many I have saved now."

"What are you doing to me? You are the monster now."

"No, Harvey, I think of myself as more of the dragon slayer," Danny says as he pulls a strip of duct tape over Harvey's mouth. "I've got an extension cord here but I'm not going to strangle you with it; that would be too quick an end for all the years of suffering you have inflicted on me and who knows how many others. I've cut the end off of it and we will attach the bare wires to you just like that. Next step is to plug it into this timer, and I will set it for about twenty minutes. How's that? Do you think that will give you enough time to reflect on the devastation you've caused during your pathetic life once I've plugged you in?" Danny plugs the timer into the wall and fills a pitcher of water and pours it over Harvey's feet leaving a puddle around his chair. Harvey hums out muffled protests as he tries to lurch his chair out of the puddle.

"I've taken the liberty of screwing the chair to the floor, as I needed your undivided attention," Danny says as he places a chair in front of Harvey. He leaves the room returning with a mirror that he places on the chair. "As you reflect on your past deeds, I wanted you to see the monster that the rest of us had to deal with in our lives and our nightmares. I've taken five minutes of your time; I'll leave you to the fifteen you have left. Look hard in the mirror, Harvey; see if that monster looks familiar." Danny gets up from the chair. He leaves feeling resolute that he can put this nightmare behind him now, hoping that he has somehow vanquished this monster and that it will no longer chase him.

* * * * * * *

When Danny started high school, it felt like a new beginning, a fresh start that would leave the old issues of his public-school days far behind him. He would soon find that new beginnings often came with new problems. As he progressed into the year and physical changes began to occur within him, he found himself plagued with continually worsening acne. No remedy seemed to be able to contain the outbreaks of pimples that seemed to occupy every square inch of his face and spread at random down his neck, chest, shoulders and back. He found them on his arms and legs, through his hair and even showing up on the back of his fingers. No place on his body was spared. It made him self-conscious and vulnerable to a whole new brand of torment. One guy in particular by the name of Glen seemed to go out of his way to try and make Danny's days miserable, embarrassing him by yelling out "hey zit face," as he passed him in the hall. Sometimes Danny would have particularly bad flare ups of acne up along his spine. The pressure from the lumps would be so painful that he couldn't sit at his desk with his back against the chair back. Glen would pound him on the back, saying, "Hey zit face. Let's pop some pimples today."

One day Glen hit a lump on his spine and Danny spun around in pain saying, "Fuck off, Glen, or I'll drill you one." The teacher sent Danny to the office, and he ended up in detention for not being able to control himself. After he got home, to his embarrassment, he discovered that blood spots had soaked through the back of his t-shirt. He was mortified that he had been walking around all day like that. Glen was having a good laugh at his expense. He hated getting changed in gym class and would try to do so quickly, as Glen would bring everyone's attention to his skin condition. Any attempt by Danny to get him to back off with his incessant attacks would only cause Glen to escalate his actions.

Danny struck up a friendship with an attractive girl who seemed to be interested in him. Cindy didn't seem to mind the complexion that he was so self-conscious of turning girls off with. She smiled at him, and he forgot all his problems and self-conscious worries. Cindy told him that Glen's behaviour was just a sign of his own insecurity that he was trying to overcompensate for. She had built Danny's confidence up so much that he finally got the nerve up to ask her to be his date at the high school dance. She said yes.

This was Danny's first dance and really his first real date. He had been cleansing and steaming and medicating his face meticulously for days leading up to the big night. He prayed there would be no last-minute flareups. The last thing he wanted was a new big pimple on the end of his nose when he would greet Cindy. He changed his outfit three times before deciding that blue would definitely be the colour that would most impress her and would match his jacket the best. He fussed with his hair and checked in the mirror one more time for any signs of a new face invader; he was safe for now.

The night was warm with almost a full moon in a cloudless star-scattered sky. A whisper of a breeze would make it perfect for a romantic night walk after the dance. There was a small park close by with plenty of benches where you could just sit and talk in the moonlight or just keep walking through the night air. Danny knew the exact bench he would pick to stop at if they decided to sit for a while. It was near a big maple tree where they could sit and gaze at the moon while they talked and shared undiscovered things about each other. There was a small flowerbed right beside the bench where the wildflowers were in full bloom. He would make sure he sat on that side of the bench where he could spontaneously reach over and pick the perfect flower to delight Cindy with. He was getting ahead of himself, but he planned it all out in his mind how perfect the night would be. They had agreed to meet outside the auditorium doors as Danny wasn't old enough to drive and Cindy would have to be chauffeured in by her father or mother. Danny was excited and nervous at the same time, so full of anticipation that he could barely stand still. He shifted the pink carnation from left to right hand as if they couldn't agree on which one could best present it. The cars pulled into the lane, stopping to discharge their excited passengers, then leaving again to make room for the next arrivals. Chatter filled the air as Danny scanned the laneway for Cindy's beaming smile standing out amongst the happy faces coming towards him. He had practiced in the mirror to perfect the most flattering compliment he would greet her with and settled on "You look beautiful tonight." That would sound the sincerest, as he didn't want to overstate, or worse still, become tongue-tied. The expectation of that first joyous embrace was so thrilling that he almost couldn't stand the wait any longer. He could hear a new arrival of car doors slamming shut. His heartbeat rapidly now, as he eagerly stood on his toes to peer through the busy crowd merging towards him. There would be no way he could miss her engaging appearance. She would stand out from the crowd, she would be glowing, she would be breath-taking, she would be magically floating towards him. Suddenly, there she was coming towards him, arm in arm – with Glen.

Danny's heels hit the sidewalk with a resounding thud, glued to the ground. He stared out blinking in disbelief, not understanding, trying to make some sense of what he was witnessing before him. He had to be dreaming, this had to be some kind of a nightmare that he was going to wake up from. He would wake up, get out of bed, go through his day and get himself ready for the dance, for the perfect night he had planned for. Cindy would excitedly greet him at the door, they would dance the night away, and then after they would walk off together hand in hand into the moonlight. It would be the best night of his life. The stabbing pain in his heart was too real, the anguish he was feeling slapped him with the reality that this wasn't a dream. There had to be a reasonable logical explanation for what he was seeing. Maybe Glen didn't have a ride to the dance and had just arranged to be picked up along the way. Maybe in appreciation he was just escorting her to the door and pretending he was her date just to get him going. That would be just like Glen to do something like that. He would walk up to him, let go of her arm and say, "Boy I bet I sure had you worried for a minute there. Cindy's a good sport to go along with my prank." There were a dozen scenarios racing through Danny's mind, trying to rationalize what he shouldn't be seeing. As they approached the door he could see and hear them laughing through the fluttering in his ears. Danny forced a smile on his face. The complimentary greeting, he had so earnestly prepared didn't seem appropriate to deliver at this moment. They walked up to him at the door. Danny kept the smile pasted to his face, ready to understand. Neither one of them made the attempt to unlock their arms.

"Hello, zit face, are you the doorman here tonight?" Glen callously said. Cindy put her hand to her mouth and let out a giggle. It wasn't Glen's rude comment that hurt Danny – it was the giggle that came after. He ignored Glen and fixed his gaze on Cindy.

"Cindy, I don't understand, what's going on, I thought we had a date?"

"You got to be dreaming, pimple head; you think a girl like this is going to date you?" Cindy let out another half giggle. Danny doesn't look at Glen, his focus still on Cindy. He doesn't let on that his heart is tumbling down into an abyss.

"I thought we were friends in school."

"I've been dating Glen. He put me up to this; we thought it would be really funny when he came up with the idea to pull this joke on you and see if you would fall for it." Danny couldn't believe what he was hearing. Were those words that he had just heard actually falling out of her mouth?

"So, you pretended to be my friend to go along with this guy's sick sense of humour. You still think it's funny?"

"I guess so," Cindy says as she shrugs her shoulders. Danny doesn't know who he is talking to anymore. He doesn't recognize this actor, this pretender, this accomplice who participated in a warped deception to inflict abuse into another person's life. He won't even call it a joke or a prank. It was subterfuge deployed with the most cold-hearted intent.

"I think it's a riot," Glen says as he chuckles out loud.

"You would because you're a real fucking piece of work," Danny says, finally addressing Glen.

Glen laughs as if it were almost a compliment. "Nice carnation. Too bad you don't have a date to give it to," he laughs as he holds Cindy's arm and proceeds into the dance.

Danny walks off into the night, the hum of the auditorium fading behind his footsteps. He walks through the park past the large maple, past the small bed of wildflowers, past the moonlit bench which is perfect for intimate conversations. Without stopping, he tosses the pink carnation onto the seat and keeps walking as there is but a whisper of breeze making it a perfect night for a romantic walk. His solo journey is without romance, without conversation, the only sound is the repetition of his shoes hitting the dark pavement. He walks through the empty park, and it is a long walk home, but not long enough to walk off the rage that is churning inside him. He may never be able to walk that off.

Danny made his way through the hallway to class and passed Cindy along the way. He made eye contact with her, and she said hello to him, but then he looked away without saying a word. How she could even face him after what she did was beyond him. It may have been a feeble attempt to initiate forgiveness from him to ease her conscience – if she had one – or it could be the lead up to another cruel scheme. Danny wasn't interested or going to be fooled twice. Anything he had felt was gone, evaporated into the air that night and replaced with what he couldn't walk off.

Glen sat behind him in biology class as usual, and he attempted to get his attention. Danny wasn't interested in engaging him to be the target of his name calling and insults so just ignored him. Suddenly Danny felt the sharp jab of Glen's pen into his back, hitting a swollen blister of acne. He spun around in pain to face Glen's stupid guffaws and, without saying a word, spun back, raising his left arm. His fist caught the side of Glen's head in a left hook, knocking him out of his seat and onto the floor. The next thing he knew, he was reporting to the principal's office. It would mean a week's detention, but, this time, Glen would be joining him as well; it was worth it. Glen seemed to back off tormenting him after that day, but his demeaning treatment would stay permanently cemented within Danny; the damage had already been done. Danny wasn't surprised at his reaction in class that day with Glen; it was a long time coming. Sometimes the time it takes to make things right is a long time coming.

CHAPTER SIX

Casey drums his fingers on his desk as he looks over the report for the fifth time. "My assumption was right. There wasn't a print we could lift off the car or anywhere else that was a damn bit useful."

"What about the key fob or door handle?" Kent says.

"Only Adams's prints were on the fob. The rest of the car had so many other prints on it from people helping her in with gifts at the party that nothing is clean enough to use. The killer would have used gloves; wouldn't make that obvious a mistake, same with Brown's car. He or she had to drive Brown's car to the location to blow him up. The explosion destroyed or contaminated any traces they might have left behind. Adams drove herself home. No reason for the killer to be inside the car. Just lifted her in and opened the windows, even turned the key by just leaning in through the open doors."

"He had to go in the house to get the card," Kent said. "Maybe he was waiting for her in the house and followed her into the garage. There were traces of the same drug in their blood that he used to knock them out."

"That's the connecting clue, but the other clue is that the same rope was found on both victims, so we have the same killer by the looks of things."

"Hard to trace the rope or duct tape; there's a hundred places he could have bought it. Video surveillance is bad; at the best of times, the footage frames would be long gone before we could see them all," Kent said.

"No, don't waste your time; he or she will slip up and leave us a traceable clue sooner or later. They always do. What about Adams's co-workers? Any disgruntled teachers passed over for advancement that may have been jealous of her retirement?

"No, she didn't seem to have made any enemies along the way. Although, she may have quite a few revengeful students; she apparently was tough with the discipline," Kent said.

"Well, that should be easy. We just have to go back forty years or so and check every student that misbehaved in class, track them down, question them asking if they ever wanted to kill their teacher, and if they say yes, we arrest them for suspicion of murder; piece of cake. That's a career in itself if it were even possible," Casey laughed.

"You laugh at how ludicrous that would be, but the reality is that one of them most likely did it." Casey brings up on his phone the picture he snapped of the greeting card.

"I've been thinking about this greeting card. Why this one? Was it random, or does it have some significance?"

"Sunny days ahead for your retirement," Kent reads aloud. "We checked the obvious, it was a family member that gave it to her, no motive there to murder her."

"The killer wanted her to study this card, see what she was missing, see what he was depriving her of. He or she was possibly seeking revenge for something she deprived them of. There was no robbery."

"The only thing a teacher could deprive you of is an education," Kent says. "Someone could've had it in for her because they got expelled from school, it screwed up their lives and now they were blaming her."

"It's a long shot but see if the school would have records going back on anyone in her classes that got expelled; there couldn't be that many. We can comprise a list, eliminate all the successful students off of it and see who's left who may be struggling or still had a connection to her that wasn't healthy."

"Failing that, we are just going to have to follow the rope and see where the other end leads us to," Kent said.

"Excuse me." Casey takes a call and puts his phone up to his ear. Kent watches his eyebrows shift up and down and the changing expressions on his face as he intently listens. She can tell by his expressions that the call is engaging, disturbing, and commands his full attention. The call ends and he put the phone down.

"I can tell by the expression on your face that wasn't a good news phone call," Kent says.

"No, I'm afraid the one-sided conversations never are. Looks like our duct tape and rope killer has struck again."

"Man or woman this time?"

"Middle-aged man killed in his own home," Casey says as he grabs his coat.

"Do they know the cause of death yet?" Kent asks as she gets up from her chair.

"Yep, are you ready for it? The killer fried him."

"He was set on fire?" Kent says.

"No, he was electrocuted in his own kitchen."

"Oh, that sounds like a nasty end for him; wonder why the killer chose that."

"Maybe we're about to find out," Casey said.

The lingering odour of burnt flesh crept into their noses as they entered Harvey's kitchen. They circle the chair that Harvey is slumped over in, giving a wide berth to the forensic team working in the room.

"He was wired up to a timer, cooked like a pot roast," Casey observes.

"This chair and mirror set up in front of him is consistent with the other crime scenes," Kent says. "The death is delayed giving the victims time to reflect on whatever brought about their demise. Interesting that he was forced to look at himself, watch his own execution; that is a little morbid."

"Not so morbid, judging by these pictures he has collected, and there're probably plenty more lying around where these came from. The killer is making him pay for being a child molester by the looks of it. He is judge, jury and executioner, death by electric chair of sorts. Figures he is doing society a favour."

"Maybe it's payback as well, "Kent says. "Maybe Harvey here molested the killer when he was young or someone the killer knew."

"That's a good possibility. By the looks of the rope, I'd say we had the same killer on our hands. Probably a male suspect."

"You don't think a female is capable of these murders?" Kent says.

"Anyone is capable. It would just be more difficult for a woman to commit these murders."

"You don't think I could be cold blooded enough to torture or blow someone up or kill my teacher if I was motivated enough? Don't you think I would have the strength to move these bodies around and tie them up? Do you doubt that I would hesitate to screw Harvey to the kitchen floor, wire him up and fry his nuts off if he molested me as a child?" The two forensic officers glance over at Kent then quickly look back to their work.

"I don't doubt your capabilities or any woman's ability for one second. I'm not completely ruling a woman out, but the probability of it being a male is leaning more towards me concluding that. However, the frog angle plays into it in Brown's murder: most women have little interest in amphibians. Most kids that ever got into trouble when I went to school were usually boys, and judging by these pictures that Harvey collected, most of them are of boys as well. I'm just saying that most of the evidence is pointing in that direction."

"I guess you're right; it's not a question of ability. It always boils down to who would have the strongest motive to carry the crime out," Kent relented.

"Now that's not to say that Brown got on the bad side of a herpetologist that got into trouble in Adams's class as a young student and is now avenging her brother's sexual assault by Harvey."

"Glad you're keeping an open mind, detective. Anything's possible, but I think our efforts would be better spent focusing on a male suspect."

"You know I was being facetious," Casey said.

"I know; so was I."

"So how was Harvey able to stay under the radar all these years carrying out his perverted interests and not get caught?" Casey said.

"He never tried to abduct anybody, as far as we know. His actions were a crime of opportunity. These guys put themselves in a position or take the opportunity to exploit vulnerable kids. They gain their confidence, then betray it. The victims are usually so confused, scared or intimidated, especially if it's someone they know, that they keep it to themselves. They live their lives ashamed and embarrassed, emotionally traumatised, and may only get the courage to speak out about it as adults. These guys know how to manipulate their perversion and can carry out their reign of destroying lives indefinitely, unfortunately."

"Until a victim catches up with them and evens the score," Casey says.

"So how many more murders is it going to take before this killer has evened his scores? Is it going to stop with Harvey, is this going to be the end of it?" Kent wonders.

"It depends on how many wrongs he has to make right in his mind. These are definitely not thrill killings, nor do they involve robbery. The killer doesn't even stick around to watch them die; that isn't the purpose. He leaves them time to ponder why he is doing this, to understand what wrong he is trying to right. He is teaching them a lesson and punishing them at the same time. Their last living moments are spent in regret, guilt, and terror. He wants them to suffer the way they have made him suffer all his life from whatever they have done to him. He settles his score, sets their fate, delays their inevitable death and it gives him time to get away. It's perfect. All he leaves behind is some rope and duct tape. When are the murders going to end? That depends on how rough a time this killer had growing up.

If the world was unkind to him, we aren't going to see an end to it anytime soon."

"It can only end one of two ways, then," Kent says. "Either he settles all of his scores, or we catch him."

"I don't like the sound of that," Casey says. "This guy might have had a pretty rough life. As for catching him, I don't like the way the score is adding up on that either: so far, three to nothing. We got our work cut out for us."

* * * * * * *

Danny was able to get himself a part-time job working after school a few days through the week and on the weekends at a small local grocery store. Smith's Fresh Market sold a bit of everything that the bigger stores carried, and it competed by having slightly lower prices to draw its customers through the doors. The owner Frank Smith was a bit of a gruff character who always seemed temperamental even on his good days. Danny couldn't tell if Frank was this way by nature or if long years running the business had made him this way; maybe it was a little of both. Frank didn't ask Danny too many questions when he hired him, he only demanded that Danny show up on time and said that if he found himself with nothing to do, he wasn't in the right store.

"Are you afraid of hard work?" Frank asked.

"No sir" Danny replied.

"Can you be here on time?"

"Yes sir."

"Can you work every day after school when we're busy?"

"I guess so," Danny replied.

"You want the job or not?"

"Yes sir, I can work those busy days," Danny quickly said.

"Good. You can start next Saturday."

"What will I be doing?"

"Everything that Carl tells you to do."

Danny wondered if most kids even showed for their first day after Frank's blunt interview. Frank probably screened out a lot of the unsuitable candidates using this method. Carl was Frank's store, grocery and department manager, and he made sure Danny always had more to do than he could possibly finish in one shift. There was no risk of him winding up with nothing to do under Carl's watch. Danny wasn't afraid of hard work; he just didn't like getting pulled in four directions at one time. He would be stocking shelves and Carl would tell him to go collect the carts. In the middle of collecting the carts he would stop him.

"Why aren't the shelves stocked up?" Carl asked.

"You told me to collect the carts."

"Then why aren't all the carts collected?"

"You told me to broom the aisles."

"How come you didn't finish the aisles?"

"You stopped me and told me to finish stocking the shelves."

"You're going to have to learn how to multitask if you want to keep this job." Danny just figured that this was some sort of frustrating initiation process that Carl was putting him through, but it went on at random for months. He realized that Carl enjoyed the control, bossed him around just because he could, made him look bad to make himself feel good. Danny thought of quitting several times, but he liked having the extra spending money and wasn't going to let Carl push him out. He didn't want to complain to Frank either, as that wouldn't go over well or get him very far. It would only make things worse. He would endure Carl's torment and keep the job for now.

CHAPTER SEVEN

It never ceased to amaze Danny how people were such creatures of habit, how predictable they could be. The daily predictable routines of Cindy West changed very little if at all. Every Thursday after work, she would stop by the gym for an hour on her way home. Once she was finished, there she would stop briefly and treat herself to a sherbet, a small reward perhaps for putting herself through that one-hour workout. She would then proceed to the supermarket, Save A Bundle, to pick up her groceries for the week. Save A Bundle didn't always have the best prices on everything she needed, but it was convenient for her because it didn't take her out of her way on the drive home. She always parked in the west parking lot as it was handy to the cart corral where she delivered her cart when she was done. It was farther from the store but easier to find parking around, and she didn't mind walking the guilt off from her sherbet indulgence. The shopping trip through the store, checking out and the trek back to the car took almost forty-five minutes, so she was usually finished around eight o'clock – you could almost set your watch by it. She would always fit a few bulky items into the cluttered trunk and then open the rear driver's side door, leaning in to place the remaining bags on the back seat. How easy it would be to walk up from behind, administer the injection and push her into the back seat, close the door, return the cart and drive off. How easy it was to take the cross-town bus, then changes buses and get off at the stop a short walk from Save A Bundle. Twice before, he had had to abort his plan and keep walking past the car. Once, someone was sitting close by in their car on their phone, and another time, someone was too close loading groceries into their car. Those opportunities were too risky – but there would be other Thursdays.

It wasn't hard planning a murder. The hard part was planning a murder you could get away with. It was like making an exotic dessert. It took skill, it took patience, it took planning. There had to be a covert way in and out without any witnesses, without any trace. No clues left behind unless you wanted there to be.

Danny lifted Cindy out of the car and pulled her inside, her heels dragging on the ground as they went. He sits her limp body down in the heavy wood chair, tying her upper torso to the chair back and her left arm to the arm of the chair. The chair sits adjacent but halfway ahead of another chair facing towards her. The other body is bound to that chair at the ankles, arms and upper torso. Both their heads are slumped forward, and both chins are at rest on their collar bones. The body beside Cindy has a sheet draped over it. Cindy's eyes flutter open as her chin raises off of her chest. Startled by her strange surroundings, she lets out a frightened shriek. The loud shriek stirs movement under the sheet beside her, and as a head moves upright under the sheet, she looks over and screams again.

"Now Cindy, don't alarm yourself," she hears a vaguely familiar voice say. She snaps her head around to the direction of the voice and studies the face for a long moment. Suddenly, she can put a name to it.

"You're Danny from high school."

"It took you a minute, but that's probably because my face cleared up."

"What are you doing; what's going on here?"

"Ah, yes, that's the question I once asked a long time ago. It's very unsettling not to know what's going on, isn't it? Believe me, I remember that feeling just like it was yesterday."

"Danny, that was a long time ago. I was just playing along."

"So, you do remember our date, or charade is a more appropriate term. You were playing me, and you were very good, building up my confidence, building up my hopes. I was an insecure, tormented teenaged kid thinking I'd finally met someone who cared, who understood, who would be there for me, but instead, you targeted me to play out some sick plan. You took all my hope and anticipation and crushed it like a discarded cigarette butt ground into the street."

"Danny, I'm...."

"Don't even try to pretend you're sorry. You saw how devastated I was that night. You had a chance to apologise then, but nothing, you just shrugged your shoulders and walked away. You felt nothing, you couldn't give a rat's ass."

"It was a mean thing to do; I shouldn't have done it."

"I want you to meet someone here, Cindy. It will be just like old times," Danny says, pulling the sheet away.

"Oh my God," Cindy gasps.

"Glen, you remember Cindy, don't you? Of course, you do, how could you forget an old girlfriend or, should I say, accomplice."

"What are you trying to do here?" Glen nervously asks.

"I'm just trying to bring back old times, Glen; you know, when turds like you just wanted to have a laugh at other people's expense. Only, this time, I'm not going to be the victim. Cindy here is going to be your date again for the night, but this time I'm not going to mind, as she is going to be the date from hell." Danny slides a pink carnation corsage onto Cindy's wrist. "I took the liberty of picking this carnation up for you, Glen, as I know you weren't in any condition to get one when I picked you up. Unfortunately, there won't be any dancing tonight, but that's okay since I don't have a date anyway. Brings back old memories, doesn't it?"

"Danny, you don't have to do this," Glen says.

"I don't have to, but I want to, to make things right. Cindy here is going to learn what it feels like to have her night go terribly wrong, the horror of things happening that she totally didn't plan on. As for you, Glen, let's just say you're going to feel my pain." Danny tapes the handle of a heating element around Cindy's free right hand, the element sticking out eight inches from the handle. He plugs the cord into the wall and the element begins to instantly warm, increasing in intensity to a dull and then a full glow of hot orange. "Now, Cindy: touch the element to Glen's face."

"No, I won't do it, I can't do it," she cries, looking at the intense glow at the end of the wand.

"You're crazy, man," Glen yells out.

"You will do it," Danny commands as he lights a propane torch and holds it near Cindy's face. "It's either his face or yours."

"I can't."

"Do it!" Danny yells, waving the torch closer, singeing her hair. Cindy closes her eyes and swings the element into Glen's cheek. "Again," Danny yells as she pokes the wand forward. "Again, again, again." Cindy jabs the wand wildly, hitting Glen's forehead, cheeks, and neck. Glen screams out in agony as the element sizzles into his skin, the burning stink of his face filling the air. Cindy opens her eyes and sees the horrific burn marks and blisters welting up on Glen's face and neck. She starts to involuntarily tremble.

"Fuckin' stop, stop, stop," Glen screams out.

"Again," Danny yells, bringing the blaze of the torch beside her cheek. Cindy thrusts the element into Glen's chin. She stares out in a glassy glare, unblinking, Danny's commands barely audible. She robotically strikes out, repeatedly hitting Glen's chest, nose, neck, forehead, and cheeks. Glen is in a nonstop scream. Danny grabs the cord and yanks it from the wall. He grabs Cindy's wrist and pulls her arm down to the arm of the chair, ripping the tape off and releasing the element from her grasp. She quietly looks up at Danny and back over at Glen, then fixes her stare to the floor. It takes her a minute, and then another, and then she is back again.

Danny straightens the pink carnation on her wrist. Glen has stopped screaming now, his voice simmered down to a continual audible groan. His head is dizzy from hyperventilating, but the pace of his breathing gradually slows now. His head, neck and chest blister, ooze and burn.

"So, how is your date going so far tonight, Glen? Probably not as well as you had hoped; I know the feeling; I've been there." Danny holds a mirror up in front of him. "What did you expect? Did you think a girl like this would be happy dating someone that looks like you?" Glen looks at his ravaged face in the mirror. "Now you know how it feels to look scarred, disfigured, to look like what you referred to as a zit face or pimple head as you liked to say. Not so hilarious when it's your face looking back at you in the mirror, is it, Glen? Now imagine looking like that at the most self-conscious stage of your life. Walking through the school hallways feeling insecure, doubting any of the girls would give you a second glance because of the way you look. Then have someone single you out, make a spectacle of you, embarrass and humiliate you daily. But all of a sudden, a girl takes an interest in you. You're elated and on top of the world. You feel accepted and anticipate the biggest night of your life only to find out it was all a joke at your expense. I should have Cindy burn your back and then pound on it to give you the full treatment, but I think that I've made my point."

Glen realises this has gone way past the point of no return. The abuse and humiliation he had heaped on Danny was still spilling out of him as fresh as the day he had poured it into him.

"You'll never get away with this, Rosen. If you kill us, they'll catch you and you'll rot in prison and then you'll burn in hell."

"Maybe so, maybe not. But if I do wind up in hell, you're going to be waiting there to welcome me." Danny pulls a clear bag over Glen's head. "Tell you what, though: I'll make an interesting proposition for both of you because I'm a reasonable fellow. Once I tighten the string on this bag, you have about five minutes as Cindy watches you suffocate. If she lets you die, she saves herself and walks away. If she pulls the string and lets you live, then we flip a coin – heads she lives, and you still die, tales she dies, and you walk away. She trades her one hundred percent chance of living for a fifty percent chance by giving you half a chance as well. Kind of a personality test."

"How do we know you won't just kill us both after?" Glen asks.

"You don't, but you have no other choice."

"How do you know one of us won't go to the police after?"

"I don't, but I have an accomplice who will make you and your families disappear if I get arrested."

"How do we know that's not just bullshit?"

"You don't, but are you going to take the chance? We are all going on trust here."

"Why are you giving me a chance now?" Glen asks.

"It's not much of a chance, Glen, she did just save her face." Danny ties the string and leaves the room.

Five minutes go by, and Danny re-enters the room. The room is quiet as he approaches Cindy and Glen. He observes that Glen's head is pitched forward resting on his chin with the drawstring still tied tightly around his neck. "Just as I figured, Cindy, you weren't going to take the risk by giving Glen a chance just for old times' sake. No love lost there was there, Cindy....Cindy?" Danny feels her neck for a pulse. "Son of a bitch, Glen, I think she's had a heart attack. Sorry about your luck."

CHAPTER EIGHT

Danny had mostly worked only two days through the week and Saturdays at Smith's Market, which was fine since it wasn't interfering with his homework. He wasn't sure if they would ever get busy enough to need him every day after school or if that was just Frank's way of testing his commitment. He never felt that he could completely trust Carl, as, besides his bossy nature, he had the type of personality that could turn from friendly to hostile in an instant. One day Danny was in the back breaking down cardboard and putting it in the compactor, and Carl seemed to be in a good mood, even joking around with him. The next minute, he came back yelling at him, telling him to get his ass out on the floor to load sale bins, calling him a moron because he should have had the cardboard finished sooner. Carl seemed to enjoy causing conflict just so he would have somebody to bark at and push around. Danny was the youngest stock boy in the store, so Carl always seemed to have him in his sights. He continually pulled him off of one thing to start another and then berated him for not getting back to finish what he started.

Danny worked the aisles, pulling product that was at its expiration date. He placed items from the meat cooler on his cart and then pushed it into the back room, leaving it near where Carl was working. He grabbed a new cart, and back out into the aisles he went. When he took the second cart back into, the stock room, he noticed Carl re-wrapping the meat trays he had previously left and placing new date stickers on them.

"Don't look so shocked, kid, I'm just giving these trays a little extended life; they will all be gone by the weekend."

"Isn't that unsafe, won't that make someone sick?" Danny said.

"Not likely. If something does go bad, people will either throw it out or bring it back."

"What if they eat it?"

"It's not going to kill them. Look, kid, if it bothers you, just look the other way. Sometimes in life, you just need to look the other way." Danny stood there transfixed, unsettled by this new discovery. "Better still, come over here and put these new date stickers on as I wrap up the trays." Danny reluctantly walks over to the counter.

"Does Frank know that you're doing this?"

"Frank has other things to concern himself with. Let me explain something to you, kid. We don't stay in business and compete here by throwing everything out. My bonus depends on the store making money. If there's no profit, there's no bonus, get it? When you're done here, you can take those packages of cookies and other dry goods out of their expired packages, put them into plastic bags and wheel them out to the bulk food bins. No one will know the difference. Your hands will be just as dirty as mine then and you won't feel so righteous after."

"I'll know the difference," Danny muttered. As he stuck the new 'best before' tags on the meat, he wondered if this was what Frank had meant by "do everything Carl tells you to do."

His parents shopped at this store sometimes, and he wondered now about those times in the past when his stomach had acted up out of the blue and when he had woken up in the middle of the night with cramps and had had to make a beeline to the bathroom. He wondered how many other people had suffered from Carl's self-guaranteed-bonus-plan. *Fresh Market, what a joke*, he thought.

Danny pushed his cart though the store towards the bulk food bins. He felt awkward, like he was deceiving customers, and Carl was right, his hands felt dirty, and so did his conscience. He unloaded all of the items into the bins and returned with the cart into the back room. Carl instructed him to restock the paper goods section next. Danny pushed his cart alongside the towering pile of paper towel boxes and stopped to look around for a push ladder to reach the top boxes over his head. Suddenly, the wall of boxes was crashing over him like a giant cardboard wave. He held his hands up as the weight of the boxes knocked him backwards, falling onto the floor with the steel cart falling over against his shins. He jerked his legs back in pain as he pushed the boxes away from his chest. The next instant, the boxes rolled off of him and there was Carl looking down at him. Carl helped him up as he steadied himself, trying to limp the pain out of his throbbing shins.

"You're lucky I was close by, kid; that could have been a lot worse. That shows you what can unexpectedly happen if you suddenly got an urge to wag your tongue in an attempt to clear your conscience. If an accident like that were to happen again, you might not get off so lucky as just boxes of paper towels."

"Don't call it an accident," Danny said, pulling his arm away.

"You better get this mess cleaned up, kid, before Frank happens by and sees it." Danny rights the cart on its wheels and starts to re-stack the boxes. Whatever animosity he had simmering for Carl was bubbling up to a steady boil now. Danny never gave Carl an easy opportunity to give him grief, as he always kept busy, was never late for work and worked any extra time that was asked of him. Still, Carl had it in for him, and Danny figured it was because he kept his nose clean, worked with a conscience and paid attention to what he was doing. Any other boss would be thrilled with that, but Carl needed someone to give grief to. He didn't feel satisfied, it seemed, unless he was correcting and scolding someone. He was just the type of person who needed someone to crap on all the time. Danny deprived him of those opportunities, and it frustrated him to have him around even though Danny did a good job. Carl continued to fabricate the conflict he craved by trying to pull Danny in four directions at once. Danny was getting faster and better at covering his ass, which frustrated Carl even more. Danny thought Carl was starting to get nervous having him know about his date switching and all the other questionable tactics he did daily.

The next thing Danny noticed was that he was missing hours on his pay that Carl had asked him to work extra time for. It started adding up, and when Danny asked him about it, he would always put him off, saying he would check on it. Danny was surprised one day when Carl said he wanted him to learn how to cover the express cash register. He became adept at it after a few days and was put on the register mainly on Saturdays. Carl hadn't made good on his missing pay. Then, late one Saturday afternoon, Carl called him into his back office. Danny figured he was finally going to square up for the hours he owed him and quickly came to the office.

"Looks like there's a hundred dollars missing from your till kid."

"Excuse me?" Danny replied with a blank stare.

"Your till is short a hundred bucks."

"I didn't take any money from the till."

"That's not what the till says." Danny knew what was going on. Carl wanted him gone and Danny had become bulletproof on the stock floor. By putting him on cash he knew he could target him. He had been set up.

"You know I didn't take the money. We both know that, Carl."

"Sorry it didn't work out, kid; that's life." Danny stood up and walked out the door. He knew he was innocent; he knew he did a good job; he knew he worked hard, and he knew he got screwed in the end.

CHAPTER NINE

"So, Harvey has no record of arrest for sexual offences. That eliminates having knowledge of any of his victims who might come back to do him in for us," Casey sighs.

"No; anything he did for however long he did it stayed under the radar," Kent said.

"The rope is common to all three murders, the duct tape for the last two. I'd say we have the same killer for sure."

"Same drug in his blood as well, for sure. The electrocution stopped his heart," Kent said.

"The killer probably brought the extension cord and timer, and the mirror was one of Harvey's. Other than that, nothing else was disturbed except the pictures that were found in the kitchen. The place is clean. He was careful not to step in the water, not a footprint."

"He couldn't even leave his card with his name and phone number to give us a break," Kent says.

"His rope and knockout drug are his only calling cards so far." Casey slaps another folder down on the desk. "Now things are escalating with this new case."

"I know, just what we needed: a double homicide," Kent said.

"So, we find the victim in the front passenger seat of her car, report says she died of a heart attack. The male victim is in the back seat behind her with multiple burns to his head, neck and chest. The elevated CO_2 level in his blood and his bloodshot eyes indicated death by asphyxiation. They both died within minutes of each other, and there is no rope or duct tape at the scene. The car was parked in the same parking lot of the store the victim does her shopping at. The groceries are still in the car from the night before, the time on the receipt 8:02 pm and that is it in a nutshell," Casey says, slapping his hand down on the report.

"There was no need for the killer to tie and gag them, as they were already dead when he left them in the parking lot. There were rope marks on their skin from being tied, especially on the male, Glen Sweet. He would have to have been tied down for those burns to be inflicted. The kicker is that the female victim, Cindy West, had traces of Glen's DNA on her right arm and no rope marks on that arm. Her hair was also singed on the left side, though. What's your theory, detective? I've got the feeling she was the one who burned him."

"Records show that both victims attended the same high school at the same time, so they may have known each other. Whether there was any relationship between them, no one knows for sure. I've talked to both parents. Cindy's father vaguely recalled a few brief dates, but that's all, no names. She ended up marrying a college sweetheart, and that ended in divorce, so no love triangle there."

"People's memories aren't dependable as witnesses after a few weeks, never mind several decades," Kent says.

"Exactly. It would have had to have been a long-term romance to remember it. Who's going to remember the flavour of the month? But sometimes you get lucky by asking," Casey says. "There still must have been a connection between the two, though; why else would he have grabbed the both of them at once?"

"Yes, our killer is really upping the ante grabbing two people the same night."

"Cindy was the first grab; Glen was the bonus. If he couldn't have grabbed Glen that night for some reason, he would have come back and gotten him another time. He knows his victims, he stalks them. He knows their routines, their every move, then he strikes like a snake and has them before they know it. He's had a long time to plan his moves. That's why he is so difficult to catch, and his memory is clearer than most. He is calculating his every move with a vengeful memory that doesn't forget."

"A lone wolf who can only count on himself, what's your take on this?" Kent says.

"The killer is waiting for her in the parking lot. He already knows when she will be coming to her car. There are only security cameras inside the store entrance, nothing in the parking lot; he knows this. He knocks her out in the car and drives off to Devan Plastics. That's where Sweet works his nine P.M. shift, and he waits for him to show up there. He drugs Sweet as he is getting out of his car, puts him in Cindy's car, and drives off. Probably takes them to the same location where he tortured Brown."

"If there had been a glitch grabbing Sweet, he would have just left with Cindy," Kent says.

"That's right, but it worked out. Sweet's wife doesn't miss him, knows he's at work. Now he has West tied up beside Sweet, face-to-face almost, and her right arm is free. Your deduction is correct. He forces her to burn Glen with some sort of hot iron by threatening to harm her. It's payback for something in the past."

"He has changed his technique of putting something in front of them to dwell on in their final moments, but he doesn't have to. He has replaced that by making them look at each other instead," Kent says.

"Precisely. He is getting her to do his dirty work for him, maybe even going to have her kill Glen, but then there's a glitch. She ends up having a heart attack in the process."

"The killer has to finish him off by suffocating him, can't even make it look like a murder suicide because she is already dead," Kent says.

"Right; he loads them into the car, drives them back to the Save A Bundle and disappears into the night. There's no trace of him in the car, and all the fingerprints in the car were hers. It's like chasing a ghost, a phantom killer," Casey says.

"With five murders, he is going to slip up sometime, something is going to go wrong somewhere that will lead us to him. It's just a matter of time," Kent says.

"Unfortunately for his victims, they appear to be on borrowed time if he still has some score settling to do. He may slip up, but what if he is getting better?"

"That's a possibility, but the unexpected can still happen, and when it does, that will be our break," Kent said.

Casey drummed his fingers on the pages of the report as if it would vibrate loose some precious nugget of information that had been missed, some inconspicuous detail that would leap off the page from its clandestine refuge, illuminating into his mind.

"Did you get anywhere checking the shit list at the school where Adams taught?" Casey asked.

"She only taught lower grade classes in her career; no kids were expelled at that age. The worst that could happen would be a short suspension, and the school didn't keep detailed records of those back then. A student would have had to been a major problem to get pulled from class, and none of hers were. Back in those days, a lot of what happened in the classroom stayed in the classroom. She wouldn't get away now with the tactics that she practiced back then."

"Well, that throws a log across that road, then, but it was worth a shot," Casey said. "We have a blown-up frog victim, a murdered retired teacher, an electrocuted child molester and two victims that may have been lovers decades ago. Kind of makes it hard to connect the dots, doesn't it?"

"Unfortunately, it looks like we are going to need a few more dots to connect," Kent says.

Casey purses his lips as he flips the folder closed.

* * * * * *

The sun has already set as Carl completes his end-of-the-month paperwork. The store has been closed for an hour now, and he has had enough of it eating into his Sunday. He taps the bottom of the papers in line on the desk and secures them with a paperclip. He slides the file cabinet open, inserts the pages, then slams it shut. His chair creaks as he swivels out of it, grab-bing his jacket. He taps the code into the security alarm and pushes the crash bar, exiting the steel back door into the still night air. "Son of a bitch," he calls out as he strides towards his car. He pops the trunk open, fumbles for the jack and pulls out the spare tire. The single light on the back of the store allows him just enough light to curse off the wheel nuts and replace the tire. He places the jack back into the trunk and then lifts the flat tire in. He flinches from the jab and tries to push himself out of the trunk, but his arms are turning to rubber. The dark-ness of the night turns to pitch black as the lid of the trunk slams above him.

Carl drifts back into consciousness and peers through the slit of his eyelids. His mind tries to make sense of a hundred-dollar bill laying in his lap, but it doesn't make sense. He closes his eyes for a moment, as he must be dreaming. His brain spins and shifts and reboots. He remembers the tire, remembers the open trunk. He remembers the sudden jab, and it springs his eyes open. He instinctively tries to stand, then realizes his arms and legs are bound to a chair.

"What the fuck is going on here?" Carl blurts out.

"Hello, Carl, it's been a long time; not that I missed your company."

"Who the fuck are you and what's this about?"

"I see you haven't changed, just as nasty as ever. You don't remember me; I thought the hundred dollars might jog your memory."

"I should know you for some reason?"

"You should know me for a lot of reasons. I'm that kid that you were always giving a hard time to. You went out of your way to make my job miserable for me to make yourself feel good."

"You're the kid who wound up under the pile of paper towels," Carl laughed.

Danny walks over to the wall and picks up a long-handled round-nose steel shovel and walks towards Carl. He winds up in a baseball swing, slamming the back of the shovel off of Carl's left shin. Carl yells out in pain, snapping back in the chair.

"I'm the kid who you pushed the boxes over on and threatened after. As a matter of fact, I still have the marks on my shins from your so-called accident." Danny winds up and slams the shovel into Carl's other shin. "How does it feel to be on the receiving end of it?" Carl unclenches his teeth as his legs throb from the pain.

"Maybe I was hard on you back then, but that's how I had to run things. It was just business."

"You made a choice, Carl. You chose to be a heartless prick and crap on me. You chose to deceive people for your own selfish personal gain. Don't try to justify it by calling it business. It was your slimy business only."

"Look, kid, that was a long time ago."

"So that's how you like to operate? Screw people and move on? I've got some unfinished business to take care of here to make things right. Like you say, though, it's just business, like when you screwed me on my pay to get rid of me. You thought I would quit, but I didn't. You didn't like having me around because I knew about all your schemes. I was too moral, too honest, for your liking. Then you fabricated the missing money lie to fire me, but look, there's the money sitting in your lap; you had it all the time, you lying bastard."

"That's not the money; you're crazy."

"I know it's not the money, just like you knew I didn't take the money." Danny swings the shovel and slams it into the side of Carl's head. The force of the blow spins his head; the side of his jaw bounces off his shoulder as the impact reverberates through his skull. Everything starts to go black, and then he opens his eyes and spits out the blood that has trickled from his cheek.

"Okay, okay. You didn't take the money, I set you up."

"It's too bad for you, Carl, that you didn't make that admission a long time ago. Now, after all the abuse, I'm afraid it's too late."

"What are you going to do, fuck, what are you going to do?"

"You treated me like garbage; because of you, people got sick from things that should have gone in the garbage. Your punishment should fit your crimes, and yours won't be pretty, but, like you told me, sorry it didn't work out; that's life." Danny puts the injection into Carl's arm.

Carl opens his eyes and can feel duct tape pressing across his mouth. It is dark, but small cracks of light knife in from above him. A pungent smell assaults his nostrils, and he tries to move, but his hands and feet are bound together behind him. He attempts to roll onto his side, but the movement only settles him further into the garbage bags. He is in a quicksand of garbage. His heartbeat thumps up into his ears as the drone of the diesel engine draws nearer. The truck is on schedule every Monday morning at eight P.M. for the pick-up. The engine revs higher as the steel forks jolt into the side brackets of the dumpster. In one last panicked attempt Carl desperately tries to roll onto his side as his face presses into the garbage. The container raises into the air up over the truck cab, its lids dropping open. The contents rumble out into the belly of the beast, and the compactor engages. It crushes and squeezes and pushes the load to the rear of the truck while the forks settle the empty dumpster back to the ground.

CHAPTER TEN

The summer before Ian had to move away was one of the best of times that Danny had spent building a friendship with someone. Other than their terrifying run-in with Harvey and the bad run-ins they had had with Vince, they had enjoyed their time together. Even those run-ins had strengthened their bond. They had always gotten along together, and if Ian hadn't moved away, Danny was sure they would have been friends for life. One morning during one of their many excursions around the pond, they had come upon a young cat that followed along with them. It didn't appear to be full-grown yet, but it may only have appeared that way because it was so skinny from being underfed. Danny decided to take it home, as it didn't look like anyone had been taking care of it, and they were afraid if Vince found it, he would have done it harm or worse. Danny was overjoyed when his parents said he could keep the cat, and he named her Rusty because of her orange colour. It didn't take long for him to fatten her up a bit, and with her hunting skills, she was able to catch her fair share of mice from the woods behind the houses. Danny was always afraid at first that she might run off, but Rusty always came home.

Down the street from Danny lived a miserable man: Stan Stevens. Stan lived by himself, and all the kids called him scary Stevens, as he would yell at them to get off his lawn. Danny and Ian were throwing the ball back and forth as they walked up the street. The ball rolled up on Steven's lawn, and Danny ran up to retrieve it. Stevens came out the front door, and Danny stopped dead in his tracks.

"I told you kids to stay off my lawn."

"We were just getting our ball," Danny said.

"Well, that's too bad." Stevens picked up the ball and pushes it in his pocket. "Now get off my lawn."

Danny ran off the grass and walked down the street with Ian.

"He kept our ball; we will never get it back now," Danny said.

"He's mean to everyone. I heard he catches rabbits and skins them in his basement, chops their heads off," Ian said.

"No way," Danny said.

"Yeah, it's probably true."

They quietly continued down the street, both of them picturing in their minds the gruesome sight in scary Stevens's basement.

The next run-in they had with Stevens was late that summer. Stevens had an apple tree in his backyard that he almost never picked the apples off of. Danny and Ian had just finished the laborious task of building their fort in the woods. They were famished, and they could just taste those juicy apples going to waste on the tree. They snuck along the tree line until they reached Stevens's back yard. They paused to make sure the coast was clear, and then they climbed through the cedar rail fence and ran over to the apple tree. Danny boosted Ian up to reach the apples, locking his fingers firmly under the weight of Ian's right foot. Just as Ian plucked the first red prize from the branch above him, the dreaded voice thundered across the yard.

"Hey, you kids, what the hell do you think you're doing."

Ian and Danny tumbled to the ground. They scrambled to their feet and raced towards the fence, which seemed impossibly far away now. As they climbed through, they were hauled backwards by the backs of their coats. Stevens pulled the hoods of their jackets over the fence post; they were suspended with their feet barely touching the ground. "I warned you two to stay off my property," Stevens barked, shaking his finger at them. Danny could feel the jacket zipper tight around his neck and started gasping gulps of air into his lungs. He could also hear Ian wheezing beside him. "You come here to steal my apples, you little thieves." Danny starts kicking his heels into the fence post and grabs at his zipper while Ian grabs wildly at the back of his hood. "I ought to skin you little bastards alive," Stevens threatened as he pulls their hoods off the post and drops them to the ground. "If I ever catch you here again...," Danny and Ian don't hear him finish as they clamber through the fence and disappear like rabbits into the woods. They pound the ground with their feet until they stumble into the sanctuary of their fort. They sit, leaning their backs to the wall, knees drawn up to their wrists, waiting for their lungs to catch up to the exertion of their legs. They had heard stories of little kids disappearing and wondered if it was at the hands of someone as hateful as scary Stevens.

The nights were getting cooler now, and Danny's cat Rusty wasn't staying out as long into the evening. She had become quite satisfied with the comforts of a warm home, so Danny had started to worry when she hadn't shown up as darkness started to fall. He decided to go out looking for her and crossed the backyard into the woods calling her name. He searched along the tree line, calling out into the woods while looking into the backyards along the way. He had walked as far as scary Stevens's backyard and decided to turn back, as he figured she wouldn't have wandered any farther away. He stared across Steven's yard without seeing her and noticed a light on in the basement. He had wondered about all of Ian's crazy stories, and curiosity burned inside of him. He wiggled through the cedar rail fence and crept across the backyard under the cover of darkness. A twig snapped under his foot, and he froze in place, deciding whether to make a run back for the fence or not. Scary Stevens's warning was echoing in the back of his mind, but the yellow light from the basement window was beckoning him forward. He gingerly stepped ahead and reached the back corner of the house. He steadied his hand along the siding as if he were walking along a tightrope without a safety net. The crickets silenced upon his approach, then resumed their chirping chorus behind him. Nearing the window, his hand snagged a spider web, causing him to jerk it away from the siding and quickly shake the webbing off. He knelt down by the window's glow, steadying one hand on the siding and the other in the cold dew of the grass. Danny held his breath as he peered down into the basement through the dirty glass window. His heart pounded against his ribs as he noticed scary Stevens busying himself with something in front of him, his back turned towards Danny. Danny's gaze shifted through the room across the cracked cement floor, past the dusty old furnace, then upwards to the rough wood beam spanning the room. There is where he saw it. Hanging from the beam in that cold dingy basement was a grey cat and his cat Rusty. Danny stared at the horror burning into his mind, not believing what he was seeing, not wanting to accept the finality of this terror before him. He let out a loud gasp, his hand sliding down onto the window as if he could reach through and free Rusty from that beam.

"Who's there," Stevens said, turning towards the window.

Danny pushed himself away from the window, his weight cracking the glass. He panicked across the backyard past the apple tree and through the cedar rail fence. In a blur, he was through the forest and back into his yard. He wiped the tears away as he told his parents about his horrific discovery.

"Are you sure it was Rusty you saw?" His mother asked. "I don't think Mr. Stevens would do a terrible thing like that."

"It was he's a cruel person," Danny said. The next day, Danny and his dad knocked on Stevens's door.

"Good morning, we are looking for a lost orange cat. You wouldn't have happened to see one around?" Danny's dad said.

"No, can't say that I have," Stan said.

"My son here thinks she may have wandered up this way."

"There's a lot of kids up to no good around here; someone broke my window last night," Stan says, looking down at Danny. "Maybe one of them took off with your cat."

"Just wanted to let you know she was missing," Danny's dad said.

"If I see her, I'll be sure to get her back to you," Stan says, closing the door.

"He's lying," Danny said.

"I'm sorry, son, there's not much else we can do."

Danny missed having his pet around. He missed how she would playfully capture his hand in her paws, draw it to her mouth pretending to bite as she pressed her teeth against his finger, then affectionately give it a lick. He missed having Rusty curled up on his bed at night and the comforting sound of her purring him to sleep. He couldn't get the image out of his head of her hanging from that beam in Stan Stevens's basement. That was two friendships that had been ripped away from him at the end of that summer, two losses that would haunt him forever.

*   *   *   *   *   *   *

Casey clicks through the images on his screen and makes notations on the reports scattered open on his desk. Kent knocks on his open door and comes in, sitting in the chair at the front of his desk.

"Any new insights on these murders you'd like to share?" Kent says.

"Nothing that's going to crack the cases wide open yet," Casey says. "I keep looking at these photos and shuffling things around, but the main common denominator is the same rope has been used each time. Although it's missing from the last crime scene, I'm sure the killer used the same rope when he had them tied up. His drug of choice has been present in all five victims. His motive definitely isn't money, and although the first victim and Sweet were initially somewhat mutilated, his intent isn't to torture them to death."

"No; Adams, Harvey and West weren't roughed up at all, and he made West inflict the injuries on Sweet, it appears. He's more concerned with his purpose than interested in torturing his victims. His motive seems to be revenge for some past injustice that his victims have inflicted on him," Kent says.

"Why burn Sweet, though, why get her to do it?" Casey says.

"Maybe it's symbolic. Maybe he was involved in a relationship with her and got burned emotionally when she started a relationship with Sweet. Now he has her literally burn Sweet to let them know what it feels like to get burnt in a relationship."

"Makes sense," Casey says. "That's a long time to hold a grudge, but crimes of passion have no time limits it would seem."

"If he knew them back then in school, that would make the killer about the same age," Kent says.

"Now we are getting a profile of the killer at least, and we aren't working with a random serial killer here. The victims know their killer or have known him in the past. I think it's definitely safe to assume it's him now." Casey holds his hand up. "Of course, that's not to say that a woman didn't get burned and is punishing the former boyfriend and the other woman for emotionally scarring her. As a matter of fact, that would be just as good a scenario."

"Listen, Casey, I've been meaning to say something about my feminist shout-out when we were talking about gender up to Harvey's murder; it's been on my mind. I conceded then that the murderer was more likely a male."

"Don't even give it a second thought; I haven't since," Casey says. "One of the reasons you're on these cases with me is to put your insight into it and keep me having an open mind.

I thank you for doing that. I could easily get barking up the wrong tree if left entirely to my own devices."

"So, we are both in agreement that the suspect is a male?" Kent says.

"I am totally in agreement that the killer is a male – that is, unless the evidence tells me different."

"This killer also has the resources to abduct his victims, punish or kill them in another location and deliver them to another site in their own vehicles or kill them in their own homes," Kent says.

Casey picks his phone up and listens to the call that's coming in. He puts his hand to his forehead, draws his fingers back through his hair and draws his hand down the back of his head to his neck before resting it back down on his desk. He brings the phone away from his ear.

"That's a tell, Casey; we have another victim, don't we?"

"It's coming into forensics now", Casey says.

"Into forensics?" Kent says, "what about the crime scene?"

"New location – they pulled the body out of the dump."

Kent doesn't say a word as she gets up from the desk. Casey follows her out the door.

Through their masks, they still grimace at the rancid odour that has permeated through the room. Casey has confirmed what he suspected he would see.

"Male victim bound with the same rope and duct tape across the mouth, the same as the others," Casey says.

"I'm betting it will be the same drug found in his blood as well," Kent says. "Won't be any surprise that the cause of death is crushing. I hope the victim was dead before the compactor reshaped him, but knowing how this killer operates, I'll bet the poor bastard was still alive when he was being taught his lesson."

"I've seen and smelled enough," Casey says, "let's get the hell out of here and wait for the autopsy report."

"You won't get any argument from me," Kent says.

CHAPTER ELEVEN

Casey opened his office door and flips the wall switch, bringing the flickering fluorescent lights to life. He sets his hot cup of coffee onto the desk and Kent does the same with hers as they sit down.

"The victim's car was found abandoned in a plaza parking lot; nothing unusual inside the car or anything that would indicate a struggle," Casey said.

"We have a list of the dumpster pickups that were made that day, but the killer could have dumped him in any number of them along the route the night before. He never came home from work that Sunday night or showed up for work Monday, of course, as he had been disposed of and was reported missing. The victim is a Mr. Carl Frost who was the grocery manager at Smith's Fresh Market, been there forever," Kent says.

"I questioned the owner and staff there; I got the feeling there's a lot of people that would like to have killed him. He apparently was a pretty hard guy to work for. We are looking at previous employees, but the list goes pretty far back for the number of years he has worked there," Casey said. Kent studies the report, then spins the folder back around to Casey.

"It's been confirmed that the same drug, duct tape and rope have been matched to the other murders, not that we had any doubts," Kent says. "Interesting to note that there were injuries to both shins and one side of his face from blunt force."

"Doesn't seem to be caused by the compactor."

"No, the findings were that the bruising confined to those areas was caused by impact, not crushing," Kent said.

"Then our victim wasn't just drugged and thrown into a dumpster. He was abducted, had those injuries done to him, then was brought to a dumpster after."

"Like the last murder, the killer hasn't left something in front of him to reflect on in his final moments."

"Sweet and West had each other to dwell on in the end; they were each other's lesson. In Carl's case...," Casey looks down at the report and scratches his forehead. Kent takes a sip from her cup of coffee. He looks back up at Kent and says, "Garbage — the garbage was his lesson somehow; it was all around him in his final moments.

"Garbage was the motive for murder?" Kent says.

"Symbolically, just like Sweet's burns were symbolic. Carl had some questionable business practices, according to one of the employees. Besides treating the employees badly, his actions could have made someone seriously ill, almost killing them perhaps. Now, if that person happened to be our killer or someone close to him — just a theory. Almost any possibility could set our killer off seeking retribution."

"The report noted brake dust on the victim's hands."

"I checked that out as well when I read it. The spare tire in the trunk was flat. I couldn't find a screw or nail in it but found a small puncture between the treads," Casey said.

"The killer was setting Carl up."

"He had it all planned out, as usual," Casey said. "He punctures the tire while he waits for Carl to finish in the store. Carl comes out and has to change the flat tire. Just as he is finishing up, the killer comes up from behind, knocks him out and Carl gets an economy class ride with the flat tire to wherever the killer takes his victims for their reckoning. He deals out whatever abuse he needs to Carl to make his point and brings him to the dumpster. He throws him in hog-tied so he can't get out or pull the duct tape off. Carl wakes up in the garbage and has time to think about whatever injustices he has done to the killer to face his end this way. The killer is long gone from the scene of the crime."

"What a horrific way to die," Kent says.

"Poisoning, explosion, suffocation or electrocution aren't much better; you still end up dead in the end."

"I know, but death by dumpster and then — I don't even want to think about it," Kent says.

"This is what I was afraid of; we have another dot to connect, but the puzzle isn't coming together any easier."

"Not yet," Kent says, "There's still too many pieces of the puzzle missing. Unfortunately, until we can catch up with this elusive killer, more victims will be going missing as well and showing up dead if he isn't finished yet."

"It's a cruel world, Kent; what if he's just getting started?"

"Then we will be having quite a few more of these difficult discussions I'm afraid."

Kent walks over to the microwave and puts her coffee in. She pushes the timer for a thirty-five second count down as she looks out from the second-floor window. Below in the street, a worker throws two bags into the side of the idling garbage truck. The microwave beeps and she open the door, taking her cup out just as the worker engages the crush of the compactor. She can hear the snap and pop of the squishing bags. She swings the oven door closed and quickly turns from the window and walks out of Casey's office shaking her head.

*   *   *   *   *   *   *

Every Saturday, Stan would get up at eight-thirty A.M. not because he set an alarm clock but because that was just the usual time he was used to waking up. He would make his coffee and sit at his kitchen table drinking it while he ate his English muffin. He didn't have much of an appetite, first thing in the morning. When he finished his muffin, he would wash his plate off, dry it and put it back in the cupboard. He would pour a second cup of coffee, set it on the table and go to the door to get his Saturday paper. He had warned the paper boy that if it wasn't delivered by nine A.M., he would call the newspaper office to make a complaint and cancel the paper. He also told him the same would apply if he caught him taking a shortcut across his lawn. He was miserable and set in his ways, and he didn't need to please anybody but himself. He had been mar-ried briefly a lifetime ago, but his wife had left him because of his coarse nature, and he didn't want to have any children. He didn't have the patience for them.

He read his paper at the kitchen table while drinking his coffee, waiting for most of the morning dew to burn off of his lawn. He always cut his grass Saturday morning and washed his car Sunday morning just because that was the way he had always done. By the time he finished cutting the grass, it was noon, and he came in to make himself some lunch. After lunch, he would drive to the supermarket to do his grocery shopping. After he brought the groceries home and put them away, Stan would collect his laundry and start it in the machine down in the basement. He then sat down in his living room and turned the television on to whatever game was on. He wasn't even particularly interested in sports, but he liked listening to the noise as he drifted off into a late afternoon nap. He woke up just before dinner in time to take his laundry out of the washing machine and put it in the dryer. He never prepared dinner on Saturday, as he always went out to pick up fish and chips religiously at five-thirty. He always brought them home to eat, as he felt self-conscious eating out by himself. It also irritated him to have a table of noisy and fidgety kids nearby while he was eating. Stan didn't like children anywhere near him, and he didn't make any effort to hide that fact.

Stan pulls into his driveway at almost six-fifteen on the dot. He takes the warm paper bag off the seat of his car and enters the side door of his house. Taking a plate from the kitchen cupboard, he dumps the fish and chips onto it; he refuses to eat out of the disposable takeout containers. He also uses his own ketchup and sprinkles his own salt, as he doesn't like fiddling with the little packets. The only package he will tolerate are the small plastic shells of tartar sauce that he peels back and digs out with his knife. The buzzer sounds on the dryer as he cuts into his fish. He takes a drink of the cola he has poured into a glass out of the waxy cardboard cup. He is set in his ways and has done this for as long as he can remember. He finishes his meal and takes his dishes to the sink where he quickly washes everything and puts it away.

Stan flips the basement light on, and the stairs creak as he descends into the basement. The clothes are still warm as he bends over and paddles them out of the dryer into the laundry basket. He begins to lift the basket up, but his arms no longer respond after the sharp jab that has come from behind him. His legs fold and his knees hit the cement floor as his chest comes to rest on top of the laundry basket.

Stan regains consciousness, recognizing his basement floor as he slowly rotates his gaze. He can't move his arms tied behind him nor his legs bound securely to the legs of his kitchen chair. His head raises, and he is startled to find a figure standing in his basement.

"Good evening, Stan, or should I say Mr. Stevens?"

"Who are you? What are you doing here? Why am I tied up?"

"I'm just one of the neighbourhood kids coming back to pay you a visit from the past, Stan."

"Untie me! Get out of my house."

"Now, Stan, that isn't any way to treat an old neighbour; but, then again, you never were very neighbourly to children, or pets, for that matter."

"You don't know what you're talking about."

"But I do," Danny says, shaking his finger from side to side. "I know exactly what I am talking about. Let me refresh your memory."

"I don't need to listen to any of your bullsh...," Danny swings the thick coil of rope in his hand across the side of Stan's face, knocking him and the chair over onto the floor.

"I think you do need to listen, Stan, now that I have your attention," Danny says, grabbing the chair back and righting it. A faint emergence of blood colours the abrasion on Stan's right temple. "All these years, you were so miserable you couldn't even let a kid step on your lawn to get their ball back. You couldn't even find it in yourself to offer or let a kid have an apple that you didn't give a shit about."

"Kids didn't have any business being around here."

"You made damn sure of that with your threats, didn't you? You didn't want anyone discovering what you were really up to you sadistic bastard. You remember those two kids you had choking by the hoods of their jackets on the fence post? One of them was me."

"You kids got what was coming to you."

"Just like you're going to get what is coming to you, you miserable fuck." Danny says, raising his foot and kicking Stan in the chest. His chair topples over backwards, crashing the back of his head onto the floor. "You see that beam above you? That's the same beam you hung my cat from, you sick fuck."

"I didn't know it was your cat."

"Don't even pretend you have a conscience; you didn't care whose pets they were. How many of them met their fate down here?" Danny rights the chair and throws one end of the thick rope over the beam. Stan feels a noose tightening around his neck.

"Let me out of here," Stan screams out.

"Not so pleasant when the shoe is on the other foot or, should I say, noose is on the other neck."

"Take it off me! I'm not an animal."

"I think you are, Stan. You're the worst kind of animal: an animal pretending to be a human being.

"If you do this, you will be the animal," Stan shouts out.

"Maybe I'm the wounded animal looking to heal my injured self and I can only do that by making things right, to take care of unfinished business. You're just a piece of that unfinished business, Stan."

"Take it off," Stan bellows as he sees Danny walking backwards, wrapping his grip around the rope.

"This is what it felt like when I was choking on that fence post." Danny pulls the rope, raising Stan in the chair off the floor. Stan gasps for air, the weight of his body binding the rope around his neck, and then Danny drops him to the floor. Stan chokes in some air through his beet-red face.

"Stop," he says.

"This is what it felt like when me and my friend Ian were choking on that fence post." Danny again pulls Stan off the floor, dangling him from the rope. He gurgles and his eyes bulge as saliva runs from the corner of his mouth. Danny drops the chair to the floor and Stan wheezes air into his deprived lungs.

"No more," Stan coughs out.

"That's right, Stan, there will be no more; that's why I'm here. There will be no more – that's what I've come to ensure. This is what it felt like for my cat Rusty and every other animal you hung up down here, you miserable son of a bitch." Stan shakes his head, his mouth gaping open to draw in the last breath he knows he will ever feel across his tongue. Danny pulls hard on the rope, hauling Stan in the chair halfway up to the beam. He ties the other end to a steel jack post as Stan slowly spins by his neck. "I have to take my leave now; – sorry

I couldn't have dropped by sooner. And, by the way, I will be walking on your lawn when I go."

Danny leaves by the side door under the cover of darkness. He walks across Stan's backyard, stopping to pick an apple off his tree. He reflects back to how difficult a reach it was that afternoon long ago, when he'd boosted Ian up to the same branch he so effortlessly plucked from now. He bites into the sweetness of the apple as he walks towards the old cedar rail fence. The old neighbourhood hadn't changed much from when he once lived here. The beaten path that ran through the woods and connected to the next side-street took him back the same way he came. The trees were taller, but the woods didn't seem to be as big anymore. He walked along that familiar trail and stepped from the path and walked along the street, finally arriving to where he parked his car. He drove away content, knowing that scary Stevens wasn't going to be scary any longer.

CHAPTER TWELVE

Danny's first year in high school would push him to his limit both physically and emotionally. What he had anticipated as a new beginning, a fresh start, had quickly deteriorated into unexpected turmoil. It was bad enough to struggle with his acute acne condition and Glen constantly badgering him, but his problems were only beginning. After his devastating night at the hands of Glen and Cindy, Danny felt relieved when his final confrontation with Glen caused him to back off somewhat with his torment. Danny soon had a new nemesis, Brad Parker. Brad didn't administer the verbal assaults that Glen randomly fired off; he was too busy bragging about himself. He never liked Brad from the moment he met him, as Brad was loud, obnoxious, and always tried to one up him in any sport that Danny participated in gym class. Danny didn't know why he had it in for him, but just like he had done with Vince, he went out of his way to avoid Brad whenever possible.

Danny was a good runner, and when he managed to just beat Brad in sprinting try-outs, it set the stage for a downward spiral in their association. Brad played dirty to get Danny out of his way. Twice in basketball, Brad had purposely slammed the ball into Danny's face, blackening his eye and giving him a bloody nose. Danny found it hard to concentrate on any game he was in, as he never knew when a knee or a fist was coming his way out of the blue when no one was looking. Fighting back wasn't an option, as it would mean instant disqualification from the event. For a short time, there was a punishment practiced called running the losing team through the mill. The winning team players stood face-to-face with one arm locked to the hand and wrist of their other team members, forming a tunnel. The losing team would run in a line, ducking through the tunnel while the winning team pounded on their backs with their free fist. This was especially painful for Danny with the swollen acne lumps on his back. He ran through with his team members taking their punishment as Brad on the winning team stood in the line-up waiting for his approach. As Danny ran by him, he lowered his fist to his side, drew back and slammed him in the side of his face. Danny stumbled and fell to the ground, his teammates trampling into him in a chain reaction. Nobody admitted to the vicious blow, but Danny knew exactly where it came from. After that day, the running through the mill as a punishment was stopped.

Danny was trying out for the soccer team and was manoeuvring the ball around Brad. Brad lunged forward, and instead of kicking the ball, he purposely stomped one foot down on Danny's ankle, badly injuring it. Of course, it was another one of Brad's so-called accidents involving Danny. Danny was put out of commission and could not join the soccer team; nor could he participate in sprinting for track and field. Brad had succeeded in eliminating his closest competitor. When Danny could eventually run to play football, Brad targeted a sharp blow one day with his elbow, cracking one of Danny's ribs. That effectively took Danny out of any sporting events for the rest of the school year. He moved around painfully from class to class, every motion an effort, every effort a calculated, careful manoeuvre. He had to sit motionless on the side-lines watching Brad and the rest of his classmates enjoy themselves without him. There was no punishment for Brad, no penalty. He knew what he was getting away with — don't even call it unsportsmanlike behaviour. It was vicious, premeditated, and unforgivable.

"Don't feel too bad; maybe the coach will let you be the water-boy if you're lucky," Brad said; then he laughed and walked away with a stupid grin.

Danny would never forget the undeserved pain and abuse that he had suffered. He would also never forget that smug comment or that stupid grin on Brad Parker's face.

Detective Casey fastens his seat belt, puts the key in the ignition and, with a quick flick of his wrist, starts what will be the beginning of an interesting afternoon. He had just barely finished his ham and cheese sandwich, hadn't tipped back the remaining coffee in his cup, hadn't yet wiped the errant drip of mustard from his thumb when the call came in. He flips the sun visor downward and pulls the shift into forward. It is a bright, crisp fall day just barely past August and unseason-ably cool for this time of year. The warmth of summer will sneak back in, still stubbornly holding its ground, although some of the leaves are beginning to blush, showing an early hint of red to the sharp-eyed observer. It would be a beautiful day for a picnic still, a walk in the park, a stroll around town or any other activity that didn't involve investigating a homicide.

Casey drives along the avenue, accelerating and slowing down with the flow of the traffic. He stops at the traffic light and turns onto the next street, slowing as he approaches the stationary garbage truck. A worker in a yellow and orange safety vest lobs three bags into the air, and they disappear into the side of the truck. The road is clear, so he steers around while Kent looks out the window at the idling hulk of the vehicle and turns her head away.

"It still bothers you to look at one of those trucks; you can still picture the image in your mind."

"I may never be able to look at them the same way again," Kent says, focusing out the front windshield.

"Unfortunately, that's the drawback of our line of work. You see things that you would rather forget, but you can't unstick them from your mind so easily."

"It seems our killer is having the same problem; he's having trouble unsticking things from his mind that he would rather had not happened to him in his past. I mean, who has someone crushed alive in a garbage truck?" Kent says.

"Someone who can justify paying back people for all the wrongs they've done to him; he's making it right. These people are all bad actors in his mind. Payback is a bitch, but that's the only way he can unstick whatever has happened to him in his past."

"It's a hell of a way to seek redemption," Kent says.

"Does this look familiar to you?" Casey says as he stops at the stop sign and then turns onto the tree-lined street.

"This is the same neighbourhood where our molester Harvey lived. His house was two streets over, wasn't it?"

"That's right. That makes two victims from the same neighbourhood now. We can assume the killer lived here as well at one time, or else it's one hell of a coincidence."

"At least it's another piece of the puzzle falling into place," Kent says. Casey pulls up to the curb and they exit the car, walking past the forensics van parked in the driveway. Kent and Casey step down the basement stairs, apprehensively anticipating another scene which will stick to their minds. The basement window has been opened but the smell of death still hangs heavy in the air. The flash of cameras lights up the walls as Casey unties the rope and lowers Stan to the floor.

"He's been hanging here for two days," Casey says. "He was supposed to meet his sister for lunch, and when he didn't show up, she came over to check on him. This is what she found."

"Hung up still tied to the chair. The killer wasn't interested in making it look like a suicide," Kent said.

"Not at all. They found a receipt in the trash with takeout containers marked with "5:58" and dated- Saturday night; that was the last known time he was alive. Killer was likely waiting for him when he got back. Looks like he finished his dinner and came down to get his laundry. The killer was waiting for him when he came down here."

"Could he have been murdered last night?" Kent says.

"No, the body isn't fresh enough for that short a time. Talking to the responding officers, the sister said he always washed his car on Sunday, and that never happened. She said they always went to lunch on Mondays because there were too many kids out for lunch with their parents on the weekends. Apparently, he wasn't so fond of kids."

"Looks like the killer left his calling card," Kent says. "That's the same rope used at the other murders to tie them up with. The hanging rope, that's a new touch, though, and there's no need for duct tape when someone is choking to death."

"Yes, I'm sure forensics will confirm that and find the same drug in him as well." Casey walks over to talk with the forensic agents, and Kent walks over to examine Stan closer. The agents point to the beam and back to the bench they have examined. Casey walks back over to talk to Kent.

"It doesn't appear that he was tortured, but he does have an abrasion on the side of his head," Kent points out. "As well as abrasions here on the other side of his face that would indicate some roughing up before he was hanged."

"I'm sure the killer was getting his point across very forcefully, as the impact marks on crushed Carl also indicated."

"The killer hasn't left a parting memory again for the victim to reflect on," Kent notices.

"The basement here itself is the memory," Casey says. "I don't know exactly what went on down here between Stan and the killer, but Stan had to be up to something nasty enough to set him off. Our killer could have killed him in the kitchen, living room or anywhere in the house."

"Do you suppose Stan molested him down here as a child?" Kent said.

"I doubt it; he didn't like kids enough to want to be that close to them. The agents found animal hair – likely cat hair, they said – on that beam up there and some on that workbench as well."

"Stevens didn't have a cat," Kent said.

"No, he didn't. They also pointed out traces of old blood on the workbench. They will confirm the samples in the lab, but if I were a gambling man, I would bet our killer found out what our agents are going to confirm in the lab: exactly what Stan was up to."

"Stan wasn't the only thing that was hung from that beam, then, and as for the bench—oh my god," Kent gasps.

"We're lucky we didn't come down here and find Stan carved up like a Christmas Turkey."

"It's no wonder our killer hasn't slowed down; he's had a lot of unsticking to do from his mind. I noticed Stan has significant rope burns on his neck. Is that from struggling?" Kent says.

"Partially, but the burns appear to be too wide. The rope has to have been pulled up his neck multiple times to do that. Stan didn't just get strung up and it was over with. Our killer hung him several times. He's been pulled up, choked, and let down; that was his parting memory before he got pulled up and left to dangle. Stan's transgressions have finally caught up with him, and our killer is dealing out the payback."

"So, the killer knew him well enough to know his routine or stalked him long enough to learn it," Kent said.

"All we know for sure is that the killer lived in this neighbourhood at some time decades ago, long enough to cross paths with Stan and Harvey. For all we know, he could still be living here."

"There's a lot of kids who hated Stan as much as he hated them. How do we find him?" Kent says.

"Knowing he's from the neighbourhood is another piece of the puzzle, as you say – we just don't quite know where it fits yet."

"Well, Casey, that's what I was hoping for: going from impossible to next to impossible," Kent says.

"In my book, that's what I call progress," Casey said.

CHAPTER THIRTEEN

Brad buffed the remaining wax from the curvaceous roll of the front fender. Turning the cloth over, he walked it up over the roof and down to the end of the back fender. He polished his way across the slim back bumper, stopping to admire his reflection in the shine of the chrome. He walked forward on the opposite side, gliding the white cloth back over the roof, sliding down again along the fender to the circle of the headlight. He danced the cloth across the front split bumper, circled it one more time along the fender and took two steps back. He stood there admiring the gleam of his pride and joy, a candy apple red 1972 Chevy Camaro. There wasn't enough chrome on the car, not enough flash for his liking, so he had invested in a set of five spoke bright chrome rims. He had waxed and polished those rims until his fingers hurt, but how they shimmered now. He sprayed foam on a cloth and put the shine on the sidewalls of the oversized tires, careful not to get any film on the rims. Brad had the windows tinted, as he liked the look of the black hood-stripes running into dark glass, accenting the red of the car. He stepped back once again to admire the car like he had done a hundred times or more. The black mats had dried in the sun from their washing earlier in the day, and Brad collected them up, walking with them back into the garage. Opening the driver's door, he flipped the seat back forward, placing the small mat on the floor. He pushed the seat and leaned into the freshly vacuumed interior, positioning the mat just right in its place. The dash had been wiped clean with vinyl cleaner, and a dull glow also subtly glazed the vinyl-covered doors. Closing the door, he circled the car and swung the passenger door open in turn to place the other two mats. Leaning in, he suddenly felt a twinge in his lower backside. He put his left hand on the seat to steady his weight and drew in a deep breath. He had overdone it again, pampering his car pristine, and he slowly straightened up, rubbing his lower back. He was tired, but the long hours put into this weekend ritual were worth it. He went inside, jumped into the shower, towelled off and got dressed. The day was drawing on, and he thought about grabbing something along the way but then remembered there was leftover pizza in the fridge. Sixty seconds brought his dinner to the ready, and fifteen minutes later, he was sitting behind the wheel of his beloved Camaro. He turned the key, and the engine rumbled to life. He looked approvingly at himself in the rear-view mirror as the shiny red Camaro burpled out of the garage and down the driveway. Brad turned onto the street and flexed his foot just quick enough to chirp the tires into the calm of the evening.

Saturday night was cruise night, and a showcase of classic cars had already collected in the mall parking lot. A gathering of proud owners was milling about, and several looked over in approbation while Brad parked his car. Brad gave a quick rev of the engine before turning it off just to announce his arrival in case someone hadn't noticed. He stepped out of the car with cloth in hand and carefully checked the front end for any unwanted attached bugs. Seeing he was insect-free, Brad rubbed the cloth across the front of the hood anyway and then walked around the car, placing it in the trunk. Most of the Saturday night cruisers shared their car stories, told jokes, and would generally just reminisce about the good old days. Brad would listen in and laugh out loudly at the jokes. He was short on praise for any of the other cars and would divert the conversation regularly to his own car. He was mainly there for the attention and any praise that he could soak up from his fellow enthusiasts. His character hadn't changed from his high school days and little did he know, some of these guys jokingly referred to him as Brag Parker. He was quick to go over and engage with any curious onlooker who happened to stop by and check out his car.

The night had worn on, and the cruise night gathering had started to break up. Brad wandered back to his car and joined in the procession leaving the parking lot. He followed in the customary parade of cars down Main Street and relished in the notion that all eyes were on him. Near the end of the last block, he turned off Main Street and made his way home. It was a pleasant evening, so he took it slow with the windows down and his elbow jutting out into the night air passing by. He pulled into the plaza parking lot and slowly drove by the closed stores, watching while the reflection of the glowing Camaro mirrored back at him from the store windows. The chrome rims rotated through each panel of windows, dazzling out into the night as if floating his flaming red chariot on twin spirals of silver. With a short burst from the engine, he was back out on the street again, cruising up the avenue heading for home. Brad slowly turned off the street into his driveway. In one slight press of the accelerator, he was in front of the garage. He shifts into park and gets out of the idling car. One swift pull and the garage door willingly swings up. He reaches inside the door and flicks the light switch on, but the garage remains in darkness.

"Damn, I just replaced that bulb last week," Brad mutters to himself. The headlights close in on the front wall as Brad pulls into the garage. He shifts into park, leans, and stretches over to roll up the passenger window. The reach brings the twitch in his back again, and he pauses for a moment. He finishes winding up the window and draws himself back. The twitch turns into a sharp pain, and he constricts his breathing and freezes. He tries to right himself, but his arm wobbles off the center console. The console becomes an insurmountable wall that he can't seem to scale, and he has the sensation of floating and falling at the same time. His abdomen spans the console as his head comes to rest on his outstretched arm.

Danny opens the driver's door and then walks around the car, swinging the passenger door open. He circles back, stopping to pull the garage door down, then proceeds to pull Brad out of the driver's seat, dragging him around the car. He buckles him into the passenger seat and reopens the garage door. Danny backs the Camaro out while rolling the driver's side window up, stopping to close the garage door, and then reverses down the driveway into the street. He shifts the car into drive and slowly pulls away into the night.

Brad groggily opened his eyes and raised his head, bewildered, trying to get a sense of what was happening, trying to get an idea of where he was. The fog in his mind cleared and he came to the realization that he couldn't move and that his arms were bound to the arms of the chair he was sitting in. His legs were bound tight to the chair legs. He is startled by the figure that suddenly circles around in front of him.

"Where am I? What's going on here?" Brad blurts out. Where's my car?" he says, suddenly remembering the last place he was.

"I wouldn't be so concerned about your car right now, Brad; I would be more concerned about yourself, like you usually are."

"I know you," Brad says, trying to familiarize himself with the voice and face standing in front of him.

"You certainly do. Maybe I can bring back some memories to refresh yours." Danny retrieves a basketball from behind the chair and walks back in front of Brad while bouncing it on the floor. "Remember back in high school when you viciously made use of this ball? Remember how you felt threatened by someone else's ability when all they were trying to do was play the best they could? Remember all the pain and abuse you dealt out to someone who didn't deserve an ounce of it?" Danny says while still bouncing the ball off the floor.

"You're that Rosen guy, Danny Rosen."

"Yes, I'm the guy who suffered your abuse, you selfish son of a bitch; let's play the game your way." Danny bounces the ball and hurls it at Brad's face, causing Brad's head to snap backwards and bounce off the back of the chair.

"Fuck," Brad yelps out from his split lip as blood begins to trickle out his nose. "You're holding that against me from way back then? It was just some aggressive competition."

"Don't even try to trivialize it, you conceited bastard – you stopped at nothing to make yourself look good. Here's some more of your own medicine that I had to swallow," Danny says as he blasts the ball into Brad's face again.

Brad spits blood out on the floor as his eyes blacken. "I get it, okay? I get it."

"I don't think you do; you haven't changed one bit. Apology never ever crossed your mind, not even now. You always were too self-absorbed; you didn't have it in you to look beyond yourself. Remember getting run through the mill Brad? I do, this was my fond memory," Danny says as he delivers a punch across Brad's swollen face.

"I'm, I'm ......"

"Don't even try to pretend you're sorry; don't even pretend you have regrets for what you did. Your only regret is that I caught up with you. Your only regret is having to feel all the pain you dished out coming back at you. This sets the score straight for me, for all the times it was Brad wins, Danny loses. Danny isn't going to lose anymore."

"We're even then, okay?"

"Even? Not by a long shot. Besides all your dirty blows, you also tried to break my ankle. You succeeded in putting me out of any chance of being on the soccer team. It eliminated me from track and field as well, so you could have the spotlight." Danny takes a baseball bat from the corner of the wall and swings it into Brad's ankle. Brad screams out in pain as the crack of the bat shoots agony into his body.

"My God oh my God," Brad moans out.

"How's that for aggressive competition?" Danny says. "As if that wasn't bad enough, you weren't satisfied. You made a point of putting me out of commission for the rest of the year by cracking my ribs, too, you piece of shit." Danny draws the butt of the bat back and torpedoes it into the side of Brad's ribs.

"Please, my God," Brad says, writhing in pain.

"Now you know how my year felt, asshole. I call it a walk down memory pain. The physical pain is behind me; the mental pain is about to end shortly as well."

"What are you doing? This has got to stop."

"You had a chance to stop it a long time ago, Brad, but now it's too late; the damage has already been done. You used people as steppingstones all your life, and you're right, it has got to stop." Brad lets out a yell as Danny pokes a needle into his arm.

Brad opens his eyes to the darkness of the night. He hears the familiar deep rumble of the V8 engine and realizes he is no longer restrained to the hard oak chair. Instead, he is roped securely to the passenger seat of his car, and duct tape spans his face cheek to cheek. His split lip stings under the pressure of the tape, and the drying blood has crusted in his nose. He winces as he shifts his swollen ankle, and the slightest movement spikes the pain out from his ribs. He gently turns to see Danny at the wheel and then peers out the windshield into the uncertainty of his journey.

"It was a perfect night for cruise night, everyone must have been thrilled," Danny said. "You must have been in your glory, sitting there with this car all shined up like a new silver dollar."

Brad looks out the side window, then back to the front. "Good thing the weather cooperated and didn't spoil things for everyone. That's a shame in life when other people or things come up that spoil your opportunities for you. Sometimes you never get those opportunities back, do you Brad? Once they're gone, they're gone."

Danny turns onto a narrow-, paved street that descends down to the lake. As the street nears the water's edge, the pavement becomes broken and then turns into patches of sand and gravel. Danny stops the car and shifts into park. "I'm going to give you the opportunity that you suggested to me back in school, Brad. It looks like you are going to be the water-boy now. Danny puts the car in neutral, opens the door and gets out, releasing the emergency brake. He closes the door as the red Camaro slowly rolls away, picking up momentum, and then splashes into the lake. The headlights disappear, and then the car slowly submerges as the interior fills with rising water. The roof and back window sink under, and the trunk slips under the surface. Danny walks up the road, stops and looks back to see the small spoiler and four round beady red eyes of the taillights peeking out into the night.

"Not as deep as I expected there," Danny said to himself as he resumed walking and disappeared into the cloak of darkness.

CHAPTER FOURTEEN

Danny's first year was a horrendous year in high school with the treatment he was subjected to by Cindy, Glen and Brad. The bright spot in the year was that he hit it off well with his science teacher, Rob Dover. Danny did well in science and won Rob's respect quickly. Danny liked his sense of humour and took a liking to him immediately. Danny was more than happy to help out after class and would gladly volunteer to assist with any projects. Rob appreciated Danny's help and enthusiasm and near the end of the school year asked Danny if he wanted to come and help out for a few weekends with a building project he had started on. Rob was building a house on a lot he had purchased in town and needed an extra hand moving things around and cleaning up. He couldn't afford to pay much, but it would be cash, and Danny was more than happy to help. His cracked rib was just healing up after months of taking it easy, and he was anxious to start doing more active things now.

Danny couldn't wait for the weekends to arrive. Rob would pick him up around nine-thirty in the morning, and they would head over to Rob's place. The foundation and the floor had already been completed, and the wall framing was next to be started. Danny helped Rob carry lumber up onto the floor of the house. His ribs had mostly healed, but Danny could feel a ghost of discomfort as he picked the lumber up. In his spare time, Rob was helping a contractor he had hired by the name of Bill Byrd, who operated as BB construction. Bill pulled his pickup into the gravel driveway, and Rob gave Danny a nod and tilted his head in Bill's direction. Danny walked over to Bill's truck and introduced himself.

"I'm Danny, a friend of Rob's, just here helping out. Can I give you a hand?"

"So, you're the new help here, are you?" Bill said as he lowered the tailgate. "Sure, grab those two toolboxes; don't hurt yourself."

"No problem," Danny said as he slid the toolboxes off the truck. He could feel the objection in his ribs to the weight of the toolboxes, but he didn't dare transfer the feeling to an expression on his face. He hustled the toolboxes to the floor of the house and then scooted back over to the truck.

"Slow down there, kid," Bill said. "You might be all piss and vinegar starting out but save some for later; you have a whole day ahead of you yet." Danny walked slower up to the house on his next trip. Over the next several weekends, Danny watched the walls come together, helped raise them up, cleaned up around the area, shovelled gravel and dirt and tried to keep out of Bill's way when he wasn't needed. Bill was curt and short tempered, especially on the days that things weren't going smoothly, and Danny couldn't really tell sometimes if he was being a help or a hindrance when Rob had him helping Bill. For this reason, Danny was quite surprised when Bill made an offer to him.

"What are your plans for the summer?" Bill asked him.

"I really didn't have much planned."

"How would you like to come and work for me? Things will be hopping then, and I could use some extra help. I can pay you off the books, cash money, and nobody needs to know. I might not need you every day, maybe not even all day sometimes – we'll see how it goes – but it will be some extra cash in your pocket." Danny wasn't sure how to take Bill some of the time, but he figured after the school year he had just endured that he could ride out Bill's mood swings.

"Yeah, I could do that," Danny said, making up his mind. The last weekend Danny worked helping Rob, he was sweeping up inside when he overheard a heated discussion between Rob and Bill outside. Rob had been keeping pretty close track of material expenses and was questioning the cost of materials for the project. Danny didn't know if it got resolved and didn't ask any questions, as Rob still seemed to be in a bad mood when he came back into the house. Danny finished cleaning up; Rob squared up with him and took him home.

"Thanks for all your help, Danny. I really appreciated it."

"I was happy to do it, Mr. Dover. Thanks for asking me."

"Good luck with your new job over the summer. I'm sure we'll be crossing paths."

"Thanks, I'm sure we will."

"Listen, a word of advice: I've found out since working with Bill that besides his mood I think he is a little shifty. Not to alarm you, but watch your back, okay?"

"Okay, thanks." Danny got out of the car and gave a quick wave as Rob drove off.

School was out, and Danny was standing at the curb when Bill stopped by to pick him up. The door of the dusty truck creaked as he opened it, climbed in, and pulled it shut. The black dashboard displayed a permanent shadow of grey dust across it, and the black rubber floor mats were furrowed with sand. He put his insulated lunch bag on the seat and clicked his seat belt together.

"I'll have you finish off some insulation in this house I'm completing first off today," Bill said. "The drywaller will be coming later in the week."

"Sure," Danny said. It wasn't like he had any choice in the matter. They drove through town and then pulled into the gravel driveway of the new brick bungalow. Danny went inside, took a quick look around and then slit open a bag of insulation and started fitting it in between the wall studs.

"Here's a knife you can use when you need to cut some," Bill said as he brought the knife into the room. Danny worked most of the day finishing off the insulation, and he started stapling the vapour barrier up. The homeowners weren't around like Rob had been when he was assisting in the construction of his own house. Bill poked his head into the room where Danny was stapling.

"You can leave that for now and load the rest of the insulation into the truck to take back," Bill said. Danny lugged the cumbersome bags one by one down to the truck and loaded them in upright on their ends. He barely got the tailgate closed and wondered why there had been so much left over. It seemed like a lot of wasted time and energy to have brought that much extra in just to turn around and have to lug it all out again and return it. No matter: he was getting paid by the hour, whether he was installing it in the house or taking it back to the store.

Bill also seemed to be in a bit of a hurry to stop everything and get going. Bill came down to the truck, and they headed off to the building centre.

"That's a lot of left-over insulation," Danny said.

"Happens sometimes," Bill said gruffly. Danny could tell by the tone in his voice that he didn't want to discuss it any further. They pulled into the yard of the building centre and Danny unloaded the bales of insulation while Bill took care of the paperwork. Danny finished and sat in the truck waiting for Bill. Bill came back and climbed into the truck, and Danny noticed that he threw the credit receipt into the console instead of putting it into the customers folder as he drove out of the yard.

"About that insulation, you just keep your mouth shut about it, understand? If anyone asks you anything about materials, you don't know shit, comprende?" Danny squirmed in his seat. He didn't like the way Bill did business or the way he was being talked down to. Now he understood what Rob meant about Bill being shifty, and he felt like more of an accomplice working for him.

"I will tell them just to talk to you, Bill, if they have any questions."

"That's right, my business is none of your business. You're getting a real-world education here, kid, not some textbook crap." Danny didn't like being enrolled in Bill's academy of unethical business practices, but unfortunately, he was a captive student of it now. "That teacher friend of yours, Rob Dover, is a real pain in the ass to have working around the house. Has his nose stuck up my rear end questioning almost everything I do when he's there. I'm almost sorry that I took the job on, to tell you the truth."

"Rob's a pretty good guy," Danny said in Rob's defence. "Best teacher that I ever got along with."

"Well, I'll be plenty happy when I'm finished up with him."

"Maybe Rob doesn't understand your creative accounting system," Danny said jokingly. Bill tightened his face and slammed on the brakes. The tires squealed across the pavement as the truck shuddered to a stop. He reached over and grabbed Danny's shirt at the shoulder and twisted it in his fist.

"Don't you ever talk to me like that again," Bill yelled at Danny.

"I was just making a joke," Danny said in shock.

"Never joke about that again," Bill said, releasing Danny's shirt and stepping on the gas. Danny didn't say a word as he rubbed the spot where his shirt had dug into his neck.

Danny continued to work for Bill into the summer and closely guarded what he had to say to him. He reluctantly loaded lumber from a job site, knowing full well that the customer would never get the credit for it. Sometimes, material would go directly back to the lumberyard. Sometimes, it would go into Bill's shop where there would be cases of flooring and tile piled up. Fixtures and boxes of extra hardware would sit waiting until their absence was no longer in danger of being accounted for. Bill intimidated Danny to ensure his silence. He let him know that accidents could easily happen on the job site. Unexpected things could suddenly happen, and he explained these things as veiled threats, under the guise of promoting on-the-job safety.

The humid days of August slipped steadily by. It was a strained working environment all summer between Danny and Bill, at best. Danny didn't mind the work; he just wasn't particularly fond of working for Bill. Bill's coarse nature didn't endear him to anyone, and Danny just simply endured his threats and mistreatment on Bill's abrasive days, which were more often than not. He had begun looking forward to his science classes with Rob, as he knew if it happened to be another rocky year, those classes would be the one bright spot.

They packed up the tools after lunch where they had been working, as inspections had to be done before they could proceed any further. Danny hefted the toolboxes into the back of the pickup as the sun beat down on him from a cloudless mid-August sky. His shirt stuck to his back like glass to a glossy photograph, and a slight tug on the front of his t-shirt allowed a brief pull of air across his chest. He leaned forward on the seat of the truck to loosen the laces of his work boots and let the sweaty heat escape from his burning feet. A welcome breeze fanned in from the open windows as they drove over to Rob Dover's house. Bill never put the air conditioning on in the truck. He said for the temporary relief that you got from it that it would only make the heat feel that much worse when you had to go back out in it. Might as well get used to it. They had been over to work at Rob's house on previous occasions, and Danny had overheard several heated exchanges between Rob and Bill over missing materials and various building discrepancies over the summer.

Bill backed the pickup into the driveway and was already irritable from the heat and humidity. The house was nearing completion, and Danny was hoping that the two of them had come to some agreement on the issues they had been battling out over the summer. Danny waved to Rob and began carrying trim into the house from the back of the truck. Bill and Rob walked room to room discussing deficiencies that would need to be attended to. They walked into the kitchen as Danny stood by the sink running the tap to fill up his empty water bottle.

"Guess I'll be seeing you back in the classroom in a few weeks," Rob said to Danny.

"Yes, I've been thinking about that. I'm really looking forward to class again," Danny said.

"Try and enjoy the rest of your summer; it will go fast."

"Thanks, Mr. Dover, I plan to. I'm only working for one more week."

Rob and Bill went outside to examine the exterior of the house. From the open kitchen window, Danny could hear their voices escalate but could only catch bits and pieces of the conversations as they walked around the house. Danny could hear the words "fraud" and "lawsuit" and "lawyer" and realized things hadn't been worked out between them but had definitely gotten worse. He heard the sound of an aluminium ladder being extended out to the second story roof and then the muffled thunk of footsteps across the shingles. Danny walked out the door to make one last trip to the truck and heard the ladder rattling on the side of house as footsteps rapidly descended its rungs. He stopped to hear Bill's panicked voice on his phone.

"Send an ambulance! There's been an accident, 18 Palmer Street." Danny ran around to the side of the house to find Bill kneeling beside Rob's motionless body on the ground.

"What happened?" Danny yelled out. "He's not breathing; we have to help him."

"Take it easy, kid, we can't move him; I think his neck is broken."

"We can't just leave him."

"I hear the siren. The ambulance will be right here," Bill said. Danny ran to the corner of the house and waved frantically as the ambulance pulled up. The paramedics rushed up as the police pulled in beside the ambulance.

"We were up inspecting the roof, and we never should have gone up there in this heat," Bill explained to the police. "He started bending over for the ladder to come down and he must have passed out and just gone right over the edge. I was dizzy myself and just steps behind him, but he went over so fast there was nothing I could do."

"Where were you, son, when this happened?" the officer asked Danny.

"I was inside the house still," Danny said. The paramedic looked up at the officer and shook his head. The tears welled up in Danny's eyes and then spilled out down his cheeks as he watched the paramedics carry Rob to the ambulance and slide him in. Danny stood there in shock, watching the ambulance pull away. He couldn't believe that just moments before, he had been talking to Rob, and that now, he was gone. How could it be possible that he was out of his life forever now? How could it be real? But it was as real as the pain that knifed its way through his heart was.

"Come on, Danny, I'll take you home now," Bill said. Danny walked to the truck, got in and flattened his back against the seat. Numbness crept through his body until it completely filled him up. He no longer felt the heat or the humidity or the wind that blew past him. He only felt a hollowness in the pit of his stomach. A hollowness that pushed out from the inside like a twisting fist.

"I'm sorry about your teacher friend." Bill's words simply dissolved against his numbness as Danny turned his head and silently stared out the side window.

The last week Danny worked for Bill, he was dejected, merely going through the motions that filled the hours of his day. Rob's fall was deemed an unfortunate accident that no one was going to be held accountable for. Bill never brought the incident up, and Danny watched him as he worked, indifferent, unconcerned, as if nothing had happened, blowing it off as if it were a crooked nail, he could simply yank out of a board and continue on his day. Danny had a strong suspicion at first, but now he was certain. The more he watched Bill, the more the sickening feeling grew in his gut. It wasn't just a feeling anymore; it was screaming out "murderer." He wanted to accuse Bill right then and there. Danny thought, "*How could you be so black-hearted and just push someone off the roof? How could you do that to my friend? What kind of animal are you?*" Although Bill had the world fooled, he wanted to let Bill know that he hadn't fooled him. He wanted to unleash his outrage. He wanted to pound it into him with a hammer. Danny could prove nothing. He had only heard a few heated words. He had seen nothing. Bill had gotten away with murder, and there was nothing he could do about it. To Bill, it was a problem that he had simply taken care of and wouldn't give a second thought. To Danny, it was a nightmare he would have to live with every day. He would struggle and push himself through every day of this week, loathing this abomination of a human being. His anticipated last-week pleasures of August would now have their simple joys wrung dry from them and left shrivelled. The one bright spot of going back to Rob's class that he so looked forward to now been snatched away from him by Bill, ripped out like a weed from a garden. Danny was reminded of that crater Bill created within him every time he passed Rob Dover's picture in the hallway.

CHAPTER FIFTEEN

"Care for a donut?" Casey offered as Kent took a seat at the front of his desk.

"No, thank you; it's a little early for me, I'm good with my coffee," Kent said. "My sweet tooth doesn't wake up until after lunch."

"Mine never goes to sleep," Casey said as he takes a bite out of his chocolate glazed donut.

"So, the lab report confirmed what we already suspected. Same drug in his blood, same rope was used to tie him up as the other victims and strangulation from hanging was definitely the cause of death."

"No surprises there," Casey says. "The blood on Stan's workbench was definitely from various animals; looks like children weren't the only thing he wasn't fond of."

"Looks like our killer took exception to Stan's treatment of animals, maybe his and other neighbourhood animals disappeared by Stan's hand. Like a lot of other kids, he probably had several run-ins with him as well. Thank God missing children didn't end up down there."

"Our killer has certainly had his share of run-ins with-less-than-ideal model citizens," Casey said. "Stan's killer has dispensed his own medicine back to him; thank goodness he stopped at hanging him."

"That seems to be his victims' fate; he's making sure they die by the sword they lived by," Kent said. Casey puts his donut down, thumbs the napkin between his two fingers and picks up his phone.

"Casey here." He listens intently and then pockets his phone.

"Let me guess, it's someone calling with the feel-good story of the day," Kent says, taking her coffee over to the microwave.

"Not quite," Casey says.

"Someone is calling with your morning smile?"

"You're not even trying; your coffee is getting warmer than you are."

"I'm stumped, then," Kent says, taking her coffee out.

"How about they just winched a classic Camaro out of the lake this morning with a body tied to the passenger seat, and it's coming in right now as we speak."

"I wasn't even close," Kent says.

"You didn't even try," Casey says, finishing his donut and grabbing his coffee.

"This will be the eighth victim if it's our killer's handiwork," Kent said as their footsteps echoed down the stairs. Descending those stairs was a familiar journey that Casey had apprehensively travelled more than he would have liked. He knew each step that he took was bringing him closer to face the darkness of deeds devoid of humanity. He would swallow that apprehension and temper it to strengthen his resolve to make sense of a senseless world — his world.

"I'm willing to bet my last doughnut that it is our killer, and that's not a bet I make lightly," Casey says, opening the lower entry door.

"Nice car," Kent says. "He sure wasn't driving it himself."

"Two fishermen found it this morning while launching their boat. The spoiler was just jutting out of the water, and if it hadn't been, they would have hit it, they said," Casey said as he walked around to the passenger side of the car.

"Car must have gone into the lake last night; by how it looks, it hasn't been in there very long."

"There's our same rope and probably the same duct tape," Casey says. "I would say that our victim here is our killer's eighth victim without a doubt; I'm sure the forensics report will confirm that." Kent answers her phone and scribbles a note in her notepad.

"We have an address from the plate, Casey. Looks like this is a fellow by the name of Brad Parker; we can head over there now." Casey takes one more look into the car.

"Sure, not much more we can do here. We'll get the report when they're done here."

Casey pulls his car into Brad's driveway. "I didn't notice any parting keepsake memory left for the victim in the car," Casey said.

"Judging by the last several murder locations, this one looks like it was symbolic again, if the killer was trying to make a point. It either had to be the car or the water that symbolized something to the killer." Kent and Casey get out of the car and walk up to the house.

"Door is unlocked," Casey says as he pushes it open. Kent goes down to check the basement as Casey walks around the main floor looking into the bedrooms. They meet back in the kitchen, where the chairs are neatly pushed under the table.

"Everything seems to be neatly in its place. No sign of a struggle in here. If Parker got roughed up at all, it sure wasn't in here."

"It's just like all the other victims' houses: no sign of a crime unless they were murdered there like Harvey and Stan." They both walk outside, and Casey opens the garage door.

"It's probably cleaner in here than it is inside the house," Casey says, eyeing all the car care products neatly in line along the shelves.

"This is where he probably spent most of his time taking care of his baby," Kent said. Casey notices the light switch in the *on* position and walks over to flick it back off and on again.

"Burnt out bulb?" Kent says.

"Maybe." Casey walks over and gets a stepladder off the wall. He places it under the bulb and climbs up, taking a handkerchief out of his pocket. He turns the bulb, and it comes on. Then, he unscrews it from the socket.

"Think you'll find some fingerprints?"

"I've gotten lucky before," Casey said. "Maybe we'll get lucky here. When we get back, see what you can dig up in Parker's history. I'll do some snooping around, see if I can trace his whereabouts up to last night." Casey swings the garage door back down, and they head back to the car.

"Did you have a chance to read all of the report?" Casey asked Kent as he pulls his out to sit down.

"I did. Parker died from drowning, and he was likely alive until the end, just like all the other victims. The other pieces of evidence also match the other murders, so our killer definitely left his calling card. Any luck with the lightbulb?"

"The only prints on it were Parker's."

"That's too bad. I was hoping that would be our big break."

"It was worth a shot. I did some checking with the neighbours, and one of them said Parker usually goes to the weekly cruise night at the mall. I went up there the next cruise night and asked around. A couple of the guys said he was definitely there that night, but that's the last time anyone saw him. The neighbour said he heard him come back about nine-thirty he can hear the car rumble inside his house. He said he heard him go right back out but never heard him come back."

"Hard to come back when you're parked in the lake," Kent said. There was no physical damage to the car, but Parker had a split lip, contusions to his face and a broken nose as well. His ankle was badly swollen, and his ribs were cracked on his left side."

"The killer abducted him from his garage, it looks like," Kent said.

"He was waiting there for Parker to get home; he knew that he went to the cruise nights. He unscrewed the bulb and drugged him inside the dark garage and then drove off with him. He took him to another location and inflicted those injuries on him and then drove him to the lake and turned the Camaro into a red submarine with Parker still alive inside," Casey said.

"He's subjecting his victims to their own custom terror, payback for whatever grief they caused him years ago. Talk about holding a grudge," Kent says.

"Exactly; they aren't even being roughed up the same. The injuries are specific to each victim. He is making them relive whatever trauma he has endured in the past."

"Parker is the same age as Sweet and West, attended the same high school as well. No way of knowing if he had any association with them. The killer most likely did, and he definitely would have to be about the same age, then," Kent said.

"That makes all his victims approximately the same age as him or much older, both the males and females. He doesn't seem to be playing favourites, that's for sure."

"Let's just hope he hasn't made any more enemies in high school in his past," Kent says. "Or anywhere else, for that matter."

"No, it's a bad combination when you have a long memory about bad events and a short fuse, as in our killer's case," Casey says.

"He's either going to run out of old scores to settle, or we'll catch up to him first."

"His motives seem to have originated a long time ago. Unfortunately for us, he has about a twenty-year head start on us," Casey said.

CHAPTER SIXTEEN

Bill walks down to his truck and slides his toolboxes in. Things have slowed down for the season, and he still has enough work to keep himself busy. Somebody will call sooner or later with a repair to do or a basement to finish; they always do. He's been doing this long enough that he's not worried – he doesn't even think about it. He had a guy working for him for the summer, but they had words, and he quit on him. Fuck um. He didn't really need him anymore; and he was going to lay him off anyway. This house was almost done now. Bill had hung all the doors and had just finished up the trim work. He had over-ordered on the trim he needed, just like he always did. He could calculate what he needed for the whole job right down to the last foot, but he always padded it. He carried the leftover trim and put it in the back of his truck. The customer had already paid for it, but he would return it and put the refund right into his pocket. The customer had paid him good money for this job, but there was always room to make more. They wouldn't know any different anyway, so fuck um. They would whine and cry about some minor deficiencies, and he would eventually get back and attend to them. They would convince themselves that they got good value, but they paid a pretty penny for it – how they paid for it.

Bill climbed into his truck and started the engine. He rolled down the window and cleared his throat, spitting out onto the ground. He shifted into drive and headed over to the building supply store. He figured he had over two hundred dollars' worth of trim to return, a nice little profit, a bonus for his efforts. He got a cart and loaded the trim onto it and headed to the return desk. He watched as the clerk scanned the trim tags one by one and thought, boy, how he would like to bend that over.

"Two hundred and thirty-two eighty is your refund, sir," she said.

"Thanks," Bill said as he nodded. Then, he walked out the door.

Bill headed home tired. It was pushing on into the evening, as he had stayed late in the day to finish off the trim work. He turns into his yard and then backs his truck up to unload it into his shop. Walking around the truck, he pulls the tailgate down and pulls the portable air compressor back onto the tailgate. Turning around, he pulls the shop keys from his pocket and puts a key into the door lock, noticing that there is a note on the door. He opens the envelope, unfolds the paper, and reads the note aloud.

"*Sometimes, your past comes back to haunt you. When it does, it's time to pay the piper.* "What the fuck is this all about," Bill says as he suddenly feels a sharp jab behind him. He reactively turns, and he feels himself falling, being directed onto the tailgate, and it goes dark, darker than it is outside.

Bill wakes up confused, disoriented. He thinks he is sitting in his dining room chair, but, as his head clears, he realizes he is in his workshop. His arms and legs are bound to the arms and legs of the chair. He shifts his weight, but the chair doesn't budge, as the back of it has been screwed into his work bench. He turns his head, becoming aware that someone is in the shop behind him.

"Who's there?" Bill demands.

"I've been waiting for you to come to," Danny says as he walked around from behind the work bench.

"Who are you; why am I tied up?"

"I see you are still accumulating surplus material from your job sites, Bill."

"What's going on here?"

"That's a question I'm sure a lot of people who you've stolen from ask."

"Who are you to accuse me of that?"

"Who am I? I'm somebody who knows as well as anyone who worked for you what you've always been up to. I used to have to help you rip stuff off and haul it in here. I'm the kid who you grabbed by the shirt and threatened with the promise of consequences if I opened my mouth about your creative accounting, as I called it. You remember that, Bill?"

"You're the kid I hired one summer a long time ago, had that schoolteacher friend."

"Now you're starting to remember. I was afraid that you had fucked over so many people over the years that it was all just one big blur. How many people's trust did you betray? How many people did you threaten into silence who worked for you? I'll bet it was everyone. It made me feel sick to be an accomplice in stealing from all those good people. You didn't care about anything as long as you could feed your greed, not even human life."

"Your teacher friend had a bad accident."

"That's what you wanted everyone to think. You didn't think I heard the arguments and the accusations? He was going to take you to court and sue you, wasn't he? You saw the opportunity to silence him, and you took it, you coldblooded bastard. I should have told him what you were doing with your customers."

"It was ruled an accident."

Danny takes the nail gun and pops two nails into Bill's arm, and they stick into the arm of the chair. Bill screams out in pain as his blood drips from the arm of the chair and turns the sawdust on the floor crimson.

"That was an accident. You always warned me that accidents could easily happen on the job site if I didn't keep my mouth shut."

"I didn't kill him." Danny shoots two more nails into Bill's leg and one into his foot.

"Keep telling me that, you lying bastard, and I'll nail you up like a piece of trim." Danny takes the nail gun and holds it to Bill's shoulder.

"Okay, okay," Bill wails out. "I admit it, I pushed him off the roof. He wouldn't back off; he was going to take me to court."

"So, you just conveniently killed my friend."

"I couldn't risk it hurting my business starting out. Other customers would have heard about it."

"It was worth another person's life to you. Maybe you shouldn't have been stealing from your customers. You still are, you still haven't learned. Rob died for nothing."

"If you plan on killing me, it won't bring your friend back."

"Sadly, it won't, but it will bring me closure. You told me your business was none of my business, but it is now. It's my business to see to it that you won't be screwing anybody else now. It's my business to make things right for Rob and for me. Your business is my unfinished business."

"What are you going to do?" Bill said in agony, the nails impaling him like red-hot daggers.

"By rights, I should be hauling your miserable ass up and throwing it off the roof, but that would be cumbersome, too quick, and you need time to absorb the gravity of what you've done as you are faced with the same fate. I've been busy while you were passed out. If you look up and straight ahead of you near the ceiling, you'll notice there are two cement blocks suspended there. I tied them together and suspended them from a rope above your head, and they line up perfectly with — well, let's just say you'll see them coming. I tied another rope on the back of them and pulled them straight back, almost up to the ceiling. You'll notice that that rope goes over a makeshift handle on the wall and is tied off at the bottom. I've taken the liberty of borrowing your reciprocating saw and have used steel banding to secure it to the wall, so the rope runs over the saw blade. The saw is plugged into that timer, and the trigger on the saw is taped open to run. So, when the power comes on it's showtime, Bill. The blade cuts through the rope and the bricks will swing down like a hundred-pound wrecking ball. I don't think it will take your head off, but then I don't know; I've never done this before. That would be overkill – I just want you to end up the same way you had Rob end up."

"You're insane! Let me out."

"I was hoping you'd say I was innovative, but I understand. I'll just rope your chest and shoulders to the chair, so everything goes as planned." Danny ties Bill tight to the chair and duct tapes his mouth. Walking over to the wall, he sets the timer and plugs it in. "You've got twenty minutes to think about what you did to Rob and everyone else in your sorry life. That's more time than Rob had when you pushed him over the edge. Goodbye, Bill; I'll leave you with your thoughts now." Danny walks out of the shop and closes the door. He doesn't need to be there to watch the finality of his plan of justice in motion or the aftermath. He will be content in knowing that a balance has been restored in his life. Another correction that will help him move on from the ghosts haunting his past.

*   *   *   *   *   *   *

On his tenth birthday, Danny would get the surprise of his life. He hadn't asked for anything special, his parents acted like they didn't even remember it was his birthday. Other than shoes, socks, and underwear, everything else he got was hand-me-downs from his brother. He didn't even expect new, and when he did get something new, it was quite a surprise. He was riding his brother's old bike. The chain would come off at ran-dom, causing a painful landing on the crossbar; the nut holding the split seat was stripped, letting the seat rock back and forth if you sat down on it too hard, and the handle grips turned loosely and had to be shoved back onto the handlebars repeatedly. The paint was faded, and the fenders were starting to rust at the bottom; the back reflector was long gone. The rubber on the pedals had been shoed smooth, some of the spokes were bent and the tires only had a scribble of tread left on them. Still, Danny treated that bike with respect and rode it proudly through the neighbourhood.

After he polished off his favourite dinner of lasagne and garlic bread, the kitchen lights were flicked off, and a glowing birthday cake was placed in front of him. After *Happy Birthday* was sung to him and the cake was half devoured, he unwrapped a new shirt and a new baseball glove and ball, to his delight. His old glove had previously been his brother's and was well worn and slowly pulling apart. He slid his hand into the glove and tossed the ball firmly into its pocket with a resounding thunk.

"You better break that in outside," his dad said.

"Okay," Danny said as he slid off the chair.

"Don't you want to try your shirt on?" his mom said.

"Later."

Danny headed out the back door, the glove still glued to his hand. As the door closed behind him, he stopped dead in his tracks. There it was gleaming on its kickstand, a spanking new emerald bicycle. The handle grips were matching green, and the seat was green and white. It had a gold rectangular reflector on the front and a red one under the seat in the back. He marvelled at the deep black channel of the tread on the tires and couldn't imagine it ever wearing off like the old bike. Danny's mom and dad watched him out the back door, smiling. He stepped back from the bike, throwing the baseball repeatedly into his glove. He wanted to take it all in, sitting there motionless, shining in all its newness, letting it register that it was his bike, his present. He tossed the ball into the air and snapped it into his glove on its return. He ran into the house and hugged his parents.

"Thanks, mom, thanks, dad." He slipped the glove off into his dad's hand and pushed the back door open again. The kickstand sprang up with a snap of its new spring. Danny firmly pushed the pedals, the oil-soaked chain silently rounding the spinning sprocket faster and faster. The wind pushed past his beaming face as he rode faster than he had ever rode before, proud in his moment of glory, king of the road. Danny rode to the end of the block, then around the next one, circling back through the streets and back home again. He coasted into the driveway, lifting one leg over the seat, and finished coasting in with one foot on a pedal. He hopped off, walking the bike along the walkway. He was the master of his new machine now.

Danny sat on the seat of the school bus, looking out the window as the other kids boarded. Sometimes somebody would sit down beside him, and sometimes he would ride the bus all the way home with the seat to himself. On this particular day, a new face plopped down beside him that he hadn't noticed before.

"Hi. I'm Ben."

"I'm Danny," he said, sizing up this new acquaintance beside him.

"I've seen you riding around the neighbourhood. That's a nice bike you have."

"I got it for my birthday."

"We can go out riding some time if you like; I'll show you where I live." Ben lived about a block past Ian's old house, and it was a quick ride by bike. Ben lived with his dad, and Danny never saw his mom around when he first started going over to get together with him. He felt awkward asking about where she was and decided if Ben wasn't going to bring it up, then he wasn't either. They rode their bikes around the neighbourhood, often stopping at the park to play on the equipment or play catch with Danny's new baseball.

One afternoon on his way over to Ben's house, Danny stopped his bike at the stop sign and waited for a car to pass by. He glanced over to see Vince walking towards him on the sidewalk. As the car crossed the intersection, Danny lifted his foot off the ground and pushed down on the pedal with the other. As the bike rolled forward, he quickly put his other foot on the pedal and pushed down hard. He heard the footsteps running up behind him as his legs propelled the bike forward, and then he felt it slow as Vince's hand gripped the bottom of the seat.

"Slow down there, buddy; what's your big hurry?" Danny's bike tilted over, and he put his foot on the ground. "Nice bike. Where'd you steal that from?"

"I didn't steal it, I got it for my birthday."

"Looks pretty slick. I'm going to have to try it on for size," Vince says, grabbing the handlebar and pushing Danny off the bike.

"You're too big for it," Danny said.

"It feels pretty good. I just might take it for a little spin."

"I'm not supposed to lend it."

"I won't tell," Vince says as he peddles down the street.

"Come back with my bike," Danny yells, running after him. Vince stops the bike.

"If you want it, come and get it." Danny runs up to the bike, and Vince takes off again. Danny slows to a walk, and Vince stops the bike again. "What are you waiting for?" Danny runs towards his bike and Vince peddles it away, stopping a short distance away. Danny keeps running, and Vince peddles the bike through the tall grass and down towards the pond. Danny runs through the grass and then slows down, walking towards the bike out of breath.

"Give it back."

"If you want it, go and get it." Vince swings the bike around and throws it into the pond, laughing as he walks away. Danny wades into the pond just past his knees. He can see the white of the seat through the murky water and reaches down, lifting on the seat. He stands the bike up and pushes it out of the water and through the high grass and rides it home, his seething contempt for Vince burning through him. He knew one day he would get back at Vince for everything he had done. He didn't know how yet, but one day, Vince would be sorry for the rest of his life.

Danny and Ben rode together on the school bus most days. Danny had related to Ben about his run-ins with Vince, and Ben told Danny that he had also had his share of bullying from crossing paths with him. Danny would play over at Ben's house frequently, as Ben had a treehouse in his backyard. Ben's dad had a friend by the name of Art come over often on the weekends. They would help work on each other's cars or just hang out in the garage having a few beers. The more Art drank, the more intolerant he became towards Ben and Danny, yelling at them to quiet down or settle down if he thought they were getting too rambunctious.

"Lay off the kids," Ben's dad would say, but Art would only start at them again after a short time. Danny would reluctantly engage Art after he called them over to participate in one of his many abusive games. Art would hold out both his closed hands telling Danny to pick the one that held the surprise. No matter which one he picked, it was always empty. Art would quickly open his hand and slap Danny across the face, saying "surprise" and then having a good laugh. Sometimes the surprise would be a stomp on the foot or a quick punch in the stomach. When Ben's dad caught him and said he was being too rough with the kids, Art would reply, "You got to toughen these kids up." Art would grab either Ben or Danny at random inside the house and dangle them by their ankles over the railing of the stairs leading down to the landing, threatening to drop them. Once, he lost his grip on one of Danny's ankles, and Danny's head slammed into the wall before he could regain his grip and pull him back up. He had almost dropped him. Ben would pull his pant leg or shirt sleeve up to reveal to Danny the bruises from Art's attempts to toughen him up. One rainy morning while playing dodgeball in the basement, they knocked a toolbox over, spilling the tools onto the floor. Danny and Ben scrambled to pick them up as Art stomped down the stairs after hearing the crash. He flew into a rage, taking his belt off and swinging it wildly at them. Danny and Ben jumped and spun, trying to elude the flailing strap as it stung across their backs and their legs and the sides of their arms. Ben was able to make it to the stairs and clamber up them. Art turned standing between the stairs and Danny with the belt dangling from his raised hand. Danny stepped backward until his back hit the cold cement of the basement wall. Art stepped forward, raising his hand higher.

"That's enough, Art," Ben's dad yelled from the stairs. Art froze and lowered the belt as sanity slowly returned to his vacant eyes. Danny dashed for the stairs and up past Ben's dad. He and Ben ran outside and scurried up to the sanctuary of the tree fort like two squirrels evading a frenzied dog. They sat shaking as the rain pattered on the roof of the fort. Danny vowed he would never go in the house again when Art was in there.

When Danny came over to Ben's house, it would be strictly to play in the treehouse or the yard if Art was there. Ben's dad and Art were tinkering with Art's car in the driveway, and Ben's dad had to go and get a part they needed. Art worked under the hood while Danny and Ben threw the baseball to each other in the yard. Danny's glove was well broken in, and he easily grabbed Ben's pitches as they sailed towards him. Ben threw an extra hard toss, and Danny reached high over his head for it. He stood on his toes, and the ball bounced off the top of his mitt and then off the front fender of Art's car.

"Get over here, you two," Art yelled. They walked over to the side of the car.

"We're sorry," Danny and Ben said.

"Look at the dent you put in my fender now from your carelessness."

"We didn't mean to."

"You never mean to, but stuff always happens with you two, doesn't it?" Art grabs them by the arm and pulls them around to the back of the car, opening the trunk. "Now get in there and think about it," he says while forcing them in and shutting the lid. Danny and Ben lay frightened in the darkness of the cramped trunk.

"Let us out," Danny yells.

"He's never going to let us out," Ben says, and he begins to cry.

"He has to, don't cry. Let us out," Danny yells again as he bangs on the lid of the trunk. Ben and Danny take turns alternately yelling, the inside of the trunk getting increasingly hotter. Fifteen minutes go by, and it feels like hours have passed. They get claustrophobic as the hot air becomes difficult to breathe, as if it is thickening inside the trunk. Another ten minutes go by as they panic and bang and kick. Then they hear a car pull up and the slam of the car door. They furiously bang, and both scream out at the same time. There are voices just outside the trunk now.

"You put them in the trunk? What the hell is wrong with you, Art?"

"They needed to have a lesson scared into them."

"Dad, dad," Ben screams out. They hear keys rattling in the lock, and then blinding sunlight pours into the trunk. Ben and Danny pull themselves out of the trunk, their eyes wet with tears.

"See? They're okay," Art laughs. Danny lets out a yell and runs at Art, swinging and kicking as Art holds him off. "See? I made a fighter out of this one," Art says, smiling.

"Go on, boys, go get yourself a drink," Ben's dad says. They pick up their baseball gloves and go inside the house.

"Your dad's friend is a mean bastard," Danny says.

"I know," Ben said.

The next afternoon Danny rode over to Ben's house to call on him to go bike riding. He rode up the driveway and parked his bike along the wall of the house and then walked over to the side door and rang the doorbell. He had washed his bike that morning, and he stood there admiring the shine as he waited by the door. The next moment, Art was pulling into the driveway, and Danny rang the doorbell again. The back tire of Art's car bounced as it went abruptly over the curb. Art had been drinking before he came over, and he veered the car over as soon as he felt it hit the curb. The car drifted towards the house, and Danny pushed the door open and jumped inside as the car barely missed the door where he had been standing. Ben's dad came outside to see the car parked partly on the grass. He walked over and opened the door, helping Art out and into the house, holding one of his arms around his shoulder. Danny walked over to his bike with Ben and picked it up off the driveway. Art had hit it with his car and knocked it into the wall. The handlebar grip and seat were scraped, and the paint had been scraped along the back fender. Ben stared at the bike, then over at Danny.

"He should pay for that," Ben said. Danny said nothing, as he felt an anger seeping through his bones. He quietly got on his bike and rode down the driveway. Ben was right. Danny knew Art would pay for everything; one way or another, he would pay.

CHAPTER SEVENTEEN

"So, Parker's car never did give up any clues," Kent said.
"No, it was cleaner than his house and his garage. Nothing but water and sediment," Casey said as he grabbed his coat.

"I'm not surprised. Even when the murders are messier, like in Steven's or Harvey's case, there aren't many clues left behind other than the same rope and duct tape and the same drug used to knock them out."

"Yes, it's a shame Parker's car was full of water that washed away traces of anything that possibly could have been in there. He kept it immaculate, would have been a clean slate to work with." Kent opens the door to Casey's car and gets in.

"I just automatically grab my coat when your phone rings now," Kent said. "I know it's not going to be good news." Casey starts the car and pulls away from the curb.

"No, I'm afraid this is going to be victim number nine. Since these murders started, I seem to only get two kinds of calls: bad news and worse news."

"Are we headed to the killer's old neighbourhood?" Kent said.

"No, it's an older victim this time, doesn't live in that neighbourhood. A person by the name of Bill Byrd, ran BB construction. A courier found him this morning while making a delivery, saw his truck backed up to his shop. He knocked on the door thinking he was working inside, and when he didn't answer, he went inside with the package, found him tied up and called in the emergency."

"He found him dead?"

"He knew he was dead for sure. He apparently had his face rearranged from some cement blocks, a concrete makeover; it's not going to be pretty."

"These murder scenes rarely are," Kent said. "Sounds like it might be more of our killer's handiwork." Casey slows and turns into the yard, parking next to the shop.

"We'll know for sure when we go inside. He could have had a disgruntled customer or an ex-employee."

"Someone mad enough to kill him?"

"Our killer could have been one or the other or both. When it comes to money, you never know what people are capable of. Our victim Bill could have made a few enemies over the years in his construction business." Kent opens the shop door, and Casey follows in behind her. Kent momentarily stops, taking in the grisly scene before her. Casey takes a few steps past her and also stops to survey what's before him. The cement blocks dangle motionless from the ceiling a foot away from Bill's mangled face. The blood from his face runs down his neck, soaking the front of his shirt as his head limply hangs forward like a puppet thrown into a toy box. Casey follows the trailing rope back to the wall where the end of it is still looped over the wall handle.

"Look at this," Casey says. "It is our same killer. He's got the saw hooked up to the timer to delay the killing, just like he did when he electrocuted Harvey." He looks at the frayed rope ends and back over to the cement blocks. "Amazing: our killer has gone to a lot of trouble to stage this murder. He doesn't want to simply kill his victims; as usual, he is making some sort of a point to them to justify their execution."

"His trademark rope is here binding the victim, and I'm sure that that blood-soaked duct tape will be the same as on the other victims," Kent says. "The victim's neck is definitely broken – it's a wonder those blocks didn't take his head off."

"Our killer is very resourceful. His intention wasn't to decapitate Byrd. He could have fixed a blade to those blocks and accomplished that if he wanted to. Breaking his neck was enough. Bill knowing, he was going to have his neck broken was enough. He accomplished the punishment that provided whatever restitution he needed. He doesn't need or want to stick around to witness the murder. He is satisfied in knowing that his victims know they are getting what's coming to them for whatever has happened to him in his past."

"There is no parting memento left again," Kent said.

"Knowing those blocks were going to come smashing into him was all the memento that Bill needed. Something drastic has happened between Bill and our killer in the past for the debt to be settled this way. Bill has certainly paid for it with interest."

"I'd say so, by the looks of those nails fired into him," Kent said. "He could have turned him into a pin cushion."

"Just part of his process again, making the victim's punishment fit the crime, just like all the others."

"I don't know how far back they will go, but we can check his employment records for past employees who worked for him. Maybe the killer's name will be on that list. We won't know what name it is, but at least it will give us a list of possible suspects. If a name comes up in any future investigations that matches one on the list, then that will be our lucky day."

"You're implying that it won't stop with Bill here, and you expect there to be more murders," Casey said.

"My gut feeling is that the killer hasn't resolved all his past issues with everyone just yet; don't ask me why, but I don't think we've seen the last of his victims, I'm sorry to say."

"You're probably right. I don't want you to be right, but you probably are. We'll let forensics finish up in here; let's go take a look in the house. I imagine it will be just like Parker's place, not a thing disturbed except this dining room chair which will be missing from the table." Kent takes one last glance at Bill's ghastly crushed-in face and quickly turns away, afraid that it's one more image she won't be able to unstick from her mind.

CHAPTER EIGHTEEN

Danny stands behind the tree and watches as the morning sun filters through the forked branches. He raises his rifle and steadies its sight on the rough bark. The side of the tree is still damp from the morning dew. Peering down the barrel, he exhales and slowly squeezes the trigger. The sound of the rifle breaks the calm of the forest as a tranquilizer dart sticks into a startled bear that runs across the clearing, slows, and lists over onto the ground. Danny lowers the rifle and walks over to the bear. He clips a tag onto the bear's ear, checks his breathing and makes a notation in his notebook. He picks up his rifle and walks back to the road where his truck is parked. The distinctive emblem and bright yellow lettering of the conservation authority stand out boldly on the truck doors. He opens the door and puts the gun back in its case. This is the third bear he has tranquilized and tagged this week. He is familiar with this area and doesn't expect to find anymore to tag. Unscrewing the lid from his thermos, he pours a small slosh of coffee into a metal cup and bites into a granola bar. He watches as a red-tailed hawk glides overhead scanning the span between the road and the tree line and looking for a late morning breakfast. He pops the last bite of the bar into his mouth and takes the last swig from the cup. Spinning the lid back onto his thermos, he looks at his watch, walks back up through the trees and makes his way to the clearing. Danny watches as the bear clumsily rises from the ground and scampers off into the bush. The bear was about average size and he had measured out the potent cocktail perfectly. The sedative had worked quickly and had lasted for as long as he had needed.

Danny walks back to the truck and climbs behind the wheel. He is only about ten minutes away from his cabin and decides to stop in and check on things. He doesn't pass any other cars on the winding road, and he slows the truck as he turns onto the single-lane gravel driveway. The dust kicked up by the truck becomes airborne and settles on the leaves as Danny pulls up to his cabin. He closes the truck door and takes a walk around the cabin, picking up a few small fallen branches and throwing them into the fire pit. He hadn't changed much in the cabin all the years he owned it. The two bedrooms were adequate, and it still had the original woodstove which made the living room a warm and cozy place to be on a damp and rainy day. You could nestle yourself into the thick cushions on the couch and read the evening away. Danny spent many a night on the comfortable couch lulled to sleep by the crackling sound of the fire before he had made it to the end of a chapter. The pine plank flooring that ran through the entire cabin was solid, and he had replaced the old chrome-legged kitchen table with a solid pine table and chairs to match and make it feel more rustic. He had replaced the tired old front door with a new solid wood one and had re-shingled the roof.

Danny went back to the truck and retrieved his lunch tote and thermos. Unlocking the front door of the cabin, he went in and sat down at the kitchen table. His coffee steamed in the cup as he unwrapped a sandwich from the tote while settling into the comfort of the welcoming kitchen. He admired the scented candle center piece that Linda had crafted for the table. The scent of ginger peach, her favourite, was delicately fragrant in the air. The round glass holder was surrounded by small birch branch sections she had cut at various lengths that were bound tight on their ends to the glass by hemp rope surrounding them. It sat on a round birch slab he had cut evenly for her with his chop saw. They enjoyed their weekend getaways at the cabin when Linda wasn't covering weekend shifts at the hospital. Danny devoured his sandwich and chased it down with his coffee. Lunch just seemed to taste better somehow in the cabin than when he had to eat it in the truck. He packed up his tote and locked the door of the cabin, noticing that he had left a rake leaning against the wall. He stopped by the truck to put his tote and thermos inside and proceeded to take the rake to the large shed at the end of the driveway.

The shed was more of a small outbuilding and was the only major addition that he had added to the property. It was solidly built and well insulated, with one door and no windows. Danny unlocked the door and put the rake inside beside the round-nose shovel. There were a baseball bat and a basketball in the corner, and a chainsaw sat on the floor. The two heavy oak chairs sat against the far wall. It was a room that would allow for ample storage, or it could be turned into an excellent workshop. The room kept the firewood dry and the mice out. It was a room that stored the axe and the rope and the pail and the lawn chairs and still had plenty of space to spare. It was a room where nobody could hear you scream once someone closed the door. Danny locked the door and returned to the truck. It was a forty-minute drive from the cabin back to the conservation authority yard. Danny had done some field surveillance in the afternoon and returned to the yard. After finishing up some paperwork, he got into his car and drove home.

"You're home a little early," Linda said.

"Yeah, didn't have a ton of paperwork to finish up today. I tagged a bear up near the cabin today, went there to have my lunch."

"That's nice. Everything okay up there?"

"Yeah, everything looked good. Saw a couple of mice running around though."

"What? There better not be, you got to get rid of them."

"No, I'm just kidding," Danny laughed.

"Ugh, don't tell me that. I'm working next weekend; are you going up to the cabin? You usually do that when I'm working sometimes."

"We'll see; I haven't decided yet. I don't know how I'm doing it yet."

"Doing what?" Linda says as she takes two plates out of the cupboard.

"Sorry, did I say how? I don't know where my brain is at; I meant to say I don't know what I'm doing yet," Danny corrects himself as they sit down at the table.

"Well, I don't know what you do up there all weekend by yourself," Linda said.

"Putter around, clean up, read sometimes, put on a fire, probably chop some wood, you know, cabin stuff. I might just go up there overnight; we'll see."

"Well, whatever you decide, I'm just letting you know when I'm working. You asked me to let you know when I had to work the weekends."

"Yes. Thanks."

"Butter, please," Linda said.

"Huh?"

"The butter; could you pass the butter, please? Your mind seems to be preoccupied."

"Yeah, I guess I'm just a bit tired, and I have a few things on my mind."

"They released the name of the guy who was murdered. It was all over the news today," Linda said.

"I didn't hear."

"Some local contractor. I forget his name, but I remember them mentioning BB Construction."

"Probably some shady contractor who made a few enemies along the way. Somebody wasn't too happy with him."

"They didn't release any other details about the murder, but they are calling the murderer the red rope killer."

"Why's that?" Danny says.

"On account of he uses a braided rope that has a red fleck pattern running through it to tie his victims up with. It's been used on all of his victims."

"Any other details about the killer?" Danny said.

"No, they just said that the investigations were still pending. They probably don't want to release too much information in case the killer changes the clues they are following."

"He likely wouldn't anyway. He probably likes the way the rope works, and if it works well, why change it? I know I wouldn't if it were me," Danny said as he takes the plates to the counter and washes out his thermos.

"If it, were you! That's funny coming from the great animal saver," Linda said.

"Maybe if he keeps on using that same rope, they will catch him red-handed with it."

"Ha ha, very funny," Linda says as she smacks Danny with the oven mitt.

"Well, you did marry me for my sense of humour, didn't you?"

"I married you for your money and your funny," Linda says, wrapping her arms around him.

"Oh, yeah? How's that been working for you?"

"You're big on the funny; I'm still waiting for the money."

"Sorry to disappoint you, but you might be waiting a long time," Danny says, giving Linda a big squeeze.

"I don't mind the company I'm keeping while I'm waiting; I'll wait." Linda looked up into Danny's eyes, and they kissed. It was the same way she looked into his eyes on that warm spring afternoon when they had been dating. It was a beautiful afternoon, too beautiful not to be out walking through the park. They held hands, walking, laughing, and talking as the warmth of the sun ignited their spirits while they followed the winding walkway through the expansive park. Danny pulled Linda's hand, directing her off the walkway and over to the grassy knoll where they stood looking out over the sweeping expanse of the ravine. He pointed over to a beaver dam down below in the creek that cut its way through the ravine. He held her hand tight as they stepped down the steep slope towards the dam.

The new growth of green grass spiked skyward through the faded yellow carpet of straw lying bent to the ground. Halfway to the bottom of the slope, the momentum of their steps became a slide on the dead straw shafts, then a slip. They fell against each other, solidly bumping heads together, and slid the rest of the way down the slope.

"Are you okay?" Danny asked.

"That hurt," Linda said. Then, they both looked at each other sitting there rubbing their heads and fell backwards into the grassy slope laughing. Danny sat up and plucked a daisy from the grass beside him. He leaned over Linda and placed it in the flow of her silky dark hair. Linda looked into his eyes and reached up, softly caressing the hair on the back of his neck. They gazed into each other's eyes, falling, sliding into each other's souls faster than they had down the slippery straw slope. Linda knew right at that moment that her destiny was being fulfilled, that there could be no other. Danny drifted down, and their lips met in a passionate kiss, time standing still for the etching of this irreplaceable moment. Danny lifted his head and caressed the side of Linda's soft cheek.

"I love you," Danny whispered.

"I love you more," Linda whispered back. Danny smiled and stood, taking her hands, and pulling her up from the grass. They walked past the beaver dam and then found a spot where the slope wasn't as steep past the knoll, to walk back up. They made their way back to the walkway holding hands. They didn't speak as they walked through the park. Their hearts filled with each other's love as it seemed to flow through their fingertips, filling each other up. They didn't need to say a word, only to be at each other's sides. The magic of that spring afternoon walk bonded them closer together than they had ever been before. Whenever Linda looked deeply into Danny's eyes, it took her back. Back to that warm spring afternoon in the park when they were two passionate young lovers lost in the moment, lying in the soft grass. Back to the moment she knew he would be the one woven into her heart for eternity.

"We won't get these pots washed if we stand here all night like two starry-eyed lovers," Danny said.

"You sure know how to romance the moment," Linda said.

"I know I have that romantic touch. Are you washing or drying?"

"I just might let you do both," Linda said, picking up the towel.

"Listen, make sure you keep the doors locked when you're at home until they catch up with that rope killer or whatever they call him."

"I don't think he's just prowling the neighbourhoods looking for victims, do you?"

"Probably not, but it's better to be safe just in case."

"I never thought I would have to worry about something like this living here," Linda said.

"This could happen anywhere you live; you never know. I don't mean to worry you; it would just be a good habit to get into."

"I suppose you're right."

"Those are words I always like to hear," Danny said.

"Just this time. Don't let it go to your head." The doorbell rings, and Linda goes to the door to find her sister there. "Hi,

Connie. Oh my god, come in here." Connie walks in holding back tears with a split lip and a dark crescent under one eye. Linda brings her into the kitchen, and she sits down.

"What the hell?" Danny says.

"Gary got angry at me again. I had to leave so he could cool down. I'm sorry, I shouldn't have bothered you."

"No, it's okay, Connie. You did the right thing," Linda said, getting a cold cloth for Connie's eye.

"Son of a bitch," Danny says, getting his coat from the closet.

"No, Danny, please don't," Connie said. "He won't like that I came here; he'll get angry again."

"Don't go over there," Linda says, and he puts his coat back in the closet.

"Connie, he's done this to you several times before. He's not going to change," Linda said as she dabbled some salve on Connie's lip.

"I know, I told him maybe we shouldn't be together anymore, and he went into a rage."

"I never did like that guy," Danny said.

"You've been living with him and putting up with his abuse for almost two years now. You can't keep living like this, Connie."

"I thought that he might change, but I'm afraid he's getting worse. If I left him, I think he would come after me. Just mentioning it made him so angry."

"Call the police and have him charged with assault. That would give him something to think about," Danny said.

"I think he would kill me if I did that. I try to please him and not make him angry, but he gets so jealous for no reason. I can't reason with him when he gets that way."

"Nothing you do will be enough to please him. He is always going to try and control you. We've seen the bruises before, even when you tried to hide them or make excuses for them. I've seen women come into the hospital with injuries that they were afraid to tell the truth about how they got. I don't want you to be one of those women one day."

"I should have talked to him a long time ago when we first saw this happening," Danny said. "It shouldn't have gone on this long; you don't deserve this."

"He would have only got mad and blamed me. It would have only made things worse if you confronted him."

"You could stay here with us until you find a place of your own," Linda said.

"Thank you, sis, but I don't want to cause you guys any trouble. I don't know what will set Gary off lately or what he might do. Now that I know how he reacted, I will just tell him that I'm okay with everything until I can figure out what I am going to do."

"You're on borrowed time with that guy, Connie. Don't wait too long to make a decision," Danny said.

"Thanks, guys, I appreciate everything. Thanks for being here for me "," Connie says, getting up from the table.

"You make sure that you call if you need anything – anything at all," Linda said as Connie gave her a hug and walked out the door.

CHAPTER NINETEEN

Art would putter around in his garage on Saturdays, and today, he had decided he would clean up the lawn mower, change the spark plug and take the blade off for a good sharpening. He kept a small television on his workbench and had a bar fridge in there that he would reach into at about noon. He bolted the sharpened blade back onto the lawn mower, snapped the wire back on the spark plug and gave the rope a pull. The engine revved up and then sputtered to a stop.

"Damn thing," he cursed as he unscrewed the gas cap and peered into the gas tank to discover only a thin wash of gas across the bottom. He tipped the red jerrycan for a few seconds and then quickly pulled the yellow spout out as the gas pooled up to the neck of the tank. Capping the tank, he pulled on the cord, and the engine roared to life. With a sense of satisfaction, he stopped the engine and pushed the mower over to the wall.

He remembered a friend who he hung out with for years on Saturdays, tinkering with their cars over at his place while having a few beers, and he missed those days. The friend had moved long ago, so he now mainly hung around his own place on the weekends. He had another friend, Roy, who sometimes dropped by and hung out for a while with him. But today, he was on his own so far. His car didn't need to have anything in particular fixed on it, so he spent the afternoon vacuuming it out, checking the tire pressure and topping up his oil, coolant, washer fluid and anything else that had a cap on it, all while periodically stopping to watch the TV. Closing the hood of his car, he picked up his vacuum cleaner and carried it into the garage. He took another beer out of the bar fridge and sat down to watch a little more television. He preferred to watch in his garage at this time of day as the late afternoon sun angled in through the open door and drenched him in his chair.

Hearing footsteps coming up his driveway, he turned to see the young next-door neighbour, Tommy, approach.

"Is it okay if I get my ball out of your yard, Mr. Jenkins?"

"Sure, Tommy. Go right ahead." Tommy runs over onto the grass and picks his ball up.

"Thanks, Mr. Jenkins."

"Tommy, come on over here. I have a new trick to show you." Tommy walks to the edge of the driveway and apprehensively stops. "Come on in here; it's a good trick." Tommy stares into the garage but doesn't move an inch. "Come on, come on," Art says, raising his voice and motioning him in.

"I have to go," Tommy says, bolting down the driveway with his ball like a scared rabbit. He has gotten wise to Art's tricks and surprises. He has had the bruises to show from past experiences. Art glowers as he watches Tommy peel away. He looks at his watch and surmises that Roy won't be coming by this late in the day. He finishes off his beer, folds up the lawn chair and walks over to his work bench to put his tools away. Closing the garage door, he goes into the house and stands with the fridge door open, deciding what to do for supper.

There is nothing particularly exciting in there; most of the leftovers he has already cleaned up. The bits that remain are left over from leftovers, good for the garbage. He should have taken something out of the freezer to thaw before he got involved out in the garage. There is a package of hamburger he bought two days ago; he should use that up. He opens the cupboard, and there is half a package of spaghetti, which will work just fine. The two onions he is chopping up have already begun to sprout. The frying pan and pot of water on the stove are starting to heat up. The onion and hamburger sizzle when he mixes them into the frying pan, and his stomach grumbles approvingly at the rising aroma as he opens a large can of sauce to mix in. The yellow spaghetti churns and boils in the bubbling pot and transforms into a white avalanche of steaming pasta sliding into the strainer. Art spoons a layer of sauce over a portion of noodles and sets the plate on the table.

As he sits there and spins the spaghetti around his fork, he thinks back and contemplates how things might have been different if he hadn't drunk so much. Would his wife still have been around if he hadn't disappeared on the weekends so much sometimes for whole nights? Would she still be around if he could have controlled his temper and not flown into a rage so easily? He lifts the spaghetti to his mouth and then stabs into the plate to swirl his fork again. Would she have stayed if he hadn't been so demanding and needed to be so right all the time? Would she have given him one more chance if she thought he could possibly change? Was he even capable or willing to change?? Had he been that unkind and even abusive to her and others around him? He could have been reasonable, he could have listened, he could have tried, but he didn't. He finishes his last swirl of spaghetti and puts his plate in the sink.

Art changes his pants and shirt, leaves the house and gets into his car. He pulls out of the driveway and ends up at the same place that he has always gone most Saturday nights. Parking his car, Art walks up the steps, opens the door and walks into the legion. He says hello to the same familiar faces, and the bartender knows him by name as he serves him his beer. He whiles away the next couple of hours putting away a few pints, shooting the breeze and getting up to play a few games of darts. This has become his Saturday night tradition, and he has grown accustomed to the comfort and the familiarity of it all. He yawns, looking at his watch, and decides he is going to call it a night. He heads home. He's had enough to drink that he shouldn't be driving but takes the chance anyway and arrives home without incident. He had slowed down on his drinking at the legion after he had scared himself last year when he mounted the curb on the way home.

He makes his way into the house and hangs his jacket on the back of the kitchen chair. Running some water and detergent in the sink, he washes his plate, fork, and the dirty pots from the spaghetti. As he puts the pots in the drainer to dry, the power goes out in the kitchen. The light shines in from the hallway, and Art opens the basement door to turn the light on down below. He flicks the switch, and nothing happens.

"Damn it all to hell," Art says as he goes to the kitchen drawer and fishes around for a flashlight. He switches it on and steps down the stairs into the dark basement. The beam circles along the floor and searches up the wall, locating the grey metal box. Opening the electrical panel door, he finds the tripped breaker and switches it back on. The light from the kitchen comes on and reflects off the open basement door, but the basement remains dark. "What the fuck is going on?" he says. Then, he goes silent, hearing the scuff of a shoe across the basement floor close by and realizing he isn't alone. Art tenses up from the sharp jab behind him. Spin-ning around, he shines the flashlight, and the beam captures another figure standing there. Startled, he raises the flashlight and begins to strike down at the figure, but a hand catches his wrist as his arms and legs turn to rubber. He feels the sensa-tion of the hand lowering him to the floor, and then he feels and sees nothing.

Art squints his eyes into the light as he slowly opens them, and they begin to focus. He remembers the figure in the dark, and his immediate impulse is to stand, but he can't move. He feels the pressure of his feet being bound together, and his hands are tied uncomfortably behind him. A rope circles around his chest, keeping his shoulder blades planted against the back of the chair. He looks around the basement, not see-ing anyone, and then hears footsteps coming down the stairs. He cranes his neck to see someone coming down carrying one of his belts in his hand.

"Oh, good, Art – I was hoping you were awake."

"Who the hell are you, and why am I tied up? Get this rope off me."

"I just wanted to show you a couple of tricks, Art, you know, like you like to do with all the neighbourhood kids."

"You're out of your mind; untie me."

"I don't think I'm the one out of my mind. Let me jog yours. Remember you used to come over to my friend Ben's house to hang out with his dad and play cruel jokes on us for your own entertainment?"

"I remember Ben, you were his friend. It was just harmless fun."

"You abused us. You hurt and terrified us."

"That's just how you remember it."

"I remember this trick; pick a hand." Art sits silently, not wanting to engage Danny. "Pick a fucking hand, Art," Danny screams out.

"The left one," Art says, picking the hand without the belt. Danny takes the folded belt and backhands it across the side of Art's face, and Art gasps out in pain.

"Surprise," Danny says. "Now, take another guess." Art sits quietly, not answering.

"Too slow," Danny said and swings a punch into his stomach. "Now, wasn't that fun? Those were great games to play with a kid."

"I toughened you kids up," Art says, wheezing.

"What about the day you beat us with a strap in Ben's basement? How far were you going to go with toughening us up if Ben's dad hadn't come down and stopped you?" Danny swings the strap across his other cheek. "You locked us in the trunk of your car, and we almost suffocated in the heat. This is what your toughening up felt like." He thrashes the belt across Art's shoulders and legs as Art screams out. "Maybe I should thank you for traumatizing my youth. What about the day Ben showed up on the bus with a cast on his broken arm, you bloody bastard?" Was that a result of one of your so-called jokes or just part of your toughening-up process?" Danny swings the belt down, and it smacks across Art's ear and neck.

"Stop, stop. I'm sorry I hurt you, I'm sorry I hurt all those kids."

"It does have to stop, it has to stop right here, and I'm the one who has to put a stop to your abuse. You're not sorry, and don't try to bullshit me, you'll never stop. This is unfinished business that I should have taken care of a long time ago. How many other kids have you hurt since then and left emotionally scarred?? You probably have lost count; and you probably don't even know the damage you have caused." Danny ties a rope around the middle of the other rope binding Art's feet together.

"What are you doing to me?" Art cries out, panicked.

"It stops now, Art," Danny said as he throws the other end of the rope over the support beam above his head. He pulls on the rope, and it pulls Art's feet up off the floor. He ties the end of the rope to a steel jack post several feet away and walks over to the chair. He unties the rope around Art's chest.

"Let me go, you're crazy! Let me go."

"This is your retribution for me, for Ben and all the other kids left damaged in your wake." Danny hauls down hard on the rope, and Art gets pulled off the chair up into the air.

"Let me down," he yells as he swings upside down like a pendulum. Danny winds the rope around the jack post and ties it off.

"This reminds me of one of your favourite games to toughen me up. I was terrified while you dangled me upside down over the stairs and almost dropped me in the process. I've never forgotten that day or my head crashing into the wall. I guess you did toughen me up. You made it tough for me to think of anything else other than the one day I would see you pay for everything that you did."

"Let me down, you lunatic," Art screams. Danny pulls the duct tape over Art's mouth, silencing his screams.

"This won't be nearly as quick as traditional hanging," Danny said, sitting down in the chair. "It may take a few hours, or you could be hanging here all night; either way, it will give you plenty of time to think. You see, the human body wasn't designed to be upside down for very long. The weight of your liver and other organs and intestines will slowly crush the air out of your lungs, making it difficult for you to breathe. Think of us locked in the trunk of your car while you die of asphyxiation. Maybe the blood pooling in your brain will rupture a blood vessel and you will have a brain haemorrhage. In that case, think of us hanging over the stairs by our ankles. Your heart will receive more blood than it can handle pumping, and you may end up having heart failure. So, there are lots of possibilities and lots of time to understand why you are in the position you are in now."

Art hangs motionless from the end of the rope. He already feels the pressure behind his eyes and his heart pounding in his ears as the blood rushes to his head. The weight of his body pulls the rope tight around his ankles as he strains against the rope around his wrists in a futile attempt to wiggle some slack. Danny rises from the chair. Walking towards the stairs, he stops and turns.

"By the way, I never forgot what you did to my brand-new bike. You never even apologised for that," Danny said. Then, he proceeded up the basement stairs.

CHAPTER TWENTY

Danny pulls the throttle back as he slowly approaches the shoreline. He turns the wheel and corrects the drift of his approach, lining the boat up with the trailer. A slight rock of the throttle pushes the nose of the aluminium boat up onto the partially submerged bed of the trailer. The boat slides to a stop, and he cuts the engine and tilts it up. Danny hops off the deck, clips the winch strap to the bow ring and cranks the boat snug into the front trailer guide stop. He starts the truck and pulls the trailer out of the water, then gets out and clips on the back hold-down straps. Closing the truck door, he is on his way back to the conservation authority yard. It's a small lake that he patrols, and most of the fishermen and women or fisherpersons, as he is supposed to refer to them, are usually compliant with the regulations. Today he has caught two people fishing without licences and had written them each a two-hundred-dollar fine. He could have confiscated their equipment and even their boat but only warned them of that penalty. He told them that if they were caught again disregarding the regulations, he wouldn't be so lenient. It was enough to scare them out of taking chances on any future transgressions and show them he wasn't fooling around. Quite often, he would patrol the lake and not have to write up any fines. Earlier in the week, he had written a hunter a three-hundred-dollar fine for not wearing a safety vest. He wasn't out to spoil anyone's day, but he was really protecting people from each other and themselves.

Driving into the compound, he backs the trailer up to the chain-link fence and unhitches it from the truck. He enters the office and sits down at his desk to check his email and complete his paperwork for the day. Realizing he has forgotten his thermos; he walks back out to the truck to retrieve it. Sitting back down in his chair, he tips the thermos and pours out the last half cup of coffee. He sips from the cup as he clicks through the emails and hears a buzzing noise coming from the window. A bee has followed him in and is determinately bumping its frustration along the glass, making an earnest effort to escape. Danny rolls up a sheet of paper into a cone and funnels the bee off the glass. Covering the cone, he walks to the door and releases the bee outside. It seems like a small effort, but he knows most people react by impulsively killing the bee, not realizing that one bee pollinates five thousand flowers a day. He has noticed a decline in their numbers and knows that everyone counts now more than ever. Danny looks at his watch and twists the cup back on his thermos. He folds down the screen on the laptop and swipes the light switch off as he leaves the office.

Danny turns out of the yard and heads for home. With flowers on his mind, he stops by a small shop and picks up a fresh bouquet to surprise Linda with. He steers into the driveway and is instantly delighted when he opens the front door. The aroma of lasagne and garlic bread greets him and fills the entire house. Linda knew it was one of his favourite dishes and surprised him with it often enough that he never had to miss it for very long.

"For you, Mrs. Rosen," Danny said, presenting the bouquet.

"Oh, my, thank you. You must have known I was cooking your favourite."

"No, but I like you even more now"," Danny said, giving her a kiss.

"You better more than like me," Linda said.

"I loved you even before that day we bumped our heads together," Danny said, taking a small bloom from the bouquet and poking it into Linda's hair.

"It's sweet you remembered that day," Linda said as they sat down at the table.

"You didn't think I would forget, did you?"

"Not as long as I keep making you lasagne you won't."

"Even if you stopped, I guess I'd still keep you around."

"Gee, thanks. How did work go today?"

"Nothing too exciting; patrolled the lake today. Had to write two tickets for people fishing without a licence."

"You'd think they would know better," Linda said.

"Every once in a while, you get some who try to get away without following the rules. That's why I'm out there."

"How was your lasagne?"

"Delicious and gone, thank you," Danny said, cutting another small piece.

"My goodness, you practically inhaled it."

"I worked up an appetite today. I helped five thousand flowers get pollinated."

"What? That's crazy. What are you talking about?"

"Well, I had help. Actually, I helped a wayward bee out of my office today. Did you know that's how many flowers one bee can pollinate in a day? A hive of bees has to visit two million flowers to make a pound of honey. Pretty crazy, hey."

"It is, and that's a good biology lesson, Mr. Conservation Authority."

"You can thank a bee for those flowers I brought you today."

"I appreciate their hard work as long as they stay away from me."

"You don't bother them, they won't bother you," Danny says as he clears the kitchen table. Linda hears a knock on the door and goes to answer it. She opens the door to find Connie standing there, looking down with her hand over her face. She knows without asking what has happened and she puts her arm around her and brings her in.

"Connie, not again," Linda says as she draws her hand away from her face. Linda catches her breath as she sees Connie's tears trickling into the blood that has run out from her nose. The purpling bruise on her cheek is swelling into her blackening eye as Linda directs her into the washroom. Linda runs water into the sink and dabs Connie's face with the wet cloth, realizing the disparity of how she was getting flowers while her sister was getting beaten. Connie holds the cloth over her eye and cheek as Linda pulls the kitchen chair out for her. Danny turns from the sink and stands transfixed as Linda pulls Connie's sleeves up, exposing the bruises she expects to see, and pulls them back down.

"That Goddamn bastard tried to choke you," Danny said, noticing the bruise marks on her neck.

"This has progressed far beyond abuse," Linda said with her hand Connie's shoulder. "This is violent assault."

"Gary showed up staggering – he had already been drinking. He opened a bottle and started drinking more, and I asked him to please stop. He started cursing me, and I pleaded with him to put the bottle away, I was so afraid. He grabbed my arms and shook me, screaming like he was out of his mind. He hit me across my face, and I fell on the floor," Connie said, beginning to sob. "He tried to kick me but lost his balance and fell against the counter. I ran into the bedroom and locked the door, but he kicked it open. He pushed me on the bed and started choking me."

"My God, Connie, he could have killed you," Linda said.

"He was trying to kill me. I brought my knee up into his groin, and he fell over on his side, yelling, 'You bitch, I'll kill you.' I ran out of the room and left the house and came over here, I was terrified. I didn't see him follow me out, I don't know, he might have passed out." Connie's ordeal was striking a raw nerve in Danny. The old memories he had resolved to put to rest were clawing their way back into his subconscious now. The beatings, the abuse, the outrage. Her pain was becoming his pain all over again.

"Connie, he's too volatile, too dangerous to live with; you have to get a restraining order against him," Linda said. "It's just not safe."

"That won't stop him. He won't stay away. He will always come after me. There's nowhere I can go that he won't find me. I can't live like this anymore," Connie said, weeping.

"She's right, Linda, he will never leave her alone," Danny said as he goes to the closet and puts his coat on.

"Where are you going?" Linda said.

"Where do you think I'm going,"?" Danny said, zipping up his coat.

"You can't go over there; you don't know what you're going to run into."

"That's pretty much my world every day. I'm going to see what's going on."

"Danny, don't." He closes the door behind him as he leaves.

It's a relatively short drive to Connie's house, maybe fifteen minutes if you aren't in a big hurry. It's a calm, peaceful night without much traffic to speak of. It gave you time to think, but Danny already knew what he was going to do. Gary, like so many other people in his life, left him with no other option but to do what he had to do. Even the people he had to deal with in his day-to-day job. If they fucked up, they would have to pay the penalty. If people could just be more like bees, the world would be a whole lot nicer of a place. They could just conduct themselves in a positive way so they wouldn't bother anybody, and nobody would bother them. Gary could have conducted himself better, but he fucked up big time. Sooner or later, he was going to kill Connie, and, like Danny had warned her, she was on borrowed time, and that time was running out fast.

Danny parked on the street about half a block from Connie's house. He walked up the sidewalk and then approached the door of the house, putting on the skin-tight gloves. Opening the door, he saw that the light was still on in the kitchen and the whisky bottle was sitting two thirds full on the kitchen table. Danny walked over to the wide-open bedroom door and noticed the split doorframe. He looked in and saw that Gary was passed out sideways on the bed. He pulled him around to get his head slightly raised up on the pillow. Gary stirred and, without opening his eyes, slurred some incoherent profanities. Danny went to the kitchen and brought back the whisky bottle. He tilted Gary's head slightly and stuck the neck of the bottle into his throat and tipped it up. The whisky gurgled down Gary's throat, and Danny pulled it back when he began to cough and sputter. He pushed it back in, holding Gary's head, and emptied most of the contents into his stomach.

"That's right. Drink it all up; it will be the last drink you ever have; it will be the last time you ever beat Connie again," Danny said, laying the bottle on the bed beside Gary's hand. He waited and watched as Gary's skin turned pale and his breathing started to become irregular. Stepping out the door and walking briskly to his car, Danny got in and drove home. Shutting off the engine in his driveway, he pulled off the gloves and then went inside the house.

"Thank goodness you're back; we were worried about you," Linda said.

"No need to worry. He was passed out when I got there. He hit that bottle pretty hard."

"He was in a drunken rage. I'm terrified of that bastard," Connie said.

"We were talking while you were gone, and we decided it's not safe for Connie to go back there even if we get a restraining order. She fears for her life. She can stay here for now."

"You won't have to do that, Connie. I've got some bad news, or maybe it isn't such bad news. Gary wasn't breathing when I went over there; you won't have to worry about him anymore."

"Oh my God," Connie said.

"Alcohol poisoning; he drank himself to death."

"My God, what am I going to do? Did you call someone?"

"Calm down; this is what you have to do. I can't be involved with this it will look suspicious, too many questions. You understand? You're going to drive back over there and call 911. You tell them what happened, the same thing you told us. You tell the police you came over here in a panic, we'll tell them the same thing if they come and ask. You don't mention a word about me being over there, you understand? You tell them we talked you into staying here for a while. You went back there to get some of your clothes and things, knowing he'd be sleeping it off, and you found him not breathing. They'll see what he did to you, they won't have any questions. I know this is a lot, but you don't have to fear for your safety anymore. You have your life back now. You understand?"

"Danny is right, Connie. This is a terrible thing, but it is a blessing in disguise. Go and make the call, and if you want to come back and spend the night here, we'll be here for you."

"Thanks, I don't know what I'd do without you guys." Linda walks her out to her car.

"Call me and let me know," she said.

Linda comes back into the kitchen and makes a cup of tea to calm herself. She sits at the table with her hands around the warm cup, watching Danny as he hangs his jacket in the closet. She bites her bottom lip and then brings the cup up to take a sip.

"Gary was still breathing when you went to the house, wasn't he?" Danny walks back into the kitchen and puts the dishes in the cupboard. "Danny?" He closes the cupboard door, turns to face Linda, and puts his hands on the counter on each side of him.

"As I go through my day, I make sure everyone is conducting themselves the way they should, and I keep them as safe as I can. I protect all the wildlife and help them along whenever I can. I do my job to the best of my ability, but sometimes, despite my best efforts, I come upon situations with wildlife, where I can't help. They have gotten themselves into trouble or the circumstances are such that I can't save them. The solution isn't a pleasant one, but it is the only solution that will put an end to the difficult circumstances they are in. I am faced with the difficult decision that I have to make, but it is the only option that is going to put an end to their situation becoming worse. I have no choice but to execute that decision and find solace in knowing it was the only resolution. Those are the days I don't tell you about."

"Danny, oh my God."

"Connie was in a bad situation she had no way out of. Gary was in a downward spiral and would have taken her with him on his way out. His end was inevitable. I just tipped the bottle and helped to speed it up before Connie became one of his casualties."

Linda gets up from the table and hugs Danny, putting her head on his shoulder. "Thank you for saving my sister's life."

CHAPTER TWENTY-ONE

"Thanks for the coffee," Kent said. "Are those donuts supposed to be lunch or dessert?"

"I had a late breakfast," Casey said. "I think they are going to be both. I picked up some apple fritters this time, figured they would be healthier than the double chocolate."

"I don't think anything classified as a donut can be considered healthy. I don't even think that can even be considered as healthy fruit."

"I'm just going to pretend it's better for me, then," Casey said, taking a bite into the fritter. "Care for one?" he said, pushing the bag closer to Kent. Kent pensively peeks into the bag as if there should be a warning label attached to each one.

"Oh, what the hell," she said, reaching into the bag. "It's close enough to noon."

"You say that like you're taking your first drink of the day."

"It's almost the same thing to me."

"I'm looking at this autopsy report on Bill Byrd, and it says he died from blunt trauma to the head. His skull was shattered, his neck broken, and a massive haemorrhage formed in his brain; pick your favourite."

"I was going to try and eat this donut; thanks for the memory," Kent said.

"Sorry, he might as well have tried to headbutt a wrecking ball."

"He had the same drug in him as all the others, but he was alive until he took the hit," Kent said, finally biting into her fritter and taking a swig of coffee.

"How did you make out with gathering up names for previous employees that worked for him?" Casey asked.

"I have a list of names, but it only goes back so far, and it's not exhaustive. I found out he hired part-time workers and paid them cash, so there are no records of them working for him."

"Well, we can work with what we have. If any names come up in the future, at least we have something to go by."

"That was a pretty elaborate set-up for Byrd's delayed execution. Someone would need to have construction experience or be pretty handy to set that up accurately."

"I know if it were me, I would have missed by a mile," Casey said. "Somebody knew what they were doing. They either worked for him, or it was a competitor getting him out of the way, or else it was a very disgruntled customer or a business partner he screwed; somebody had a reason to have it in for him big time."

"There didn't seem to be any indication of him having an ongoing feud with any of his competition; he didn't score any big contracts that anyone had sour grapes over. He never had a business partner who he could double cross. He had always been on his own, and he didn't owe anyone a debt that he reneged on, as far as we know. He did have some minor lawsuits that were settled, so no one would have come after him from those for revenge, so that rules everything out except the disgruntled employee angle. I did find dating way back in the records that the owner of a house he was finishing died in an accident on site.

"Byrd charged with anything?"

"No, the owner fell from the roof, and it was ruled as accidental."

"A bereaved family member could have held him accountable and come after him, but that wouldn't make any sense toward connecting them to the other murders. No witnesses, I suppose."

"No, I checked the employee records, and they don't go back that far, and, again, it could have been a cash worker if he even had one. The owner had Byrd paid up on the house, so why would he want to kill him anyway? Byrd would have just taken him to court if he didn't pay him. Byrd wasn't under suspicion; the case was closed.

"Somebody worked for him who had it in for him then; somebody got screwed," Casey said. Kent hears Casey's phone ring and finishes her donut. She'd be surprised if the call was anything different than what she expects it to be. She walks over and microwaves her coffee as Casey writes an address down and then puts the phone in his pocket.

"If it weren't for bad news, I wouldn't get any news at all," Casey said.

"Let me guess we are about to meet victim number ten."

"I'm afraid you were right when you suspected our killer hadn't evened all his scores."

"I was trying to stay positive, not to grab my coat when your phone rang, but I guess it was just wishful thinking," Kent said as she walks over with her coffee to pick up her coat.

Casey starts his car as Kent fastens her seatbelt and picks her cup up from the cup holder. He shifts into drive and checks his mirror as he signals his way into traffic.

"Are we headed to the killer's old neighbourhood this time?" Kent said.

"No. Actually, to the other side of town."

"Our killer certainly likes to get around."

"It's a male victim again, by the name of Art Jenkins," Casey says, merging onto the expressway. "They found him hanging in the basement of his house."

"Our killer isn't being as creative this time. He's using one of his previous methods."

"Only, this time, the victim has been strung up by his feet, hung upside down."

"Okay, I take it back. I'm forgetting that he's making them suffer for their own specific past transgressions."

"Now you're getting with the program. You're starting to think like the killer; that's good," Casey said.

"Wonderful. Are you trying to make me feel better or worse?"

"If you think like him, you can understand him; if you can understand him, you can profile him; if you can profile him, you can identify him; and if you can identify him, you can catch him, so keep thinking like him."

"So, who found Art upside down? Did he live on his own?"

"He was on his own. Forensics is over there now. Apparently, he's been hanging there about thirty-six hours, they say. Died sometime Saturday night."

"Another Saturday night killing," Kent said.

"Seems so. He frequents the legion Saturday nights usually that's where he was last seen. Looks like our killer was waiting for him when he got home. Strung him upside down, and he likely died of asphyxiation or a heart attack sometime through the night."

"He died a slow death. Gave him time to think about what he did to our killer. No need for a timer this time," Kent said.

"That's right," Casey said, exiting onto the ramp. "A buddy of his by the name of Roy usually stops by on Saturdays, sometimes goes to the legion with him. Roy was out of town for the weekend. He stopped by this morning to visit Art and Art was in no position to answer the door, of course. Seeing Art's car there, he went into the house to check on him and found him in the basement." Casey pulls up to the curb in front of Art's house, and they exit the car and proceed inside.

"Not a thing disturbed in here to indicate any struggle went on, just like all the other victims' homes," Kent said as they proceed through the kitchen on their way to the basement. The odour of Art's decomposing body rises to assault their noses as they descend the basement stairs. They take pause at the foot of the stairs, observing the disturbing sight of Art's suspended corpse. Bodily fluids have foamed out through his nose, leaked across his face, and dripped from his forehead, pooling onto the floor. Kent walks to the left, Casey to the right of the suspended corpse, taking in the unsettling scene before them.

"He's been tied off to the post the same as Stevens was, and there's the trademark red-flecked rope on his wrists and ankles. It's our same killer for sure at work here," Casey observed.

"If they've taken the pictures that they need, let's get him down," Kent said. Casey unties the rope, lowering Art to the floor.

"Looks like there was some reckoning here that Art was subjected to," Casey said, noticing the welt marks remaining on Art's face and neck and the belt laying on the floor. "He no doubt had him tied to that chair before he pulled him up to the beam and gave him a thrashing. Like his other victims, he's not as much interested in torturing them as he is in trying to make them relive what they exposed him to in the past. He is working through his own personal hell, it seems."

"He's lured him down here by cutting the power," Kent said, noticing the panel door open and the flashlight laying on the floor. "He knows his victims' routines, knew that Art would be at the legion Saturday night, he was waiting down here for him to get back."

"We may never know what his relationship was with Art, but it wasn't a healthy one – that's for sure. It doesn't look like Art was up to anything underhanded down here. You can check out the rest of the house; I'm going to take a look out in the garage."

Casey walks up the stairs and goes outside and pulls the garage door up. It immediately becomes obvious to him that he wouldn't be finding any signs of foul play in the neatly organized garage. He opens the door of the well-stocked bar fridge for a look and does the same with the cupboards above the workbench. Hearing a shuffle behind him, he turns to see a young boy standing outside the garage door.

"Can I get my ball out of the yard, mister?" Casey walks to the garage door and looks into the backyard.

"Sure, son, go ahead." Tommy runs to retrieve his ball and comes back to the garage.

"Where's Mr. Jenkins?" he asks.

"Mr. Jenkins had an accident, son. What's your name?"

"My name's Tommy. Are you the police?"

"Yes, I am, Tommy. Were you friends with Mr. Jenkins?"

"I was afraid of him."

"Why was that son? Was he mean to you?"

"He played mean games I didn't like."

"What kind of games, Tommy?"

"Games that tricked me and hurt me." Tommy's mom called him, and he twisted around to the sound of her voice.

"Bye, I gotta go," he said as he took off down the driveway. Casey closed the garage door and went back into the house, meeting Kent in the kitchen.

"Did you come up with anything in the house?"

"Nothing out of the ordinary in here," Kent said. "There were some old wedding pictures; looks like he had a wife a long time ago. How about you?"

"Same in the garage; no discoveries in there. I did have an interesting conversation with a little fellow named Tommy from next door. Seems like Art wasn't his most favourite person in the world."

"He didn't molest him, did he?"

"No. Looks like Art tended to be somewhat abusive with the kids. Played games and tricks on them, and they ended up getting hurt. Tommy was afraid of him, actually."

"I wonder what the circumstance was for him to be hung upside down and left to die," Kent said.

"Art did something to traumatize the killer long ago."

"He must have gone too far with the murderer in his youth; maybe he had a real mean streak in him. Of course, the method of execution is representative of what the killer endured long ago. Our slayer must have had one hell of a childhood growing up."

"We're making progress, Kent; now you are beginning to understand our killer."

CHAPTER TWENTY-TWO

Danny drove the four-wheel-drive along the countryside road, small round stones churning and jumping up from behind the spinning tires biting into the gravel road. Stopping at the bend in the road, he walked behind the truck and opened the tailgate. He pulled the lifelike deer decoy from the bed of the truck and carried it across a wide ditch to the edge of the tree line. Planting it on the ground under a low tree branch, he angled it to face the road, appearing like it was coming out of the woods. Getting back into the truck, he reversed down the road and veered off, backing the pick-up across the ditch and up out of sight into the trees. He had parked further down the road the day before and had waited all afternoon without any luck. There had been several complaints about unsafe hunting in the area, and he wanted to try and resolve it before someone got hurt. He spun his cup off the thermos and filled it full to sit back for what could be a long wait.

As he looked down the road at the convincing decoy, a recurring troubling memory echoed from the past, refusing to stay buried like so many others, before he had put them to rest permanently. The sequence of events had traumatized him, given him nightmares, and shaken the innocence of his childhood. He was only four years old, but the experience stayed with him, spun into the corner of his mind like a cocoon. The details were as fresh as the day they had happened, gripping his mind like a clenched eagle claw.

*   *   *   *   *   *   *

It was his parents' tenth anniversary, and they had plans for a celebration dinner. His brother Eric had gone over to one of his friends' houses for a sleepover. Danny looked forward to his babysitter Susan coming over; although she had only been there a few times, she had played games and entertained him the whole night every time she had come. They played snakes and ladders and hide and go seek, and she showed him new card games and magic tricks. Susan had gotten a part time job and was called into work at the last minute. She had phoned Danny's parents and told them that she had made arrangements with another girl who babysat and who had agreed to take her place. His parents were thrilled that their plans hadn't been ruined. This new girl, named Gail Evans, was polite and respectful when she met his parents, smiling and waving at him while she talked to them. But as soon as his parents left, the smiles disappeared. As young as he was, Danny knew this person Gail was nothing like Susan. She half-warmed his dinner and threw the plate down in front of him, not saying a word. Danny took a mouthful and poked through the food.

"Are you going to eat that or not? I'm not standing here all night," Gail snapped at him.

"The potatoes are still cold," Danny said.

"Eat it or don't eat it, I don't give a shit," she said, storming off into the living room. He sat there alone in the kitchen taking a few more bites from the plate. Susan never left him alone. He pushed the food around in his plate and slid off the seat of the chair. He walked into the living room and stood beside the couch. Gail was slouched back on the couch with her feet up on the coffee table. Susan never did that.

"Why are you just standing there, what do you want?

"Can we play a game?" Danny asked.

"Can't you see I'm on the phone, you little pain in the ass? Here, watch the TV," Gail said, pressing the remote's power button and throwing it on the couch. Danny picked up the remote and clicked through the channels. Susan never talked to him like that; no one had ever talked to him like that. There was nothing on the television for him, and he turned it off. He reached under the coffee table and took his snakes and ladders game out. He turned to Gail holding the box in his hands.

"We could play this game," Danny said.

"I don't play fucking kids' games," Gail yelled as she grabbed the box out of his hands and swung it, hitting him across the face. Danny started to cry, and she stood up, seizing his arm.

"You're going into the tub," she said, pulling him down the hallway.

"I don't need to have a bath," Danny wailed.

"I don't care," Gail said, pushing him into the bathroom, turning on the water and yanking off his shirt. She pulled down his pants and underwear and dropped him into the tub. The water was barely lukewarm as Danny sat wiping his eyes.

"Now, don't you come out of there until I say so, or else," Gail threatened as she slammed the door shut. Danny sat there as tears began rolling down his cheeks again. He wanted his mom, he wanted Susan to come back, he wanted someone to hold him wrapped up warm in a towel and tell him everything was going to be alright. He sat there shaking as the water turned cold in the tub. His arm hurt from Gail pulling him so hard. Danny sat there listening as he heard voices coming from the living room now. There was talking and laughing, a man's voice he didn't know speaking to Gail. Danny's teeth began to chatter, and he couldn't stand it any longer. He crawled out of the freezing tub and wrapped a towel around his shoulders, holding it fist-closed at his chest. Opening the bathroom door, he walked down the hallway into the living room. There were muffled voices, but he couldn't see anyone as he approached the back of the couch. He walked around to the front and saw Gail laying on the couch with her shirt unbuttoned and her skirt pulled up to her waist. A boyfriend was laying on top of her with his pants pulled down to his knees. Danny stood there staring, confused, not comprehending what was going on in front of him.

"Oh, for Christ sakes," the boyfriend said, noticing Danny.

"I'm cold," Danny said, shivering under the towel.

"You want to watch, you little pervert?" Gail said as he stood there shaking, not understanding what she meant.

"I can't do this," the boyfriend said, sliding off Gail. She gets up off the couch pulling her skirt down. Grabbing the front of the towel in her fist, she pulls Danny along and pushes him into the hall closet naked and shuts the door.

"Now stay in there, you little bastard," he hears through the door. He stands in the blackness of the closet naked and trembling and begins to cry. The darkness scares him, and he begins to panic.

"Let me out," he screams over and over as he pounds on the door.

"Shut the fuck up," he hears Gail yell out.

"I'm out of here," he hears the boyfriend say. Danny begins to yell and bang on the door frantically again. Suddenly, the door opens, and Gail pulls him out by his hair. The boyfriend is gone as Gail leads him down the hallway still grasping his hair.

"Remain in there for the rest of the night," Gail said, shov-ing Danny into his bedroom with a slap across the back of his head. Danny puts his hand on top of his sore head as she shuts his door. He puts his pyjamas on and curls up into a ball under his covers and trembles the cold away as he tries to warm up. The covers are pulled up to his nose as he stares at the wall and tries to process why this terror has come into his night. It's too much for a little boy to understand and more than he will ever forget.

The bedroom wall turns into a cloud of dust as a sliver pickup truck speeds by him and pulls over to the side of the road. He watches as the driver opens his door and stands behind it is, steadying his rifle through the open truck window. As he hears the crack of the rifle, Danny starts his engine and pulls his truck out of the trees. He bounces across the ditch and fishtails onto the gravel road, sliding his truck to a stop behind the silver pickup as the hunter throws his rifle onto the seat of his truck.

"You're illegally shooting across a roadway from your truck. There've been complaints of unsafe hunting around here," Danny said, confronting the hunter.

"This is the first time I've ever fired from my truck; guess I got a little excited and lost my head." Danny had heard the first time excuse many times before. Maybe it was true and maybe it wasn't, but it didn't matter; this was a serious offence, and any responsible hunter knew better.

"Hopefully, it will be the last time as well. I'm writing you a fine for unsafe use of a firearm, and I'm seizing your rifle. You'll lose your hunting licence for a year and will have to take the hunter's safety course again." Danny handed him the fine, took his rifle and got back into the truck. He drove over and took pictures of the damaged decoy and then lifted it back into the bed of the pickup. Driving back to the yard, he thought about how he had been dealing with people all his life who knew better but did what they wanted to anyway. He thought about how much pain and suffering he had been unnecessarily subjected to and the trauma it had caused him as a result. Something had changed inside of him the day he decided to fight back in school. It wasn't the person he wanted to be it was the person he had to become. It was now the only way he could find peace for all the injustice that had been heaped upon his life. Like the offending hunter, he would see to it that all those people who had rained terror down on his life would receive retribution and thus cease to haunt his memory and no longer hurt anyone else.

Driving into the yard, Danny backed the truck up to the storage shed. Unlocking the shed door, he dropped the tailgate and slid the deer decoy out of the truck bed. He placed the damaged decoy into shed. He would have to deal with repairing it another time. Locking the shed, he swung the truck door open and took his thermos off the seat. He wasn't going into his office at this hour; he decided to call it a day and headed over to his car. He was deep in thought during the drive home, and, before he knew it, he was pulling up in front of his garage.

Linda was setting the table as Danny walked in and hung his jacket in the closet.

"Good timing," she said. "Dinner is almost ready. How was your day?"

"It was a little exciting. I caught a hunter shooting up my decoy from his truck."

"That sounds dangerous, what is wrong with people?"

"It is dangerous. He's got a year to think about it, and it cost him plenty. He won't be making that mistake again."

"Just letting you know, I'm working Thursday, Friday and Saturday this weekend if you're thinking of going up to the cabin."

"I might; we'll see."

"Connie has invited us over to dinner on Sunday."

"What's the occasion?" Danny said.

"Nothing special, she just wants to show her appreciation for us being there for her during her crisis with Gary."

"She doesn't have to do that."

"You saved her life, Danny. Give yourself some credit."

"She doesn't owe me anything. You didn't tell her anything about what I did that night, did you?"

"No, she never questioned what you told her. She has accepted what happened and is trying to put it behind her. We won't bring anything up about it, but us going over there might help give her some closure."

Danny hadn't thought any more about the events of that evening; he had already gotten his closure that night. Connie had gone back to the house and called 911 like he had told her to. It had been very unsettling to her to find Gary aspirated and lying there dead. After the police had taken her statement and the ambulance left, she had come back and stayed with them overnight. An officer had shown up, and they had verified Connie's story. Linda had gone over the next day and helped her clean up. It took a while to sink in, but she finally realized that her nightmare was over.

"Yes, it will be good for her. I'll take some glue and clamps over and fix that door frame for her."

"She'll appreciate that. You'll see a big difference in her. She looks like she has the weight of the world taken off her shoulders."

Danny finished off his dinner and sat back in his chair. He knew what that feeling felt like. He knew what it felt like to have something freed from your mind that had been weighing on it for years. He knew what it felt like to finally have some of the demons and terrors of his past finally vanquished from his soul. Connie's demon was behind her now. He had spared her the burden of carrying that weight.

The end of the week crept up, and Linda had dressed for her eight P.M. shift at the hospital. Danny was unloading the dishwasher as she entered the kitchen.

"One shift down and two more to go," she said. "Are you going to the cabin tonight?"

"Either tonight or tomorrow morning. I haven't decided yet."

"Don't forget about dinner at Connie's on Sunday."

"No, I haven't; I'll be back in plenty of time."

"Maybe you could pick up a bottle of wine to take over."

"Way ahead of you. I've already got one."

"Good job, glad to see you're on top of things."

"The important things, anyway."

"Well, I'd better be on my way. Safe trip. Love you," Linda said, kissing his cheek.

"Love you too, have a good night." Danny waves at the kitchen window as he watches Linda drive off down the street. He goes into the garage and packs a bag with some of the essentials he'll need for the weekend — rope, duct tape, syringes.

It's a calm, pleasant night as the pole lamps scatter their ghostly light across the empty line-painted spaces of the parking lot. Oil-stained patches shadow each rectangle of asphalt now free from the day's hulking masses of metal dripping down on them. Gail ends her ten o'clock shift with a turn of the key, swinging the deadbolt firmly into the steel doorframe. For as long as she has been assistant manager at Avery Drug Mart, Friday night has been her scheduled shift. She sauntered over to her car and gets in, rolling down the window and lighting a cigarette. She puffs and blows smoke out the window through the corner of her mouth as she scrolls through her phone. Shoving the phone in her bag, she flicks the butt out the window and starts her car. Gail drives across the deserted parking lot and turns out onto the street, glancing one more time at the drug store as she pulls away. There is next to no traffic as she makes her way home on the normally bustling streets that are usually full of daytime traffic; the empty streets are the only benefit of working 'til this time of night. She has a rare Saturday off and is looking forward to sleeping in. A police car passes the other way, and she automatically checks her speed. He flashes his lights, and her heart begins to race. "Shit," she says, realizing her headlights aren't on. She quickly reaches to switch them on. She looks in her rear-view mirror slightly panicked and is relieved to see the cop continuing down the street. She had received a ticket for running a red-light last year, and the last thing she needed was another incident on her driving record.

Braking into her driveway, she hits the opener and drives into the garage. She gets out of the car and leaves her bag on the trunk as she lights up her last cigarette of the night. As she stands just outside the garage door, the smoke from the cigarette scissored between her fingers curls into the night air as she reads the text messages on her phone. She waves a mosquito away from her face and feels a sharp sting as a hand cups over her mouth and pulls her backwards into the garage.

Danny lays her limp body on the hood of the car and hits the button to close the garage door as he picks her phone up off the floor and puts it in her bag. He wedges the door to the house open and carries Gail inside.

Gail opens her eyes disoriented and confused, her head spinning. She closes them again, not sure if she is dreaming, and after giving herself a moment remembers being pulled into the garage. Her eyes spring open, and she looks down at her bare legs and realizes she is sitting tied up in her downstairs rec room in her bra and underwear. Her hands are tied behind her back, and her legs are tied at the ankles. A rope winds around her waist securing her to a wooden chair. She lets out a startled scream as she notices Danny standing beside her.

"You're not going to keep screaming, are you?" Danny said, holding up the roll of duct tape. She shakes her head no and tries to half-bend and twist herself in an attempt to conceal her exposed body.

"Don't worry, I'm not here to sexually assault you, Gail."

"How do you know me? What are you doing to me?"

"I know you're the babysitter from hell, that's how I know you."

"I never babysat for you; I don't know you."

"You were my sitter once, and believe me, once was enough to traumatize me for the rest of my life."

"This is a joke, right? You're not for real, are you?" Danny grabs her by the hair hard enough to tip the chair back.

"I don't joke; I don't play fucking games, Gail. You remember telling me that? It was very real for a four-year-old boy to be hit in the face by his babysitter." Danny let the chair fall forward back onto its legs and slaps her across the face. "That's what it felt like." He backhands her across the face again. "Snakes and ladders, you couldn't even play a game with a little kid, but you could abuse him. You left me alone to freeze in the bathtub while you cavorted with your boyfriend. Is it coming back to you now?"

"Stop, I remember. You're that little boy. I remember."

"I need you to remember all of it. You threw me naked and cold into that dark closet and then hauled me down the hall by my hair. What do you think that does to a small child? My God, what did you do to all the other kids under your care?"

"I abused them, okay? Is that what you want to hear?" Gail said as she sat there shivering.

"It's not what I want to hear, God help them, I don't even want to think how far you went with them. I couldn't even deal with the nightmares from how you treated me. My mother couldn't understand why I woke up screaming in the middle of the night. You can understand why you, can't you, Gail? You knew the terror you were subjecting me and all those other defenceless children to. You got away with it and just kept on doing it, didn't you?"

"So, you've come to punish me? Is that what this is all about? It won't change anything."

"No, it won't change the lives you've already scarred. Through three failed marriages, thank Christ for small mercies, you had no children of your own to terrorize. It will change things for me though. It will bring a past injustice in my life to rest. It will be one less demon torturing my soul, finishing unfinished business to make things right." Danny walks over to the chest freezer and begins emptying the frozen contents onto the floor.

"What are you doing, you psycho?" Gail yells. Danny unties the rope from the chair and lays her face down on the floor. He bends her legs up behind her, tying her ankles to her wrists, and starts dragging her across the floor by her hair.

"You left me naked and cold in the dark; I'm going to return the experience to you."

"You're not putting me in the fucking freezer," Gail screams.

"At least I'm sparing you the indignity of being totally naked," Danny said as he lifted her and set her inside the freezer.

"Get me out," Gail screamed.

"I also remember you giving me a cold dinner; I believe you said you didn't give a shit," Danny said as he placed some of the frozen food back into the freezer on top of and around her.

"Get me out," Gail screamed repeatedly.

"If it's any consolation, you will likely suffocate before you freeze to death. I remember it took me half the night to warm up, but you didn't know that. You never checked on me. Then again, why would you have? You didn't give a shit."

Danny closed the lid on the freezer, muffling Gail's screams. As he walked away, he knew he was silencing one more bad memory screaming out from the past in his own mind. Climbing the stairs, he turned off the lights and closed the door of the house. He walked down the quiet street past the sleepy dark windows, got into his car and headed off to the cabin.

CHAPTER TWENTY-THREE

Danny drove up the narrow driveway, the tires bobbing in and out of the gravel-starved potholes of his laneway. The headlights lit up the trees standing along the road like late-night sentinels, and then came to rest on the shed wall facing the cabin. The absence of a moon made the ground shadowless and left the stars solo to sparkle like diamonds poked into the night sky. Switching off his lights, he collected his bag and unlocked the cabin door in the beam of his keychain light. Turning on the kitchen light, he set his bag on the chair and touched a match to the wick of Linda's centrepiece. The aroma of ginger peach rose from the candle's glow as he dropped a teabag into a mug and put water on to boil. The sealed cabin had remained cool, prompting Danny to put a fire on in the woodstove. Heat began to radiate out into the living room and slowly crept through the cabin. Picking up his mug, he blew out the candle and drifted into the living room where he sunk into the welcoming comfort of the couch. The room was filled with the scent of ginger peach and burning hardwood that relaxed him and comforted his senses as he sipped his hot tea. It also comforted him to know that he had ousted one more demon from his past, one more ghost that had haunted him since his childhood; one more injustice had been resolved.

The fire warmed him and murmured out the hypnotic crackle and hum of its burn as he melted into the soft back cushion of the couch. His mind drifted back to his childhood, back to when he was in the treehouse with Ben. They were sitting on an old piece of carpet that offered a meagre layer of comfort over the rough plywood floor. They were playing Go Fish and had to quickly slap their hands down to hold the cards to the carpet when an occasional gust of wind whistled through the treehouse. The agitated bark of a dog several backyards away piqued their curiosity, and they stood up to have a look from their treehouse view. They could see someone come out of the house and stride quickly towards the dog. The dog was tied to a tree with a length of rope and bounded out of their sight beside a backyard shed as the owner approached. The barking stopped with a sharp yelp, and the owner walked back into his house.

"That dog looked like one of those German Shepherd dogs," Danny said.

"Is that like one of those police dogs?" Ben said.

"I think so; maybe he's barking because he's hungry."

"I think that man hurt him," Ben said. They picked up their cookies and scrambled down the ladder to the ground. Danny and Ben snuck through the backyards and approached the shed. The dog appeared from around the shed and bared its teeth, growling at them. Danny and Ben froze on the spot.

"It's okay, boy, it's okay," Danny said, reaching into his pocket. The dog barked and continued to growl. Danny threw a cookie, and the dog gobbled it down. He threw another, and the dog snapped it up.

"Here you go, boy," Ben said as he threw him his cookies. The shepherd chomped them up and sniffed in the grass, licking up the crumbs.

"He was starving," Danny said.

"Sorry, boy, we don't have anymore," Ben said, holding out his empty hands. The shepherd looked at him, giving his tail half a wag.

"Hey! You kids get away from that dog," a voice bellowed across the yard. They looked over to see the dog's owner storming towards them, and they began backing away. The shepherd strained at his rope, barking excitedly after them. "Duke, get over here," he said, lashing the dog with a stick. Danny and Ben turned and ran as fast as they could back to Ben's house. Ben's dad was coming out the door as they thundered back into the yard.

"What in God's name are you boys up to?"

"We heard a dog get hurt over there," Ben said, pointing back over the yards.

"Over at Reynolds's place? You boys best not be going back over there; that's none of your concern."

"But dad, he...."

"That's final," he said, and he walked into the garage.

The next day was a scorcher; Danny and Ben sheltered up in the shade of the treehouse. They each ate half a sandwich as they looked out over the backyards. Duke was lying under a tree panting in the heat, his tongue drooping out of his mouth.

"He's dying of thirst," Danny said.

"I'm saving this other half of sandwich for him," Ben said.

"Me too," Danny said. "I'm too hot to eat anyway. He's got to have some water." Danny sees Reynolds come out, get into his car, and back down the driveway. "Get a dish for Duke," he tells Ben.

They climb down, and Ben runs into the house and comes back out with a plastic margarine container.

"We're not supposed to go over there. We'll get in trouble," Ben says, filling the container from the outside tap and snapping the lid on.

"We'll give him this quick and leave," Danny said. They scrabble along the backyards, and Duke pulls at the end of his rope, growling as they approach.

"He's going to bite you," Ben said as Danny sets the tub down just out of reach and removes the lid. He picks up a long stick to push the water closer. The shepherd slants back his ears and starts to viciously bark.

"He thinks you're going to hit him with it," Ben said. Danny drops the stick, and Duke's ears perk back up. He picks the water up and circles away from Ben with the shepherd stalking his every step.

"Throw him a sandwich," Danny said. Ben unwraps a sandwich-half and swings his hand forward.

"Here, Duke," he calls as he tosses the sandwich onto the grass and the dog comes over to wolf it down. Danny steps forward and quickly places the water on the ground, retreating backwards as the shepherd runs over to the container. He watches as Duke laps the water up into his parched mouth. He has never seen a dog drink so fast in his life. Duke licks the last drop from the empty container, tipping it on its side.

"It wasn't enough; he's still thirsty," Danny said, looking over at the hose hanging on the house. "Tease him over with the other sandwich." Ben waves the half-sandwich in the air, and Duke eagerly runs over to him while Danny retrieves the small tub. Spinning the tap, warm water gushes out of the hose, and then Danny slows the stream as cooler water flows into the plastic tub. Ben tosses the second half, and Duke snaps it out of the air as Danny sets the tub down and backs away. Duke trots over and chomps the water back as fast as the first time, pushing the tub along the grass as he licks the bottom dry.

"The tub's too small. He wants more," Ben said.

"Maybe there's a bucket in the shed," Danny said as he walked over beside Ben.

"We'll be in trouble going in there," Ben said.

"That mean Reynolds is probably gone all day and forgot about Duke. It's too hot for him with no water," Danny said as they both stared at the dog standing there with his tongue hanging out. Duke wags his tail and comes over to lie down in front of them and begins to whine. Danny and Ben pulled open the heavy doors, and a wall of heat poured out of the shed. They stepped inside as the hum of the neighbourhood air conditioners drowned out the sound of Reynolds's car pulling into the driveway. They looked at the shelves cluttered with old half-filled Mason jars and forgotten cans of paint. Ben looked behind some scrap pieces of plywood leaning against the wall in front of an aging grass-dusted lawnmower. Danny slid aside two faded-red gas cans that were blocking a bottom shelf. He peered underneath and then slid the cans back out of the way. Hearing Duke begin to bark, they lift a weathered tarp bunched into the back corner of the shed.

"There's a pail," Ben said excitedly as he reaches for the handle while Danny held up the tarp. They hear the roll and slam of the shed doors, and they spin around and run to the front of the shed. Pulling on the doors, they hear the smack of the fold-over latch securing them shut.

"You kids are going to learn your lesson once and for all, by Jesus," they heard Reynold's yell through the closed door. Danny pulled himself up by his fingertips to peer out the dirty, hazed window as Duke's frenzied barking turned to high-pitched yelps.

"What's happening, what do you see?" Ben asked. Danny watched as Reynolds brought the stick down repeatedly, thrashing the distressed shepherd. He could feel every blow as he relived the sting of the strap Art had wildly swung in the basement. Duke turned and snarled as Reynolds raised the stick again, and then he backed away, cowering by the tree. Danny let go of the ledge and dropped to the floor with an outrage swelling up in him from what he had witnessed.

"He whipped him with the stick," Danny said with tears cresting up in his eyes.

They pounded and pushed on the solid wood doors but couldn't budge them. Sweat ran down their faces and dripped onto the floor as the temperature rose inside the shed. The sun blazed in through the cobwebbed window like a heat ray through a magnifying glass.

"Do you think he forgot about us?" Ben said.

"Mr. Reynolds, let us out," Danny yells, but he hears nothing but the drone of the air conditioners outside. They begin to get dizzy and sit down on the floor. The air seems to thicken, and it becomes hard to breathe. Their hair is soaked, and their shirts are wallpapered to their skin. Ben's face is so wet that Danny can't tell if its sweat or tears. He realizes it's some of both. They can hear Duke scratching at the side of the shed, alternating between whining and panting as the heat parches him on the outside and roasts them on the inside.

"Get away from there," they suddenly hear a voice say outside. The latch clanks back, and the doors slide open as they wobble to their feet.

"You little bastards had enough to learn your lesson yet?" Reynolds says as they step out into the blistering sun. Danny and Ben noticed the stick in his hand and begin to run on their shaky legs. Danny feels the sting across his back as Reynolds swings again and whips the stick across Ben's rear end. "Don't you let me catch you messing around here again," he yells as Duke barks, pulling against his rope. Reynolds turns and raises the stick in the air, and Duke heads over to the tree. Danny and Ben stumble into the yard and clamber up into the treehouse. Their chests heave as they sit with their backs against the wall. They open their canteens and gulp mouthfuls of water down their parched throats as the sting of their lashing burns across their skin. Danny didn't feel sorry for himself. He felt sorry for what happened to Ben, but he felt the sorriest for Duke. He didn't feel sorry at all for what he was wishing upon Mr. Reynolds.

The heat wave passed, and, despite their terrifying run-in with Mr. Reynolds, Danny and Ben would sneak over to his yard and throw Duke whatever leftovers they could scrounge. He wouldn't growl or bark at them now, and they weren't afraid of him at all. They rode their bikes throughout the neighbourhood, and one evening after dinner, they stopped in front of Reynolds's driveway. Reynolds's car wasn't there, and they sat on their bikes looking up the driveway into the backyard. There was Duke tied up to the tree as usual.

"Hey, Duke," Danny called out. Duke walked the length of his rope, let out a bark and stood there wagging his tail.

"Sit, Duke, sit," Ben hollered, and Duke sat on the ground immediately. They had taught Duke how to sit when they had brought treats over for him on the days that Reynolds wasn't home.

"Don't tell him that," Danny said. "We don't have anything to give him."

"Good boy, I'll bring something later," Ben shouted. Duke cocked his head as if trying to understand; Danny and Ben laughed at him.

They straightened their handlebars to take off, and a hand grabs the back of each of their shirts.

"Going for an evening ride, maybe?" Vince said, walking around to the front of their bicycles.

"We just want to get going," Danny said.

"You'll get going when I say you'll get going," Vince said, grabbing their handlebars.

"Just leave us alone," Ben said.

"How about taking a ride backwards," Vince said, shoving them back. Ben's bike starts tipping, and he falls off onto the driveway. Danny steps back on his peddle to catch his balance, and the front wheel rises as the bicycle braked. The bike tips towards Vince as Danny jumps off, the front wheel bolt coming down and scraping Vince's shin. Vince winces in pain and looks down to see blood oozing out of the scrape. Danny and Ben take-off up the driveway as Vince drops the bicycles and chases after them.

"You're going to pay for this," Vince yelled out. Danny and Ben glance back and see Vince pull his pocketknife out of his pocket as he charged up the driveway. They run across the backyard with Vince closing in on them.

"Over this way," Danny shouted to Ben as they run behind the tree Duke is secured to and spun around its trunk. Duke barks out savagely as Vince skids to a stop in his tracks. He swings his knife out, and Duke lunges forward, stretching his rope like a guitar string. He snarls and snaps as Vince slowly backs away.

"You little fuckers are lucky this time," he said, shaking his knife at them. They both watch him as he crosses the yard and disappears down the street.

"Good boy," Danny and Ben say as they stroked Duke's head. Duke soaked up the attention and affection like a thirsty sponge. His interactions with Danny and Ben were the only acts of kindness he had ever known. He watched after them as they made their way back to the driveway.

"Bye, Duke. See you later," Danny and Ben said as they turned and waved. They untangle their bikes as Reynolds turns into the driveway blaring his horn. Danny glares at him like the beam of a headlight as he and Ben mount their bikes and ride off to Ben's house. Ben digs through the fridge and comes up with half a baked potato and a steak bone with a bit of meat and some fat still attached to it.

"Duke is going to love this," Ben said as he dropped the find into a used bread bag. They steal across the backyards and scan Reynolds's yard for any sign of him. Duke pads over, wagging his tail, happy to see them again as they take cover behind the shed.

"Sit, Duke," Danny said as he takes the potato from the bag and tosses it towards him. Duke catches it before it hits the ground, and in three bites, it's gone. They peek around from the back of the shed to make sure the coast is still clear. Ben pulls the steak bone out of the bag and holds it out in front of him.

"Lie down, Duke," Ben said. Duke sits there transfixed on the bone, licking his chops.

"Lie down, Duke," Danny said, kneeling and patting the ground. Duke lowers himself down and stares back up at the bone.

"He did it! Good boy, Duke," Ben said excitedly as he throws the bone to him.

"Shhh… not so loud," Danny said, looking over at the house as Duke gnaws on the bone. They creep back around the side of the shed. Danny sees the whipping stick leaning against the shed and takes it. Back in Ben's yard, Ben stands on one end of the stick while Danny picks up the other end, bending it up and over, waiting for the snap.

The loud snap of a red-hot coal in the woodstove jars Danny awake. A quarter cup of tea slants cold in the tilted mug between his legs, his two fingers still hooked through the handle. His watch tells him it is almost one thirty in the morning. He levers the door of the stove open and puts two more logs on the fire. The glowing orange coals quickly kindle the logs ablaze, and he closes the door as a wisp of smoke curls out. Turning out the living room light, he enters the kitchen and pours the remaining tea out, leaving his mug in the sink. He goes into the bathroom and takes his toothbrush out of the medicine cabinet, swinging the door closed. The silver on the mirror has flaked away in the bottom corners, and there is a slight bit of rust on the back edge of the aging metal cabinet that is as old as the cabin itself. He has thought about replacing it, but it has been that way for years and hasn't seemed to get any worse. He also knows that once you replace something with new, it makes the old around it look worse somehow. But after all, it was only a cabin. If it just made the cabin feel more rustic or it wasn't broken, he wasn't in a big hurry to replace it. Besides, Linda would let him know when it started to bother her, or else there would simply be a new one sitting there in a box when he got home one day. He retrieved his bag off the kitchen chair and climbed into bed listening to the distant yip of the coyotes and the crackle from the fire lull him to sleep.

Morning seemed to come in the blink of an eye. He always slept soundly at the cabin with no sirens or honking horns to disturb his sleep. There were no city lights filtering in through the windows to keep you awake. Once the cabin lights were out, if there wasn't a full moon, darkness would cloak the cabin like a thick blanket. Night-time was truly night-time there; it was so black you almost had to part the night with your hands to walk through it. Danny shaved and ran a long shower on his sore back. This business of hauling and lifting uncooperative bodies around certainly had its drawbacks. He had afforded himself the luxury of installing a larger hot water tank in the cabin. Gone were the days of the second one in having to end up finishing with a cold shower.

Danny brewed his coffee and took his toasted bagel to the table. Having been preoccupied with planning his previous night's activities, he had forgotten to pack cream cheese. He spread strawberry jam that he left at the cabin on his bagel and ate that with his coffee. As he sat there, he noticed that dust from the driveway had accumulated on the window screen. That was one thing he would take care of today. He would clean them before the next time Linda came. He finished his breakfast and put his dishes in the sink. He washed them up as he looked out the kitchen window and watched the chickadees flit from branch to branch. His focus shifted from the birds to the police cruiser that was coming up the driveway. He wiped his hands on the towel as a cloud of dust drifted by the stopped cruiser. Danny opened the cabin door and stepped out as the officer got out of the car.

"Good morning," Danny said with a smile. "I don't get many visitors out this way."

"Good morning, sir. No, we don't usually come out this way too often." Danny walks past his car, noticing the loops of the red-flecked rope still sticking out of the bag he had thrown on the back seat. That was a crucial mistake he had made instead of putting the bag in the trunk. He leaned back against the back door window and crossed his arms.

"It's nice country out here. Gives you a nice change from city driving," Danny said.

"That it does. The reason I've stopped by is I'm just checking on properties. There's been a few break-ins in the area. Is everything good with your place here?"

"I've had no problems here, knock-on wood. I don't know about anyone else; my neighbours are pretty few and far between."

"I've noticed that driving around. You don't get too many people knocking on your door to borrow a cup of sugar out here."

"No, and that's the way I like it. It's good to know about the break-ins. I travel around a fair bit out here for the conservation authority. I'll keep my eye open."

"I thought you looked familiar. I've seen you driving around in your truck. I'll appreciate the extra set of eyes."

"No problem"," Danny said.

The officer walked past Danny, stopped and took a look around. "That's a nice storage building you have there."

"Thanks."

"You keep that locked up all the time?"

"Sure do; not much of value to steal out of there though. Just a chainsaw maybe. They wouldn't want anything else from in there."

"I wouldn't be so sure. The buggers would steal your grandmother's smile if they thought they could sell it."

"I suppose they would," Danny laughed.

"I'll let you get on with the rest of your day. Give us a call if you see anything suspicious."

"I'll be sure to." As the officer pulled away, Danny took the bag out of the car and put it in his trunk. He opens the shed and, climbing the ladder, screws a large eye hook into the ceiling. Then he drops a rope down from it. Most people would think it's a strange addition to a shed, but Danny knows it will serve its purpose in the future. He puts the ladder away and closes the door to the building. He doesn't need any prying eyes looking in, on surprise visits. The rest of the day Danny spends cleaning all the window screens and chopping wood. He takes two armfuls into the cabin and dumps them into the wood box. The rest he takes and piles in the shed. He thinks about how a saying about wood is ringing true as he stops to wipe his brow. The saying was that wood warms you three times — once while you're chopping it, once while you're piling it and once while you're burning it. He puts the axe away in the shed and locks the door.

Danny slides the plastic container into the microwave and taps the time into the keypad. He hadn't taken the time to stop for lunch, and he was starving. He had burned up every crumb of energy from his morning bagel and couldn't wait to dig into the stew Linda had prepared. The knife carved off thick pieces of the fresh French stick he had picked up on his way to the cabin. Once slightly warmed, the butter crept into the bread, and he anticipated every bite. Swirling the bread along the bottom of the container, every trace of gravy had been mopped up. He hadn't bothered to dirty a plate, as his empty stomach didn't intend to leave anything behind. Wrapping up the bread, he fished the teabag out of the steaming mug and retired into the living room. He placed a birch log into position over a bed of kindling and touched a match to the curling white bark. The flame licked around the dry log and ignited the nest of kindling into a roaring fire. Danny sat down into the comforting embrace of the couch, his back sore, body tired and belly full. He was done like dinner. He sipped his tea as the heat from the woodstove washed over him, making him drowsy. His body felt like lead, and the couch seemed to suck him in even further. His eyelids became heavy, and he thought he would close them just for a minute. The minute was long enough for his mind to wander back and reawaken the memory from his past. Back to a time when unthinkable realities reared their ugly heads like mythical poisonous serpents striking out unconscionable truths.

He was enjoying the best part of his school day, working happily away in Bob Dover's science class. It was one of his best classes that he could easily maintain a consistent high-grade point average in without even trying, it seemed. While a few of the other students struggled along with it, the subject came naturally to Danny. Well into the year, Danny was packing up his books at the end of a class. As the other students filed out of the classroom, Rob looked over his way.

"Danny, could you just hold up there for a moment if you don't mind?" Rob asked. Danny didn't think anything of it, as Rob had asked him on previous occasions to help out after class on various projects.

"Did you need me for something?" Danny said, walking up to the front of the classroom.

"I've got a big favour to ask you."

"Sure, Mr. Dover, what do you need?"

"You know Gloria Baker, the nice red-haired girl who sits one row over from you?"

"Yes, I know who you're talking about."

"Keep this between me and you. She tries really hard, but she still seems to struggle along in class. I don't know what it is, but it seems that she has trouble focusing on the material sometimes. Her marks are just borderline, and if they drop, I'm afraid I won't be able to pass her – and she needs this credit. I think she will be able to relate better with someone her own age. I've seen her asking you some questions sometimes, and she seems comfortable with you. This big project coming up accounts for a large portion of your marks this term, and I'd like to pair you up with her. I want you to help her so she can get a passing grade."

"Sure, I can help her," Danny said.

"That's great. Thanks. I'll tell her tomorrow that you'll be working with her."

Danny came into class the next day to find that Rob had arranged the desks together in groups of two. He sat down beside Gloria, and she seemed thrilled that he was working with her. Rob sat there amazed as Danny worked with her, explaining the material like he was talking about the weather. Rob had assigned some homework and gave Danny a wink as he left the classroom with Gloria. Danny walked with Gloria, wondering if he was boring her talking about science, a subject that he could ramble on about all day.

"Do you want to come over to my house and get this homework done?" Danny asked.

"I can't. I'm not allowed to go over to boys' homes."

"My mom will be there," Danny said, thinking that she didn't trust him suddenly.

"It's not you. My mom wouldn't mind, but my stepfather won't let me." Danny found it odd that her stepfather would have such a strict rule, but then he didn't have a sister and thought maybe his dad would be that protective if he had a daughter.

"I'll come over and help you at your house then." Gloria was reluctant, but she knew it was the only way she would get through the homework and not fall behind in class. Danny opened the door to Gloria's house and followed her into the hallway.

"Mom, this is Danny. He is helping me with my science project at school."

"Hello, Danny," Gloria's mom said apprehensively. They walked into the kitchen where her stepfather was sitting at the table.

"This is…," Gloria began.

"I heard who the hell he is, I'm not deaf," he blurted out.

"He's helping me with homework."

"I heard that as well. What are you stupid or something? Sit here," he says, picking up his beer and going into the living room. "Get the damn dinner on, I'm getting hungry," he shouts at Gloria's mom.

Danny and Gloria sit down at the table. He opens the books and begins working through the assignment with her. Looking up at her mom, he notices bruise marks on the back of her arms, and it reminds him of the same ones he had noticed on Ben after Art had paid a visit. They spend almost an hour working when the stepfather comes into the kitchen.

"So, have you made Gloria any smarter?" he says, putting his hand on the back of her neck. She cringed and pulled aside as Gloria's mom looks away. He digs his fingers into the back of her neck and pulls her back. "Does she look any smarter to you?"

"She's smart enough as she is, Mr. Brooks," Danny said.

"You're hurting me," Gloria said as his fingers press into her neck.

"You don't know what hurt is yet, girl," he said, pulling her head back by her hair and staring down at her.

"She's just trying to do her work," Danny said.

"Well, your work is done for today," he says as he lets go of Gloria's hair.

"Maybe it's best you should go now," Gloria's mom said. Danny stands and collects his books as Gloria strides quickly out of the kitchen towards her bedroom.

"I'm sorry it's not a good day," Mrs. Brooks said as she opened the door for Danny. He walked home thinking that no day was a good day for Gloria and her mom. It was no wonder she had a hard time focusing on class; she never knew what she was coming home to.

The next day in class, Rob smiled as Gloria correctly answered some questions, he randomly asked about the homework assignment. He subtly turned his head and gave a nod of approval to Danny. Any sense of pride Danny felt in the moment quickly dissolved, as he noticed bruises on her wrists under the cuff of her blouse. He was sitting close enough to see faint bruising on the back of her neck. He knew Gloria's difficulties hadn't ended when he left the house. He worked with her and explained details in his patient, helpful manner, and Rob could see a positive change in how she responded in class.

As he walked with her towards her house, Danny noticed a change in her demeanour. Gloria hadn't confided in him about her abusive stepfather, but behind the brave facade he could see the sadness in her eyes.

"Why does your mother stay with him?" Danny directly asked.

"We have no other place to go," came the simple reply.

"I'm sorry. I see the bruises and I feel so bad, I shouldn't ask."

"I hate him, I don't even call him my dad. He's not my dad, he's a monster," Gloria shrieks out. Danny is taken aback by the outpouring of emotion. He doesn't need to ask the next question. He doesn't want to ask the question, afraid of the answer he might hear. He doesn't want to know the answer, the hard reality of her unfathomable pain. Gloria composes herself as they reach her house, and Danny is relieved to see there is no car in the driveway. Mrs. Brooks busied herself in the kitchen as they open their books on the table and go over their notes from the day. Danny notices that the bruises had faded on her arms, but he was disturbed to see the recent ones on Gloria. The peace and tranquillity in the kitchen were broken by the click of the front door handle opening. Danny sees Mr. Brooks entering the kitchen and averts his eyes. The stepfather opens the fridge and removes a can of beer. There is no warm greeting or display of affection offered to Mrs. Brooks.

"Another damn kitchen science lesson, that's just what we need," Brooks said as he walks out into the living room. Mrs. Brooks doesn't turn around, Gloria doesn't look up, there's no engagement with him, no invitation for a confrontation. They want to maintain their fragile defence of silence. Danny speaks in a low voice, turning the pages of the textbook while they take notes. The precious minutes of calm tick away like a time bomb. Gloria's mom prepares the dinner, hoping to avoid the demanding bark of her impatient husband. She turns the handle, frustrated, as the can opener skips off the uncooperative rim of the large can of vegetables. Brooks comes into the kitchen, noticing her struggle.

"What's wrong with you," he says, butting her aside with his shoulder and grabbing the opener out of her hand. He clamps it down and curses as it jumps off the rim until he finally grinds the can open. "There," he says, throwing the opener on the counter. "Don't be so useless next time."

Danny watches her pour the vegetables into a pot on the stove. As she turns, he can see that her eyes are edged with tears. The verbal abuse has taken its toll as much as the physical has.

"Are you so dumb you can't learn that book on your own?" Brooks said, turning his attention to Gloria. "You're as thick as your mother." Gloria shrinks down in her chair as if hoping it would make her invisible.

"She's doing really well, Mr. Brooks," Danny said in her defence.

"I wasn't talking to you, Mr. Schoolboy."

"This is a team project. We're working on this together because he is my partner, not because I'm stupid," Gloria said.

"With all this learning, you're still not smart enough to know I need another beer." Gloria gets up, gets another can and puts it on the table, hoping he'll leave them alone.

"Open it," he says. She leans forward and pulls the tab back. Danny can feel her humiliation. He feels it like when he was standing back in the corner with the dunce hat on in Mrs. Adams's class. If he had a butcher's knife, he felt like he could jump up and stab her stepfather right in the eye with it. "Now you're getting smarter, you're making yourself useful," he says, putting his hand on her neck and sliding his clammy fingers under the back of her collar. "Don't you feel smarter, Gloria?"

She doesn't answer as she looks down, fixing her gaze on the words in the textbook. She wishes she could crawl right in between the pages and close the cover.

"Look at me when I'm talking to you," he says, raising his voice.

"We're almost finished here," Danny said, trying to distract his attention away from Gloria.

"Let go of me," Gloria said, pulling away.

"You're finished right now," Brooks said, flying into a rage and turning the table over on its side, sending the books, notes and beer flying. Danny pushed his chair back, tipping over and crashing to the floor.

"Take your damn books and get the hell out," Brooks yelled, kicking the textbook across the floor into Danny's side. Danny crawled around picking up books and notes while Gloria ran down the hallway sobbing into her bedroom, slamming the door shut. He knew as he pushed the front door open that it would be the last time, he would be coming to her house to help her there. He would ask Rob if they could stay after class and work but would be reluctant to disclose the abuse that Gloria's stepfather was subjecting them to. He was afraid that any outside intervention attempt would bring the wrath of the stepfather down on them, making a bad situation worse. He wondered if his presence in the house helping Gloria was partially to blame for Brooks becoming agitated so easily. Feeling the pain in his right arm from it hitting the floor, he shifted the books over to his other side. As he walked down the sidewalk, he reached over, trying to rub the ache out of his elbow.

Danny's arm tingled, sandwiched between his hip and the side of the couch. The numbing sensation woke him, and he rubbed his sleeping arm, trying to massage it back to life. Tipping his cup to look inside, he saw he had finished his tea. The log in the stove had burned down to embers, making him realize without checking his watch that he had been dozing for hours. He set another log on the embers, which were determined to smoke and smoulder the curling bark to flame. He washed up the dinner dishes and then decided to take a quick shower. The spray of the warm water felt good on his sore back as he soaped the grime of his busy day down the drain. He towelled off and went into the living room to wedge one more log into the woodstove for the night. He decided to hit the sack, as he was tired from his day despite his after-dinner nap.

Danny slept soundly, barely moving a muscle, then rose to the shine of a new day. He washed his strawberry-jam-coated bagel down with two cups of coffee and then made his bed and packed up his bag. Double checking the door lock, he figured if someone wanted to get in bad enough, they could. He knew locks only kept the honest people out. Turning his car around, he drove down the pothole-pocked lane way and journeyed home. Fixing up the tire-worn driveway into the cabin would be his next project when he returned.

"There's my weekend warrior," Linda said as he set his bag on the hallway floor. "How was the cabin?"

"The cabin was great. I overdid it a bit cleaning all the screens and chopping a shitload of wood, but I slept like a log after."

"I think even when you're working up there, you're enjoying yourself."

"True enough. Doesn't seem so much like work when I'm up there. How about you? You must be tired."

"Yeah, it catches up with me on the third night, but I had a little nap before you got home. That will tide me over until this evening." Danny takes his bag upstairs while Linda settles into the couch to watch the television. He isn't up there long putting his things away and comes back down to find that Linda has dosed off. He knows how fast that can happen; she was obviously more exhausted than she thought. He quietly steps out and takes the bag containing the rope, duct tape and syringes out of the trunk. He puts the bag in a cardboard box he keeps in the garage. Linda sleeps into the afternoon and wakes to find Danny reading the paper at the kitchen table.

"Hi, sleepyhead," he said.

"My gosh, I went out like a light. You should have woken me."

"I would have if you'd slept any longer. Connie would have been wondering where we were soon."

"Look at the time," Linda said. "Let me just splash some water on my face and we'll get going."

Connie throws her arms around Danny and Linda as they come through the door.

"Smells awfully good in here," Danny said as he put the bottle of red wine on the kitchen table. "You girls go ahead and catch up. I've got some fixing to do." He pried the crack wider apart and squeezed the wood glue into the split door frame. Clamping the wood together, he tapped three finishing nails into the moulding. He glanced over to the empty bed where he had left Gary and pushed the image out of his mind.

"Danny, are you almost done? Dinner is ready," Connie called out. He washed his hands and came to the table with a big smile on his face. She had prepared a lasagne, Caesar salad and garlic bread.

"I just may have to come over and fix something every Sunday afternoon," Danny said as he poured the wine.

"You've got one woman spoiling you at home; that's more than enough," Linda said.

After dinner, Danny took the clamps off the door frame. The repair had made the split almost invisible. They thanked Connie and walked out to the car. Linda told her that next weekend, dinner would be at their place.

"It's so nice to see her smiling all the time again – what a change," Linda said.

Sitting across from him during dinner, Connie had silently mouthed the words "thank you" to Danny. He wondered if it was for fixing her door frame or for taking care of her bigger problem and changing her life. He opened the trunk and threw the clamps in. If repairing the traumatic cracks from his past were only so simple as gluing and clamping, he thought. He still had some major repairs to tend to.

CHAPTER TWENTY-FOUR

"So, the report said Art died of a heart attack and asphyxiation," Casey said, turning onto the boulevard.

"Likely had the heart attack as he was suffocating upside down, poor guy," Kent said. "Also had traces of the same sedative."

"The killer was certainly acting out some payback from his youth."

"You did say Art was abusive with kids; even Tommy said so."

"Yes, He must have had the killer in the same position, almost suffocating him years ago, among other things, and our man never forgets, unfortunately for this victim."

"You're still eating those things for breakfast," Kent said as Casey takes a donut from the bag sitting on the console.

"Just a bad habit, I guess; call it brunch, it sounds better. Help yourself."

"Thanks, but I felt guilty for the rest of the day after the last one I ate."

"Just think of it as a reward for a difficult day ahead – then there's no guilt."

"Is that what you do?"

"No, I just like them."

"I don't even know why I ask," Kent says, shaking her head.

"Looks like we have a female victim this time," Casey said, pulling into the driveway. "A Gail Evans, worked at the Avery

Drug Mart. Came home after closing last night, and that was the last time she was seen." Casey pulls up the garage door and sees the bag sitting on the trunk.

"Looks like the killer grabbed her out here," Kent says, noticing the cigarette butt on the ground. "The butt is burnt down but not crushed out, and she wouldn't have left her purse and phone out here."

"He's knocked her out and taken her into the house." They enter the house and walk downstairs to find the forensics agents pulling Gail's frozen body out of the freezer.

"Unbelievable," Kent gasps.

"Some frozen chickens, pork chops, bags of vegetables, ice cream and our frozen victim number eleven," Casey said.

"There's the same rope. The way he had her tied up, she wouldn't have been able to move in there."

"He had her stripped down to really suffer from the cold. My God, how awful that must have felt," Casey said. "She wouldn't have died of suffocation right away; he really wanted her to suffer in there."

"What in the world did she do to the killer to meet this end?"

"Maybe she locked him outside in the cold. Who knows," Casey said. "There's the interrogation chair over there. He probably worked her over tied up to it before he dumped her in the freezer."

"She could have ended up in there all weekend. Who found her?"

"Her boyfriend couldn't get a hold of her this morning and decided to drop by. He didn't find her in her bedroom, and when he saw her car in the garage, he came downstairs looking for her. He noticed the food on the floor beside the freezer and wondered what the hell was going on. He opened the lid and got the shock of his life."

"I can't even imagine," Kent said.

"This is going to be a tough one," Casey said. "We might be grasping at straws, but maybe there's something in her history that will connect her. The victim is older than our killer and doesn't have any obvious connection to him, as far as we know. The only likely motive for the murder would appear to be abuse to him as a child, as in Art's case."

"Art was left to hang upside down, and Gail here was left to freeze to death. What the hell did these victims do to the killer in his childhood to deserve this kind of payback?"

"I don't know, but whatever it was, it messed him up pretty good," Kent said. "Whatever they did has come around full circle to greet them."

"Check into her past," Casey said as they walked to the car. "We may find something connecting her to the other cases. He's killed two other women. Adams was likely his teacher, and West could have been an old girlfriend. Whatever Gail Evans was to him may not be easy to find out, but it would sure be interesting to make the connection."

Every Saturday afternoon after lunch, Stu Reynolds would back his mid-size pickup up over the backyard to the side of his shed. He kept a small aluminium fishing boat there on a trailer out of sight from the street. He hooked the trailer up to the truck, towing it across the lawn and down the driveway. He liked to go fishing on Saturdays and would stay out until late in the afternoon. He rolled the trailer into the lake, slid the boat off and parked the truck on the side of the road. With a pull of the cord, he was motoring across the water to his favourite spot. Whether the fish were biting or not, it was a good way to spend the afternoon. The repetition of casting the line out and reeling it in was very therapeutic, and the anticipation of a lucky strike kept things interesting. Other than a couple of small throwbacks, Stu wasn't having much luck. He looked at his watch, pulled up anchor and cruised into the shore. He backed the trailer into the lake and cranked the boat on to head home.

Danny parked along the street and got out of his car. He walked through the old neighbourhood, noticing the changes, and remembering what hadn't changed at all. The trees were bigger, but the yards seemed smaller. Once-smooth, -white sidewalks were now weathered down to pitted, worn, grey sections of concrete. The tired front porches appeared to be yawning out towards the street as they fronted the dated houses seemingly frozen in time.

Danny took a left turn and walked up Reynolds's empty driveway and into the backyard now secluded by the overgrown cedars bordering it. He stopped and reminisced, looking at the tree where Duke had once been tied up. He remembered how Duke had so fearlessly defended him and Ben from Vince as they stood behind the tree. He could still picture Duke at the end of his rope snapping up treats as they taught him to sit and lie down. He looked at the old shed that Reynolds had impris-oned them in on that stifling day, and remembered watching through the window as Reynolds mercilessly thrashed Duke. He walked behind the shed as he heard the truck back up the driveway.

Stu maneuvered the trailer through the backyard and parked it beside the shed. Uncoupling the tongue, he turned around and opened the tailgate. He leaned into the truck bed reaching for the lifejackets and winced at the sudden pain from behind. He tried to push himself up but felt a hand on his back holding his chest to the truck bed, then felt nothing at all. Danny lifted and pushed Stu into the truck, closing the tailgate and fastening down the tonneau cover.

The drive over the potholed laneway bounced Stu's limp body around as Danny pulled up to the front of the shed. Danny got out, dropping the tailgate, and unlocked the door of the building.

Stu groggily opened his eyes, staring at the smooth cement floor and trying to figure out what had happened and where he was. His ankles were tied together, and his arms were stretched above his head by the rope bolted to the ceiling. As he dangled there, he wondered what the hell was happening. Maybe he had slipped and hit his head and was dreaming all this. The door swung open, making that thought perish from his head.

"Well, Stu, I see that you've come around. That's good," Danny said.

"Who are you, and why have you brought me here?"

"I'm a tormented soul in the present making you face your tribulations from the past."

"I've done nothing in my past to be punished for."

"You have, Stu, you have – you've just conveniently buried it. I've had to live with it all these years."

"Live with what?"

"Live with the trauma of one of your lessons, that's what. I'm one of the two kids you locked up in that sweltering shed. We could have died in there if you had left us locked up any longer."

"You're one of the kids who was messing with that damn dog I had."

"Duke, his name was Duke. He wasn't a damn dog; he was a damn good dog."

"He was a pain in the ass just like you kids were."

"He was courageous, but all you did was beat him, you cruel bastard." Danny opens the door and brings in a flexible long green branch he had trimmed.

"It wasn't bad enough you tried to suffocate us, you had to whip us as well." Danny draws the stick back and strikes it across Reynolds's back. "That's what it felt like across my back, and this is what it felt like across my friend," Danny says as he lashes him again. Stu yells out in pain as Danny whips the stick across his chest and stomach and down his back to the backs of his knees. "That's what it felt like for Duke," he yelled as Stu slowly spins from the rope in agony.

"No more, Christ, no more," Reynold's pleas.

"I've lived with our pain, Duke's pain, but now I'm making it right. I don't have to live with it any longer. This is long overdue unfinished business, old ghosts I can finally free from my mind," Danny says, cracking the stick across Stu's shoulder blades.

"Stop! I went too far with you kids, I mistreated the dog, I admit it! Just stop."

"Mistreated him? You half-starved him, and he would have collapsed from dehydration that day if we hadn't come over. As for us, you're going to find out how bad it was for us that day," Danny says, putting an injection into Reynolds.

"What do you mean? What are you doing to me, what are...," Stu's head nods forward, and Danny duct tapes his mouth.

He lowered the rope and slid Reynolds into the bed of the pickup, closing the tailgate. Locking the shed up, Danny drives down the dark laneway and back to the city to Stu's house. Linda was called into work, and he wasn't lying to her when he said he was thinking of making a trip to the cabin. He backed up Stu's driveway and across the backyard and stopped in front of the shed. The old, shed doors groaned open, and Danny pulled Stu out of the truck and inside the aging structure, closing the doors behind him.

Stu blinks his weary eyes open, recognizing the familiar surroundings in the dim light of his shed. He can't move his legs, which are secured to the legs of the old wood chair, and his hands are also tied firmly behind the chair's back. His skin stings from the discomfort of the lashings as his body presses against the hardness of the chair.

"This brings back some bad memories being in here again," Danny said, looking around the shed. "Right where you're sitting, that's where Ben and I were starting to lose consciousness in the unbearable heat in here. You were right, though; it was a lesson for us. A lesson in the inhumanity someone is capable of inflicting. Ben and I suffered from it, Duke suffered from it and now after all these years, your day of reckoning has come." Reynolds stares blankly at Danny, unable to say a word. There is nothing he can say that would change anything, nothing that Danny wants to hear. "You've got a lot of stuff lying around in this cluttered old shed. Scraps of lumber, old paint and newspaper, oily rags lying around all over the place, a real fire hazard. You're going to experience what we felt in here that blistering summer day." Danny unscrews the caps of the two partially full gas cans on the floor. To Stu's horror, he lights a match and holds the flame below one of the greasy rags scattered along the wall.

"It won't be long before it gets unbearably hot in here. It will give you enough time to feel what two little boys suffered through in here. You'll have time to think about how Duke suffered, and then you won't have time to think about anything else but your own pain as you burn." Danny steps out of the shed and rolls the doors closed as the flame slick along the bottom of the inside wall. He gets into the truck and drives across the backyard, parking it in the driveway. He strides down the sidewalk to his car, starts the engine and pulls away from the curb. By the time he drives past Stu's house, the flames are curling out the eves of the tinder-dry shed, and he can smell the smoke in the air. He thought that if Reynolds were lucky, he would die of smoke inhalation before the flames ignited the gas cans; either way, his end would be quick.

Danny drove out of the neighbourhood and headed towards the highway, intending to make his way home. Stopped at the traffic lights, he could hear the sirens of the approaching fire trucks and waited for the lights to turn green. The trucks careened through the intersection, turning past him with their horns blaring. Danny changed his mind and turned at the lights to head up to the cabin. As he drove onto the highway, he knew that the shed was fully engulfed and that by the time the fire trucks got there, the burning roof would be collapsed onto what was left of Stu. The torturous broiling shed had imprisoned its last victim, and he had vanquished one more ghost haunting him from the past.

Danny slowed and turned off from the gravel road. His headlights searched over the potholes pressed into his laneway like giant serving spoons as the tires dipped and rolled their way to the cabin. Unlocking the door, he went into the kitchen and put the water on to boil for his tea. Linda wouldn't be home from work until the morning, and he decided he would rather kick back for the night here. The cabin soothed and relaxed him, and he could feel it pulling the stress out of him as soon as he walked through the door. Opening the woodstove door, he stacked two split logs over a nest of cedar kindling. Touching a match, the flame danced to life through the fragrant cedar and curled its way around the logs. The cabin wasn't even particularly cool but putting a fire on brought it to life as if waking it from hibernation.

Danny dropped a teabag into his mug and poured hot water in. Feeling hungry, he took the French stick he had sliced up out of the freezer. He popped two thick pieces into the toaster and gave his tea a stir. Wiggling the crusty toast out, he layered on crunchy peanut butter and coated it with honey. He set his toast and tea on the coffee table and sat down into the comfort of the waiting couch. Biting into his delicious snack couldn't have tasted better while he watched the warm glow of the fire through the glass of the woodstove door.

There was nowhere else he wanted to be at this moment. He emptied his plate and could feel his eyelids getting heavy as he finished off his tea. He knew that if he sunk back into the couch, the warmth of the fire blanketing over him would cozy him to sleep. Stoking the fire with another log, he removes his dishes to the kitchen, washes them up and decides to head to bed. He lies there staring up at the ceiling, invisible overhead in the darkness of the night, and quickly falls asleep.

The morning dawned bright and sunny as Danny woke to the chorus of chirping birds coming from the trees outside his bedroom window. The coffee brewed while he stuffed two more pieces of French stick into the toaster. It had tasted so good the night before that he was more than happy to have it again. Finishing up his breakfast, Danny took the shovel and rake from the shed and walked down the driveway. He scooped shovelfuls of gravel that had been pushed to the sides of the laneway and threw it into the potholes, raking it level. He could see as he scraped and raked how the gravel had disappeared, beaten down into the roadbed and absorbed into the dirt below it. Next time, he would bring in a load of new gravel to spread out and start the cycle all over again. Danny worked all morning and finally made it to the end of the laneway. He turned and looked approvingly up the driveway at his hard work as he leaned on the shovel and arched his sore back. It was a good fix, and it would work for now.

He walked back up the driveway with the shovel and rake over his shoulder and opened the shed. Putting the tools in the corner, he picked up the stick he had lashed Stu with and snapped it in half the same way he had done with Duke's whipping stick. He threw it into the firepit, as he didn't want any reminders of what he was able to finally put behind him.

Locking the shed, he went into the cabin and poured himself one more cup of coffee. The coffee steamed from his mug as he rested, pushing the curve of his spine into the solid back of the pine chair. His mind roller coaster through all the monsters and dragons he had slain from his past, all the nightmares that would no longer haunt him. Glancing at his watch, he washed out his mug and closed the cabin. Danny slowly drove down the flat, dentless surface of his driveway. He could feel the old torments being lifted from his past, hoping one day to have his mind free and as smooth as the laneway into his cabin now was.

CHAPTER TWENTY-FIVE

"So, there's no obvious connection between Evans and our killer that's turned up yet," Kent said as she gets into Casey's car.

"They've had to cross paths somewhere in the past for him to unleash his wrath on her."

"It doesn't seem to be because of love or money. Unless he worked with her sometime in the past, it's still a mystery."

"This next victim was some of his handiwork, I'm sure," Casey said as he pulled up to the curb. "Victim's name was Stu Reynolds."

"This is the third victim from the killer's old neighbourhood," Kent said as she gets out of the car and looks around. They walk through the backyard and stand in front of the charred remains of the shed.

"Fire marshal said that with the flammables stored inside, the shed basically became a crematorium. They weren't expecting to find a body underneath the burning rubble," Casey said.

"They had to identify him from his dental records," Kent said. "My God, I hope the killer didn't burn him alive."

"You can probably bet that he did. The killer is dealing out payback here, don't forget. Something has happened to him inside this shed sometime in the past. Reynolds has done something to him in there as a kid – there's no doubt about that. He could have easily killed him in the house; burning him out here was planned." Casey looks at the burnt-off trailer tire and burnt remains of the motor on the boat.

"There's certainly no evidence left behind here to connect our killer to the crime," Kent said, looking at the charred rubble.

"Actually, there is. Forensics went over the truck, and there were rope fibres in the bed that match the same rope used in the other murders. No sign of anything in the house, though."

"So, it was our killer at work here for certain, then."

"Judging by the recent tracks on the lawn, I'm guessing Stu was out fishing for the day and that when he got back, the killer was waiting for him here. He needed to reckon with him first but didn't want to risk doing it here, so he put him out and took him to wherever he takes his victims. He tied him up and threw him back in the truck to bring him back here to do him in. It had to be done here – the shed held some connection for the killer to the original incident."

"So, he tied Reynolds up inside still alive, set a slow burn and walked away. How horrific," Kent said.

"Yes, he would have had just enough time to walk away, and then it wouldn't have taken any time at all for an old shed to go up in flames. They said it had almost burnt to the ground by the time the fire department got here."

"Reynolds would have had just enough time to think about his plight just like all of the other killer's victims. How symbolic, how sad."

"What is sad is that we have a merciless killer on a mission still, a twelfth victim and are still not much closer solving these cases than when we started," Casey said.

"I'll check into Reynolds's background to see if there is any possible connection the killer may have had with him, but if it's anything like Evans, I'm afraid we might be coming up dry again," Kent said.

"He must have abused or burnt the kid in there. Something has to turn up, somebody has to have been charged with something along the line somewhere. There's got to be a connection somehow from the past."

"Take it easy, Casey – there's got to be a solid clue showing up sooner or later."

"That's the problem: if it's not sooner, our next victims will never see later," Casey said as they walked back to the car.

Brooks finished his lunch, plunking his knife and fork onto his plate. Pushing his chair away from the table, he walked over to the counter and slid his plate into the sink on top of his breakfast dishes.

At the front of the garage, his workbench was cluttered with an array of tools and uncompleted, disassembled projects. An old upright vacuum sat with the beater bar taken out of it, waiting for a plastic replacement clip that had broken inside. A toaster was apart and lying on its side because the lever would no longer stay down. There was a worn pot with a loose handle that needed a stripped screw to be replaced.

Brooks opened the side door of the garage and brought in an old floor lamp, setting it on the workbench. It had become wobbly, as the weighted center was no longer secure in the metal base. He tightened the bottom bolt, but the pole continued to wobble back and forth. Taking the center out, he bent the edge of the base slightly cutting his finger in the process. Pushing the center back in, he became frustrated to see that it was still loose. As the blood spotted out of his finger, Brooks lost his patience, took his hammer, and beat the living crap out of the edge of the metal base. Setting the lamp upright, the wobble was even worse now. Brooks threw his hammer on the workbench and went back inside the house.

Sitting on the living room couch, he clicked through the channels and decided to watch a Saturday afternoon football game already in progress. He could feel himself becoming drowsy and was fighting to stay awake. Soon, he was sound asleep, snoring away with his head pitched back on the couch, oblivious to the play-by-play commentary coming from the television. Snoring through the second quarter, he stirred and partially opened one eye at halftime and then slept through the third and fourth quarters of the game. The clunk of the remote hitting the floor jarred him awake. Looking at the time, he was miffed that he had fallen asleep for so long. Saturday night was his bowling night, and he wanted to get to the lanes by seven. He didn't have enough time to get involved with preparing a drawn-out meal, so a TV dinner would have to suffice. Brooks puts the dinner into the oven and washes the dishes piling up in the sink. He goes into the bedroom to change and puts on his favourite bowling shirt.

"Damn lamp," he says, looking at the cut on his finger. He wraps a bandage around the cut, hoping it won't throw off his bowling game.

Turning off the stove, Brooks takes the hot dish over to the table on top of an oven mitt. Salisbury steak: not his dinner of choice, but mostly all that was left on sale when he got to the store. It was quick and easy and would hit the spot for now. Calling it a steak was a joke, he thought as he cut the pressed hamburger with a fork and stirred the gravy into the mashed potatoes. Flipping the lid on the trash container, he dropped the black plastic tray into the bag and left the house, getting into the car. He pulled into the parking lot at the bowling alley just after seven o'clock. He could feel the weight of the ball pressing against the cut as he stepped forward swinging his arm down the lane. The ball curved to the left and knocked down two pins as he stood shaking his head at the outcome.

Danny finished cutting the lawn and tipped the lawn mower partially up on its side. Using a wooden paint stir stick, he scraped the underside of the mower deck free of the mounding layer of moist grass. Pushing the mower into the garden shed, he took out the lawn rake and cleaned up the clumps of minced grass, dumping them into a yard waste bag.

"Lawn looks good," Linda said as he came into the house.

"Yeah, you work like a bugger to get it to grow and then you wish it would slow down once it gets going."

"Are you done out there? Dinner is almost ready."

"Yes, just give me a minute to wash up," Danny said, going into the washroom. The soap lathered green as he rubbed his hands under the tap.

"You haven't forgotten I'm going into work tonight, have you?"

"No, it's been quite a while since you've had to work a Saturday."

"I know. They've needed me more through the week lately for some reason."

"My goodness, stuffed chicken breast, wild rice and creamed cauliflower," Danny said, cutting into the chicken. "Wrap these in bacon and I'd marry you all over again."

"You'd marry me again if I served you wieners and beans every night."

"That's true, but there would have to be lasagne too."

"Are you going up to the cabin to stay over tonight?"

"No, there're a few more things I would like to catch up on around here."

"I'm impressed. I know you would rather be there, even if you are working when you are up there."

"I fixed the whole driveway up last time I was there, smooth as a baby's bottom now. Everything is pretty ship-shape there; you'll have to come up with me next time you have a weekend off."

"Yes, I'd like that. It's been a while."

"It has; it will be perfect. Just you and me all cozied up on the couch in front of a roaring fire in the woodstove with a bottle of wine."

"And no mice running around, right?"

"No mice running around, guaranteed."

"It's a date, then. You better not be lying to me."

"Me? Never, but I'll hold you to that date."

"You keep looking at your watch like you have to be somewhere," Linda said, taking the dishes off the table.

"Just checking the time because I know you have to get going soon."

"As a matter of fact, I do. I should go upstairs and get changed now."

"Just leave those dishes. I'll clean up in here." Danny puts the leftovers in the refrigerator and is just tidying up as Linda comes down the stairs.

"Nice job on the kitchen. Thank you, I just might hire you full-time."

"You're such a good cook, I'll work for food," Danny said as he gives her a kiss goodbye.

"I'll see you in the morning," Linda said as she opened the door and walked out to her car. He waved and watched out the window as Linda drove down the street. Danny steps into the garage and opens the cardboard box containing his rope, syringes, and duct tape. He packs a bag, also putting a timer in. He wraps a small cardboard box slightly larger than his hand in brown paper and cuts one side out of it. Evening has crept in as Danny starts his car and pulls out into the street. This monster he must purge from his nightmares has been haunting him from the past for far too long. The justice he will serve will be final and long overdue. It has waited patiently like an arrow in its quiver to be plucked out, firmly drawn, and decisively launched.

Brooks bowled his final frame and then sat down to take his shoes off. The game he bowled wasn't so terrible; it could have been far worse. The bandage held firm on his finger, but he could feel pulsing beneath the cut. Pushing through the doors into the emptying parking lot, he got into his car and drove out down the boulevard. Pulling up to the intersection, he stopped for the red light, drumming his fingers impatiently on the steering wheel, waiting for the signal to turn green. The light changed, and the driver in front of him momentarily hesitated to move forward.

"Come on, sister, sometime this year," he yelled out the window as he honked his horn. He tailgated the car through the intersection and then stomped on the gas, steering around and passing it as he cursed. His headlights rebounded off the faded green garage door as he arrived home. He thought he had closed the side door of the garage, noticing it was slightly open as he walked to the house. Poking his head into the garage, he took a quick look and then closed the door. He fumbled the key into the side door of the house and pushed it open, going inside.

Danny snugged up beside the curb and turned off the car engine. Looping the handles of the bag around his wrist, he picked up the paper-wrapped box from the seat. Stepping onto the sidewalk and closing the car door, he was transported back to another time, taking a long look around. He remembered the familiar houses from when he walked up the same sidewalk with Gloria after school. Their old wood windows had been replaced, now encased in the shine of new vinyl frames; modern porch lights brightened the doorways, but they were the same old houses etched in time. There was the fire hydrant layered in red paint that he tied his shoe on while Gloria held his books. He walked up the driveway that he hadn't set foot on for decades, opened the aluminium storm door and knocked on the entry door. It was the same door he had so wildly swung open when making a hasty exit so many years ago. He could still hear the thud it made off the doorstop as he had pushed his way out the storm door like it was yesterday. Brooks opened the door and silently stood there staring apprehensively with his shirt half unbuttoned.

"Good evening, sir – how are you this evening?" Brooks neither moved a muscle nor said a word. "I'm in the neighbourhood with a special offer that will save you hundreds of dollars on your grocery bill."

"Goodbye, I'm not interested," Brooks grunted.

"You'd be surprised at how fast the savings add up."

"Piss off! Are you deaf?"

"I understand if this isn't a good time, sir. Please accept this free sample and my card and think it over – our gift to you." Danny holds the box up with his left hand. As Brooks reaches out, Danny pulls his other hand out of the empty box and plunges a syringe into him. Danny pushed him back into the hallway as he stepped inside the door. Brooks tries to regain his balance and push back as Danny pivots him against the wall. The strength fades from his arms as he feels himself sliding down the wall, his legs feeling like they are sinking into quicksand. The floor is cold and hard, but he is oblivious to its discomfort as Danny turns around and closes the door.

Brooks regains consciousness, his neck stiff as his chin rests pushed into his chest. He feels the discomfort of a rope binding his wrists together behind the kitchen chair he is seated on. The same rope wraps around his ankles, holding them tight to the front legs of the chair. Turning his head to the side and back, he tries to crack the stiffness out of his neck as he looks at the figure sitting at his kitchen table.

"Who the fuck are you to be coming in here and trying me up," Brooks said.

"You know, there's some interesting information in here," Danny said as he flips the pages of the textbook.

"Did you hear me?" Brooks said, louder.

"For instance, a lot of people think spiders are insects, but they're not; they are arachnids."

"Who the fuck gives a shit about bugs. Who are you?"

"Calling them bugs is incorrect as well," Danny says, turning a page."

"What the hell," Brooks says.

"An insect has three body parts. A head, thorax, and abdomen, plus two antennae. A spider only has two body parts and no antennae."

"Fuck, are you for real?"

"Six legs – an insect has six legs; a spider has eight. Can you remember that?"

"What the hell is this,"?" Brooks said.

"I guess you could say this is another one of those kitchen science lessons, Mr. Brooks."

"Who the hell are you?"

"I'm who you referred to once as Mr. Schoolboy," Danny said, slamming the textbook closed. "Do you feel any smarter now? You don't look any smarter. Do you remember those words of encouragement?" Brooks' mind stumbles and shuffles back until it grasps the familiarity of the words, drawing them forward from the past and spilling them across his memory like beads from a broken necklace.

"You're that kid that used to help Gloria here."

"I couldn't help her enough. I couldn't help her get away from you, you sick, abusive bastard."

"You don't know squat," Brooks said.

"I know the abuse you put your wife through until she finally couldn't take it anymore and got the courage up to take Gloria and leave you and move in with her sister. I sat here and watched as you dehumanised her and Gloria. I had a monster like you once try and grab me, but you're the worst kind of monster for what you did to your stepdaughter. You think I didn't know that you sick puke?" Danny takes the textbook and slams it into the side of Brooks' face so forcefully that it toppled the chair over, smashing his head onto the floor. Blood trickled from one of Brooks' nostrils as Danny pulled the chair upright.

"You don't think I knew the pain and horror you were subjecting her to,"?" he said as he swings the sharp corner of the book into the side of Brooks' ribs and Brooks lets out a gasp of pain.

"I can't take it back."

"No, you can't – that's for damn sure – and you can't go back and congratulate her. You couldn't even offer her one kind word of praise. She did a hell of a job on that project, got her credit for that class while enduring your abuse, but you couldn't give her a crumb of recognition. You just used and abused her, you sad sack of shit," Danny said as he walloped the other side of his face with the textbook, sending blood splattering up the wall.

"Stop! What's done is done," Brooks cries out.

"How's it feel to be on the receiving end of it? This is just for Mrs. Brooks' pain and suffering. We're not done, not by a long shot, yet."

"My head is splitting, I'm in so much pain," Brooks said as blood dripped off his chin onto his bowling shirt.

"You don't know what pain is yet," Danny said as he stuck a needle into Brooks. "That's what you told Gloria when I was sitting right here, but she knew what pain was. She felt the horror when she came home every day. She felt the terror when you forced yourself on her and ripped the soul right out of her body. Fuck you, you remorseless bastard." Brooks is no longer able to hold his head up as Danny tilts the chair and drags him down the hallway. The back legs of the chair shudder against the hardwood floor as they scrape a sharp turn into the bedroom. The aging hardwood had stood resilient against the footsteps of a raging monster unleashing his fury on two undeserving souls. It had been the pathway for unspeakable atrocities that no one should have had to endure. The hard grain of the hallway would never bear witness to the returning footsteps of that monster again.

Brooks opens his eyes to the brightness of the ceiling light fixture smarting into his vision. Blinking away the lambency, he feels the discomfort of rope around his wrists and ankles still, as a pillow props up the back of his head. Dried blood crusted in his nose, and a dull ache pushed its way through his brain. No longer in the chair, he is tied securely to the four posts of his bed, laid out like a starfish. Behind the sun-faded curtains, the blinds are pulled down, resting on the sills of the bedroom windows. Feeling the grip of the rope biting into him as it wraps around his waist, he looks down and is horrified to see the weight that is pressing against his groin.

"I took the liberty of borrowing your skilsaw," Danny said. "It looks brand new, doesn't look like you've used it very much."

"No, no, Christ, no," Brooks says.

"For years, I had my own monster chasing me in my dreams, molesting me in my nightmares. I was finally able to put that monster to rest permanently, but there were still other monsters that haunted me, monsters like you that wouldn't go away. The guilt also hung over me that I couldn't do anything to stop that monster from hurting Gloria when I knew she was suffering. This is unfinished business that has been eating away at me like a cancer. A final justice that needs to be dispensed. You subjected that poor girl to physical and emotional abuse and a crime so evil that a thousand punishments won't bring justice. This punishment will fit the crime, though."

"For the love of God, don't do this," Brooks yelled.

"I'm sure that's what Gloria screamed to deaf ears. By rights, I should cut you in half with a chainsaw for what you did to her."

"Please take it off," Brooks pleaded as he felt the sharp carbide-tipped blade pressing into his pants. He began to scream, and Danny duct tapes his mouth shut.

"I've locked the switch on and taped back the blade guard, so everything is ready to go. The cord is plugged into that timer on the wall. You'll have about fifteen minutes after I leave to think about how you treated your wife and what you subjected

Gloria to. What I suffered from as a result was traumatic but small in comparison to the terror she had to live through." Brooks strains at the ropes so hard his hands turn purple as he panics at his desperate situation and the inevitable outcome.

"Their pain lasted for years, and they are still struggling with it today. I know that feeling very well. Your pain will be short-lived-in comparison; bleeding to death quickly will be your saving grace." Brooks' screams muffle into the duct tape as he jerks against the grip of the rope, the saw weighing firmly into his crotch.

"I'll leave you to your thoughts, now; it will soon get messy in here. I have no need to see you suffer. I am more than satisfied knowing that justice is being delivered." Danny moves to the doorway and turns towards Brooks. "This one is for Gloria," he says as he leaves the bedroom.

As he walked down the driveway, he remembered thinking back to how he thought it was going to be the last time he was going to be able to help Gloria when he left the house so many years ago. He hoped he had now helped her again by slaying this horrific dragon from her mind, and it would give her the closure that she so desperately needed after all these years when she found out. He knew it was one less nightmare, one more monster that was banished from his past now as he got in his car and pulled away. These old houses he was driving past held many happy memories from the past. There were the tragic few that held the darkest of secrets that no one could have possibly imagined, such as the one he was driving past with the faded green garage door.

CHAPTER TWENTY-SIX

Casey turns the pages of the forensic report as he taps the tip of his pen on the desk. Drawing his fist up alongside his jaw, his thumb clicks the refill in and out of the barrel of the pen. The report frustrates him as he reads through, telling him little more than he already knew.

"That's a look of disappointment if I ever saw one," Kent said as she sets the two coffees and a brown paper bag down on the desk.

"There's not much here that will point us in any new direction," Casey said.

"I was afraid of that: burnt bodies and burnt-out crime scenes are never evidence-friendly. Other than the rope fibres found in the truck, there's not much else to connect with the other murders."

"The killer definitely took Reynolds somewhere to rough him up, but the report indicates that his fractures are from the collapse of the shed," Casey says, peeking into the bag. "What's this – no donuts?"

"Banana or blueberry muffins. Take your pick," Kent said.

"No chocolate chip?"

"No chocolate nothing for your own good today; these will be healthier for you."

"Thanks," Casey frowns as he takes a banana muffin out of the bag and bites into the side of it. "These muffins are good, but I don't think I'm quite ready yet to part ways with my donuts."

"I'm sorry to have to tell you that Reynolds didn't have any record of assaults or any other charges that would give us a lead on this case," Kent said as she breaks the top off a blueberry muffin.

"Of course, not; that might have pointed us directly to the killer. Would have made it too easy to give us the name of a possible suspect."

"Reynolds hasn't done anything bad enough to be charged with, but for the killer to do this to him, Reynolds has to have hurt or burned him bad enough for the killer to deal this kind of revenge out."

"Whatever it was he did, it definitely was our killer's motive," Casey said.

"I certainly feel your frustration, but I hadn't held out much hope of any ground-breaking clues when I saw those charred ruins," Kent said.

"So, we continue to chase after missing pieces of the puzzle," Casey said as his phone rang on his desk. Kent could see the disturbed look on his face as he listened to the details of the call sliding into his ear. She finishes her muffin, knowing it won't be long before she grabs her coffee and her coat, and she heads out the door and down the stairs. It won't be long until she closes the door to Casey's car, and they are off down the street on their way to meet the next murder victim.

Before she knows it, she will be looking at the next gruesome scene searching for some logic, some explanation to the madness that has taken place in front of her and trying afterwards to unstick the image that may forever stay branded into her mind. Casey ends the call and puts his phone down on the desk, pushing it forward as if he could distance himself somehow from the conversation that just occurred.

"By the look on your face, we are about to meet our thirteenth victim, I'm assuming." Casey lifts his cup up and takes a slow drink before answering.

"Believe me, it's unlucky number thirteen by the sounds of it. You may want to sit this one out, from what the responding officer is telling me."

"I'm in this investigation to see it through to the end with you; there's no quitting now. From what I've seen so far, I don't think anything this killer will do will phase me. My skin has grown a little thicker since we started investigating these murders. Since that first incident with the bombed-out car, I've been steeling myself against what to expect next."

"I'm just saying, no one would blame you if you took a pass on this one. I'm not even sure if I'm going to be prepared for this."

"I'm not going to lie to you and pretend these murders don't bother me. They have been some of the most disturb-ing crime scenes I have ever had to deal with in my career on the force. I could have stepped away at any time; call it pride or stubbornness, I was determined to see this investigation through to the end. No matter how much it may disturb me, I've been assigned to this investigation. I've got a job to do, Casey, and I'll be damned if I'm going to bail on you."

"There's been some challenging crime scenes, and I admire your resolve. There's no one else I would rather have working with me on these cases."

Kent looks out the car window at the familiar streets passing by and feels a slight ping of anxiety as they approach their destination. "Are we going back to the killer's old neighbourhood again?"

"We're going to be close; a good twenty-minute walk from it."

"What did they tell you they found that's got you so revved up?"

"Something we're not sure we are going to believe until we see it, so we are about to find out for ourselves," Casey said as he pulls into Brooks' driveway. Kent reaches for the door handle and takes a deep breath, swallowing back the apprehension that is creeping up her throat like a furry caterpillar.

She remembers how, as a little girl, she'd lie in bed at night, her imagination rolling, churning up her worst fears about there being a monster under her bed. She had tried to get her courage up and dare to take a look to dispel her fright, but what if she hung over the mattress looking under her the bed and found a pair of red eyes glaring back at her? What if a slimy claw reached out, grabbing her, and pulled her under the bed? If she screamed out, would her parents hear her? Would she even be able to scream out, or would her throat be so constricted with fear that nothing would come out at all? She pulled the covers up tightly over her nose, not moving or making a sound. If she didn't look, she would hope to stay safe but would lay there night after night, fearing the unknown. She laid there night after night for as long as she could remember in her childhood, fearing that unknown monster.

"Damn it, Casey, I'm going in there," Kent said, pulling the door handle and opening the door.

"You won't get any argument from me. I'll be right behind you."

Casey opens the storm door and follows in behind Kent. She picks up the blood-smeared textbook from the kitchen table and looks at the blood-spotted wall.

"Looks like the question-and-answer period started in here with Mr. Brooks," she said, setting the book back down.

"Looks like it ended back there," Casey said, noticing the scuff marks down the hallway. A forensics officer looks out from the bedroom and motions them towards the room. Casey and Kent enter the bedroom and stop inside the doorway, staring at Brooks lying in his blood-soaked bed, the skilsaw still tied between his legs. They both take a step back in shock, as if some invisible hand gave them a shove. Blood covers the saw and has rooster tailed across the room and up the wall to the ceiling. Brooks' body is pale white, lying on a sea of red sheets. The skin on his wrists is worn raw from tugging at the ropes.

"Am I seeing what I think I'm seeing?" Kent said, aghast at the sight in front of her.

"I tried to warn you," Casey said. "It's our killer's work, no doubt about that. There's his rope and the timer on the wall to delay the victim's death and give him a few minutes of terror to contemplate his past deeds, the ones he's paying the price for."

"He's obliterated his genitals with that saw," Kent said, still keeping her distance from the bed.

"That and then some I would say. I don't need to wait for the autopsy report to tell me he bled to death."

"He actually tied a saw to his groin; unbelievable."

"It's a little much to take in all of a sudden. You going to be alright?"

"I don't think either of us is going to be alright after we get through this investigation. What was Brooks, some kind of a rapist, to end up being murdered this way?"

"It's hard to say. He was bowling Saturday night; that's the last time anyone saw him. The killer must have been waiting for him when he got home, roughed him up in the kitchen and dragged him in here on the chair to rig this all up."

"How did anyone find him?"

"The saw ran Saturday night after the killer left for some time. Someone would have heard it if it ran into the night, but the timer wasn't set for very long, as the killer knew Brooks would bleed to death quickly. Even if someone had heard it and found him shortly after, it would have been too late. The cleaning service comes in every other Monday; thank goodness it was today. The woman found him this morning and was hysterical on the phone when she called in."

"My God, I imagine she was," Kent said. "There's more blood in the room than left in him, I think."

"Once again, our killer got in, set his retribution up and got out before the murder even took place."

"Brooks must have sexually assaulted the killer years ago for him to do this to him."

"Or someone he knew, possibly. Again, we'll check if Brooks had any assault charges against him, and we'll possibly get some names of victims that may have retaliated."

"I'll check, but if it's anything like Reynolds, don't get your hopes up."

"I have to hope for something to show up, or else we will just be coming to another dead end," Casey said.

"What was the significance of the killer beating him with that textbook in the kitchen? Was that just handy, or was it symbolic from the past?"

"He was too old to be in school with our killer, and he wasn't a teacher, so maybe there is a connection that will show up when we dig into his past; or maybe not. We have to follow up on any possibility; the clues are so sparse, we can't afford to allow any clue to go unchecked," Casey said.

"This is also close enough to our killer's old neighbourhood that it has to have been a part of his life growing up."

"As troubling as his life was growing up, it's all been a result of what's driving him now; we just have to connect the dots somehow."

"We best do it soon. These murders are getting more and more bizarre," Kent said. "Freezing, burning, mutilation; if they are all representative of what he went through growing, up it's a wonder he even survived his childhood."

"He survived, but he's making damn sure his victims don't survive their punishment," Casey said as he photographed the room.

"I don't think I'm ever going to forget the image this has left in my mind," Kent said. The scenes from these murders were far worse than any fears she had imagined when she was a little girl. The grisly reality of it all seeped into the corners of her mind and parked itself firmly in place. She had fearlessly flung open the doors to these grim realities and faced them head on. Every case took its toll, every horrific image wedged itself into her memory like an axe swung into a wooden stump. She no longer feared the monster under her bed; it was no longer there. It was roaming around at will and pulling itself into her mind with a slimy claw in the form of each new murder she investigated.

CHAPTER TWENTY-SEVEN

Danny unclips the winch strap from the bow hook and pushes the aluminium boat off the trailer bed. Hopping into the boat, he hits the tilt button, lowering the engine into the water. With one turn of the key, the engine fires up as lily pads bob over the wash rippling out from the hull. Water lilies explode their snowy petals out like miniature white fireworks erupting from the lake, their spidery yellow centres tickling upwards towards the sky. Danny dips his arm over the side of the boat and draws a water sample up, one of four he takes as he crosses the lake. Labelling the vials, he sets them in their cases and cruises up to the anchored fishermen nearby.

"Good afternoon, gentlemen. How's the fishing been so far today?"

"Not so good – we still have all our bait."

"Well, hopefully that will all change soon. Could I see your fishing licenses please?" They each pull out their licence, and Danny takes a quick look over the equipment in the boat. "Thanks, gents. Hope the action improves and remember your limits."

"We wish that was going to be our big concern; we can only hope." Danny gives them a wave and throttled over to check out the other boats fishing on the lake.

It was a good afternoon with everyone in compliance on the water this time around. As Danny checked out the last fishing party, he noticed some boaters paddling across the lake with their motor pulled up out of the water. The breeze had picked up, and they were fighting a light chop that was pushing them sideways as they tried to paddle their boat forward. Pushing the throttle down, he steered his boat across the short expanse of water pulling alongside of them as he slowed the engine to a purr.

"You folks look like you're having some engine trouble; or are you out of gas?"

"Lots of gas; the engine just cut out on us all of a sudden."

"Can I give you a tow to shore?"

"That would be fantastic. We are fighting a losing battle here," they said as Danny tossed them a tow rope. Danny cruises into shore and tows them to the launch dock where the grateful boaters release his line and yell out a big "thank you."

"You're welcome," Danny hollered back as he pulled in the rope. He trolled over to where he had launched and nudged the boat back on the trailer. The water gushed from the trailer as he pulled it from the lake and headed back to the conservation authority compound. Wheeling into the compound yard, he backed the trailer up beside the storage shed and uncoupled it from the truck hitch. With the water sample kit in one hand and his thermos in the other, he went into the office and sat down at his desk. He poured the last of one more cup of coffee, draining his thermos, and turned on his laptop. As the laptop booted up, he gazed out the window while putting his thumbnail to his mouth and biting at the edge of it. As his tooth scraped away at the tip of the nail, his mind drifted out through the office window and into the past.

It was his second year returning to high school, and the absence of Rob Dover hung heavy in the air. He had been well-liked by students and fellow staff, and his presence was sorely missed by all who had known him. School just didn't feel the same to Danny without Rob's smiling face greeting him into the classroom. The new science teacher didn't have Rob's charisma or flair to make the lessons entertaining or as engaging. He taught with a "here it is, get it done" style that was blunt and mechanical in its delivery, served up like half-cooked pasta on a stone-cold plate.

Danny considered himself lucky and breathed a sigh of relief when he discovered that Brad Parker wasn't in his physical education class this year. Between Brad and Glen, last year was a year of torment that he was glad he could put behind him. This year, something more insidious would rear its ugly head in the form of John Luker. John was a new physical education teacher and coach at the high school who was demanding and intimidating in his approach and too hands on as far as Danny was concerned. It was a warm day in September when Danny first felt an uncomfortable sensation waft over him. Luker had the gym class running laps around the track. Danny was fast on short sprints, but how he hated pounding his way around the hard-packed track.

"Another lap," Luker yelled out as they rounded the corner to where they'd started. Danny's heart thumped against his ribcage as his lungs burned inside his chest. He rounded the track only to hear Luker shout "again." The class staggered around the oval a third time, once again to hear Luker bark out "one more time around." Some of the boys slowed to a walk, some stopped momentarily bending over with their hands on their knees to huff air into their starving lungs. Danny slowly plodded along with his hand gripping the painful cramp in his side.

"Let's run it in, boys," Luker shouted. "Time to hit the showers." Danny climbed the steps leading to the changing rooms, his legs moving as if they were full of lead.

"Step it up, Rosen. You haven't got all day," Luker said, swinging his hand across Danny's behind. The swat surprised him; Luker's hand had remained there too long, making Danny uncomfortable as he sprang ahead out of reach.

Danny and his classmates stripped off their shorts and sweaty tee shirts and entered the large shower chamber. Standing there rinsing off in the group shower was something he could never get comfortable with. Luker came into the changing room with an arm full of towels and dumped them on the bench as the boys started to leave the shower.

"Eight minutes to bell," Luker said, poking his head into the shower entrance. Danny turned towards the shower wall as he felt Luker's gaze staring over him and the other students. The seconds ticked away feeling like an eternity until Danny finally turned around to see that Luker was no longer there staring. Danny stepped out from the shower quickly snatching up a towel from the bench. One of his classmates, Tom Becker, limped past him with his leg still cramping from the track run. The coach had him sit down on the far end of the bench while pulling a chair up in front of Tom and stretching his leg out. Danny dried off, watching as Luker steadied Tom's foot against his crotch and massaged his calf while glancing over at him while he dressed. Danny could see the awkward look on Tom's face as he felt his own embarrassment shivering through him. Tom was intimidated by the coach's authority and sat there frozen as Luker massaged up his leg to the top and underside of his thigh. Danny looked away, tying his shoes as Luker pushed at Tom's leg muscle under the towel. There was only the three of them left in the changing room, and Danny had a funny feeling about leaving Tom behind with Luker. Much to his relief, the class bell rang, and Luker pushed the chair to the corner while Becker hurriedly got dressed. They both left the changing room to go to their next class without saying a word.

Despite the new science teacher's lacklustre teaching approach, Danny still performed well in class. Science came second nature to him, and he absorbed the class lessons like he was on autopilot. Other students weren't as fortunate, and some ended up dropping the class. He knew if Rob were still here teaching the class, he would have worked diligently with those students and tried his damnedest for that not to happen. Gym class was another matter. His class was now in the gymnastics program, and John Luker's aggressive push for more performance took a lot of the fun out of it. Danny was developing his co-ordination over the long box vault when Luker decided to stack it at full height.

"Okay, Rosen, I want you to do a hand flip over the box," Luker said.

"You got to be kidding, coach. I'll never make it over at that height."

"Don't say never, just get your speed up and the momentum will take you over."

"I don't know about this, coach."

"Just go. I'll be standing at the side to spot you over." Danny looks at the box looming in front of him, almost as tall as he is. Luker stood at the side of the vaulting box, ready to push against Danny's back to help him complete the flip if needed. Danny took in a deep breath and ran towards the vault box. Reaching the box, he jumped up, diving over, and placing his outstretched hands on its vinyl-covered top. He could feel the weight of his legs dragging behind over him as the momentum of the flip waned. Luker pushed on his rear end while his other hand slid from his pelvis down onto his groin. Danny reactively pulled his knees downward, shifting his weight and throwing himself off balance. He tumbled down the side of the vaulting box, landing on his back and knocking the wind out of himself.

"Are you okay?" Luker said, running around the box. Danny laid on the floor like a stunned bird after hitting a window. Tom came running over, lifting one of Danny's arms while the coach helped him up, lifting the other.

"I've got a sharp pain in my lower back," Danny said as Tom helped him over to a chair and eased him down.

"I saw what he did to you on the vault; I saw him grope you," Tom said.

"He caused this whole accident, he's a pervert. You saw how he acted in the changing room, leering at us, and massaging your leg. What was that all about?

"I thought that was normal. I thought he was helping me, but then I didn't know what to do."

"Do about what, Tom?"

"He had my foot jammed between his legs while he worked his way up mine. I could feel him getting hard against my foot. I was freaking out, but I was in shock at the same time. I didn't know what was happening."

"I knew it. I had a funny feeling about him – that's why I didn't leave you behind in the changing room."

"Thanks, Danny. I was so afraid," Tom said, looking uncomfortably at the floor.

"Yeah, I was never so happy to hear a bell ring in my life," Danny said, looking up at Tom's vacant stare. "Are you alright?"

"He fondled me under that towel. The fucker touched me right before the bell rang."

"What do you think we should do?"

"What can we do? Nobody's going to believe us. It will just be our word against his, then what?"

"Then we will be doing laps around the track for the rest of the year," Danny said.

"When word gets out what we are trying to accuse him of, everyone's going to think we're gay or something." Danny and Tom were victims silenced by a culture that would ultimately shame them for speaking out. The only thing they could do was try and limit their vulnerability to Luker. They tried to be the first ones into the showers and the first ones out of the changing room.

Danny and Tom were doing some extra training in the weight room after school, determined to increase their upper body strength. They took turns spotting each other on the bench press, adding ten pounds to the weight bar until they could no longer push the weights all the way up off their chests.

"One hundred and sixty-five pounds for three reps, that's pretty good just starting out," Danny said as he lifted the bar off Tom's chest.

"Okay for a couple of rookies, but we've got a lot of work ahead of us." The door handle turns, and they are reluctant to see John Luker come into the room.

"I noticed that the two of you started using the room recently. Good to see you boys putting in some extra work."

"We're just having a little fun here, coach; nothing serious," Danny said.

"If you want to see results, you have to take it seriously. I've got a weight training program I want you to start right away that will get you those results." Danny knew that once the coach got involved, it would be push, push, push, and working with the coach was the last thing they wanted to do.

"It's okay, coach. We have a routine worked out that we are sticking to," Tom said.

"You have a routine? Who's the coach here, you or me?"

"You are, coach, but..."

"There are no buts about it, Tom. I'm starting with you, one-on-one. Twice a week here, Tuesday and Thursday after school, starting now, and you'll have the results you need in six weeks. Rosen: I'll work with you after I'm finished with Tom's training."

"Coach, I don't think Tom, or I intended to have an intensive program to follow when we decided to do this."

"Let me put it this way," Luker said. "If you finish this six-week program, I'll guarantee that you both have a high passing mark at the end of the year. If you don't participate, I'll guarantee that neither one of you gets a passing mark or the credit for this course for the year. Leave us to it, Rosen. I don't have all the time in the world."

The next thing Danny knew, he was standing outside the weight room door wondering what the hell had just happened. Luker had taken their simple afterschool plan and railroaded them into a situation he was manipulating for his own sordid benefit. His first instinct was to turn around, push the door open and tell Luker they weren't going to be intimidated into going along with his contemptible plan. As he pushed on the door, a click of the door lock meant Danny never had a chance and Tom's fate was sealed.

Danny bit off the sharp edge of his thumbnail and threw it into the wastepaper basket. He filled out the paperwork for the water samples, angrily carving the information into the forms with his pen. The details in the weight room that Tom had related to him over his following weeks of training were flashing back in his mind. Tom confided to him how he had been groped and fondled under his shorts. Danny was sickened to hear how Luker had exposed himself and sexually assaulted Tom in their sessions in the weight room. Danny snapped his pen in half, angry at Luker and furious at himself for letting Luker intimidate him into silence. Danny never had to endure Luker's special program. Tom never did finish the six weeks of sexual abuse; before the end of four weeks, he had committed suicide. There was no note blaming anyone, no explanation. Everyone was shocked, but nobody knew why. Luker knew why — Danny knew why. Danny knew Tom was hiding the shame and embarrassment, living with the stigma and fear of someone finding out. Luker played on those fears, intimidating Tom into silence and submission, threatening him with repercussions if he ever spoke out. Tom suffered in silence — ashamed, protecting his family from embarrassment, Danny being his only confidant.

Luker wasn't going to push his luck – he didn't bother Danny anymore. He gave Danny a passing grade for the class and a credit for it at the end of the year. Danny didn't have Luker as a teacher the following year, but he knew Luker would continue with his predatory ways. There would be new unsuspecting victims falling prey to his intimidating abuse, countless lives ruined by his career of sexual misconduct. This was evil in its purest form, as Danny saw it, an authority figure violating a position of trust with vulnerable lives. It amounted to nothing less than a reign of sexual terrorism. Even though they felt as if their hands were tied, he felt like he had failed Tom, and he felt guilty for being a survivor. Luker had made him carry that weight from the day of Tom's suicide forward. If only he could have acted, done something, had the courage to speak up, Tom might still have been alive today. If Rob Dover had still been around, he would have confided in him, and Rob would have believed them. Rob would have known what to do, but as fate would have it, tragedy would beget more tragedy. Fate would saddle him with that weight until Danny could purge it from his mind and finally make things right. He shut down the laptop, tossed the broken pen into the garbage and locked up the office for the day.

CHAPTER TWENTY-EIGHT

"Hello, beautiful. Looking lovely as ever," Danny said, wrapping his arms around Linda's waist and kissing the back of her neck."

"My, you're in a good mood. Or are you buttering me up for something?"

"No, just glad you have the weekend off with me."

"You're probably just excited about going up to the cabin."

"Well, yeah, and you're still coming up, too, aren't you?"

"I sure am we can go up tonight after dinner if you want."

"We might as well. Let's eat."

"Somebody's a little anxious to get going," Linda said as she put the chicken and rice on the table.

"The sooner we're, there the sooner the weekend starts," Danny said, looking around the kitchen.

"What are you looking for? Are you missing something?"

"Is my nose playing tricks on me, or do I smell lasagne in here?"

"No, just chicken and rice. It's just your imagination," Linda said with a grin.

"You're shitting me, I can tell by the look on your face."

"Just eat your chicken! That's all there is."

"I know when you're lying to me. Where are you hiding it?"

"Maybe it's a surprise."

"I knew it, I could smell it a block away on my way home."

"It's for tomorrow night's dinner at the cabin, so don't get excited."

"Now I'm more excited than ever to go to the cabin."

"The lasagne is in the fridge; you can put that in the car, and I'll grab the bag from upstairs."

"The house next door sold – it looks like we'll have new neighbours soon," Danny said, noticing the "sold" sign as he backed out of the driveway. Ten minutes later, they were merging onto the highway, making their way up to the cabin.

"How was your day patrolling the lake? Anything exciting happening?"

"Not really. Did some water sampling and checked several boats out. Actually, everybody was behaving themselves today."

"That's nice to hear for a change."

"Yeah, good to see everyone complying for once. Towed one breakdown into shore; that was about it for the day."

"I'll bet they were glad to see you come by."

"Were they ever. It was getting pretty choppy out there; I don't think they would have made it in under paddle power," Danny said as he turned into the laneway.

"Wow, nice job on the driveway."

"I told you, smooth as a baby's bottom. Took me half a day of shovelling and raking."

"Here I was, all ready to give you a hard time about what you got done on your trips up here," Linda said, getting out of the car.

The sun sank below the horizon, and dusk settled quietly around them as Danny opened the cabin door. He creaked open the woodstove door, laying a log on a bridge of kindling, and touched a match to the splintered wood. Watching the wood struggle to light, he took a deep breath and blew life into the smouldering stack. With a poof, the flames jumped up from their slumber, hungrily licking up the sides of the log as Danny closed the stove door. Linda walked from room to room, ritualistically checking for any sign of a furry intruder, ready to shriek Danny's name at the first sign of confirmation of her worst fear. It was only after the reassurance of this preliminary patrol that she could relax for the weekend. Danny opened a bottle of merlot on the kitchen table and poured out two glasses.

"I bought you a little present," Danny said, handing Linda a tissue-stuffed giftbag.

"How sweet, a new ginger peach candle," she said, pulling it out of the bag.

"I kind of used the other one up on my overnight trips."

"There's still some left; we can use it in the living room," Linda said, taking the used candle and lighting it on the coffee table. Danny brought in the glasses of wine, and they nestled into the couch.

"A toast to my fabulous wife and a fantastic weekend" Danny said, clicking Linda's glass with the rim of his own. They sipped the wine as the fire crackled and danced behind the glass door of the woodstove. The scent and warm glow of the ginger peach candle enchanted the air as the fire warmed the room.

"Are you ready for another glass?" Danny said, taking Linda's empty wine glass.

"Ready when you are. That first one went down way too easy." Danny went into the kitchen to fill the glasses and brought them back, setting them on the coffee table. He sat back on the couch, putting his arm around Linda's shoulders. When he sat down, he had reached under the back of his shirt collar and taken out a small stuffed mouse he had stashed there that was now cupped in his hand. It was a realistic cat play-toy he had purchased, complete with fur and two beady little eyes. He set the mouse on top of the couch back to the left of Linda's shoulder as he put his arm around Linda. Linda snuggled a little closer to Danny as he looked over at her.

"Don't move," he said in a low, serious voice.

"What do you mean, don't move?" Linda said, following his gaze to her left. She screamed and lurched away from the mouse, falling over his lap and then jumping up on her feet.

"I got him," Danny said, holding out his fist, then opening his hand. Linda screamed again and jumped back. "It's fake," Danny said, starting to laugh.

"You son of a bitch, don't you ever do that to me again," Linda yelled, picking up a pillow and beating on him with it. Danny couldn't stop laughing as he picked up another pillow, using it as a shield. "Never ever again," Linda said, swinging the pillow at him with every word. Danny reached around her waist, pulling her down against him, and held her tight against his chest.

"That was a cruel joke to play on me, you're such an ass."

"I know, I'm sorry. I saw that mouse in the store, and I couldn't help myself," Danny said as he rubbed her back. "You don't hate me now, do you?"

"I don't hate you, but I'm still mad at you for doing that."

"Don't be mad. I promise I won't do anything like that again," Danny said, getting up and throwing the mouse into the fire. He sits back down beside Linda and hands her the glass of wine from the table. "New toast. To my fabulous wife who puts up with my warped sense of humour and to no more cruel jokes."

"I can take a joke, but you scared the shit out of me."

"I know, I'm sorry. I was going to put it in the bed and let you find it when you pulled the covers back."

"Good thing you didn't; you would have been sleeping in the other bedroom after that."

Danny drew Linda closer to him as they snuggled into each other. They finished their wine as the fire radiated its ambiance, mesmerising them into a sleepy comfort.

"We should go to bed now, or we'll never make it," Linda said, catching herself drifting off against Danny.

"Look at us flaking out like a couple of old fogies," Danny said, taking her hand and helping her off the couch. She went into the bedroom and cautiously pulled the covers back, checking to make sure there were no surprises waiting for her under the sheets.

"You're a lucky man, Mr. Rosen," she said as Danny came into the bedroom.

"I may be a prankster, but I'm no fool," he said, getting into bed.

Linda awoke the next morning after a sound night's sleep. Stretching her arm out, she felt the vacant pillow beside her. The aroma of bacon and eggs and coffee brewing lassoed her and drew her out of bed.

"My, this is a treat," she said, sitting down at the table.

"I thought, after last night, I had better make it up to you. I was going to bring you breakfast in bed."

"Oh, that's sweet, but I'm over it. This will be more than enough."

"For you, my dear," Danny says as he places the breakfast plate on the table in front of her.

"Thank you. I'll have to get mad at you more often for service like this."

"I'm sure it won't be long before I end up doing something else."

"You're doing just fine. You have nothing to worry about. I couldn't ask for a better husband than the one I've got."

"I thought we might go for a little hike after breakfast if you're up to it."

"Sure, that sounds great. I would have brought better shoes if I thought we were going on an adventure."

"Just a little walk in the woods – you'll be fine. We don't have to go that far."

Danny and Linda held hands as they walked along the narrow path leading into the forest from behind the cabin. Twigs snapped under their feet, and they were careful not to stumble over the gnarly roots that insisted on snaking their way at random across the gently beaten trail. Startled black squirrels launched themselves from branch to branch like furry overhead trapeze artists of the forest. Danny pointed out a grey owl warily watching them from its lofty perch, barely distinguishable from the tree bark behind its feathers. The trail dipped and twisted through the forest around ancient oaks, under the deep green canopy of the maples and past the ghostly grey polypore-covered stumps absorbed by the forest floor. They walked into a small clearing towards a solitary wild black cherry tree as the ferns delicately brushed by their legs.

"Remember this?" Danny said, pointing to a hand-sized heart carved into the smooth bark of the tree. The heart had the initials D and L carved across its center with a small plus sign between the letters.

"I sure do. I remember you doing that the first year we bought the cabin. You said it was a good tree to mark our eternal love into because they last for two hundred and fifty years. You were such a romantic."

"Still am," Danny said, pointing to a string tied to a small nail in the trunk of the tree.

"What's this?"

"Go ahead and unwind the string." Linda unwinds the string from the nail and lets it slowly run through her fingers as a small box lowers down from the branch above her. She unties the string from the box and opens the lid. Inside is a white-gold heart with two diamonds suspended in its center.

"It's beautiful, but it isn't even our anniversary."

"It is, of sorts; it's been ten years since we first started dating."

"You're too much. I was wondering why you were up so early this morning. I love it; thank you," Linda said, hugging Danny and giving him a kiss. "You are a romantic at heart picking out something that represents you and me together."

"The two diamonds reminded me of the day we knocked our heads together in the park," Danny said as he put the necklace on Linda.

"Don't tell me that," Linda said, spinning around and frowning her face.

"I'm just joking. I picked it out because it was symbolic of both of us in an eternal heart of love."

"That's much better; that's what I wanted to hear." They walked back along the trail to the cabin as Danny chuckled to himself. "You and your sense of humour; you're really something else."

"That's why you married me – you said you liked my sense of humour."

"Maybe I was just humouring you."

"Now you're the one being funny," Danny said as they walked out of the woods to the cabin.

Linda warmed the lasagne for dinner as Danny loaded firewood into the wood box. He used the last light of the day to chop a fresh load of kindling for the woodstove.

"The lasagne is ready when you are," Linda called out the door.

"You sure don't need to call me twice," Danny said, coming into the cabin with an armful of kindling. He opens a bottle of wine as Linda lifts two squares from the glass dish.

"What?" he says, noticing Linda's stare as he cuts into his meal.

"Sometimes I wonder if I'm in a competition between you loving the lasagne and that wood stove."

"Well, the lasagne warms me inside, the stove warms me outside, and you warm the rest of my life, my dear."

"Good answer; you should have been a politician."

"No thanks. I have all three things that I love here at the same time. I'm in heaven."

Danny tops off the wine glasses and sets them on the coffee table in the living room. He packs the stove with kindling and two logs and has a roaring fire blazing as he settles back into the couch. Linda finishes in the kitchen and sits down beside Danny, placing a box in his hand with a simple green ribbon curled around it.

"Happy ten-year dating anniversary."

"You didn't have to get anything for me! I just wanted to surprise *you* today; anniversary presents are meant for the ladies."

"It's no big deal, just something simple that I thought you'd like." Danny pulls the ribbon and opens the box. He takes out a folding pocketknife with an ebony handle and the initials DR engraved on the polished steel blade.

"This is fabulous. Thank you very much," he said, putting his arm around her and giving her a big kiss.

"I was hoping you'd like it. It's not fancy."

"Are you kidding me? This is fantastic! I just love it; I would have picked the same one myself," he said, turning it in his hands as he admired it. Danny gets the wine bottle from the kitchen and sits back down on the couch, topping off the glasses again.

"You're not trying to get me drunk, are you?"

"Another toast to my fabulous wife," Danny says, clinking her glass. "To the only woman I ever want to butt heads with."

"You're such an ass, but I love you anyway," Linda said, laughing and drinking her wine. They sipped away, talking, and laughing and watching the fire dance until the wine bottle was empty. Danny opened the stove door, rolling and poking the burning logs, then positioned a new log into the fire.

"Are you going to play with that fire, or are you coming to bed?" Linda said. As he knelt before the fire, he looked over his shoulder to see Linda standing in the bedroom doorway with a sheer black nightie on that left little to the imagination.

"Wow, you're barely wearing a shadow," Danny said, standing up and almost forgetting to close the woodstove door.

"Happy ten-year dating anniversary," Linda said, sliding her hand down the door frame and disappearing into the bedroom. Danny dropped the log poker into the tool stand and ventured into the bedroom where Linda was already sitting on the bed. Shedding his clothes on the floor, he slid under the covers beside her. Leaning over, she slowly kissed him, her tongue darting against his while her fingertips caressed his chest, tickled down his stomach and slipped under the covers to meet his swelling anticipation. Flipping down the sheets, she sits on his stomach, leaning towards him. Reaching up, a short tug on the top bow lace reveals the soft curve of her cleavage. He pulls the second bow loose exposing, the perk of her firming nipples. Drawing open the loop of the third bow parts the shadowy fabric, allowing the full splendour of Linda's womanhood to come into view. Danny cups his hands around Linda's curvaceous breasts as his heart pounds blood through his excited body.

"I love y...," Danny begins to say.

"Shhhhhh," Linda says, putting her finger against Danny's lips. She rises on her knees and gently shifts back. Danny feels the warmth of her body enveloping him. The moment is silent, intimate, full of anticipation. Neither one of them says a word; the room is as quiet as a spider's whisper. They begin a slow momentum, building faster and faster as Linda squeezes tighter around Danny's feverish thrusts. She is steadied by his firm grip on her breasts as her heart pendant swings wildly back and forth from her neck. Her nightie has fallen from her shoulders and drapes across her back as their bodies move together in a rhythm of ecstasy.

"Oh my God," Danny yells out, unable to hold back his release any longer. Linda also sounds out her elation as Danny pulls their heated bodies together in a final gasp of pleasure. They lay together as one, their hearts beating to catch up with their exhilaration. Danny caresses Linda's bare shoulder as she lays against his chest.

"I don't think you have to worry about any competition from the lasagne or the woodstove; I'd say you win, hands down."

"I'd say you did pretty well yourself; maybe it's the air up here," Linda said.

"See? You'll have to come up here with me more often. Just remember to bring your new pyjamas."

"I see, you just want to bring me up here to take advantage of me."

"I'm not so sure who was taking advantage of whom; neither one of us seemed to be complaining," Danny said, circling his fingers across her back. "I'm just happy you're here with me.... Linda?" He hears a soft snore and pulls her nightie up over her shoulders. She has fallen asleep for the night with her head on his chest.

Sunday morning shines into the bedroom, and Danny quietly rolls out of bed and tiptoes into the bathroom. He shaves in the mirror of the old medicine cabinet and then opens the shower door to turn on the hot water. Adjusting the temperature, he steps in and shampoos his hair. Rinsing the soap from his head, he is startled when the shower door opens.

"Is there room enough for two in here?" Linda says, stepping into the shower.

"I guess there is now," he says, moving over.

"I woke up and there was no one to cuddle with."

"I was trying to be quiet and let you sleep in; guess you've had enough sleep. You were out like a light last night."

"I slept great, didn't wake up all night. How about you?"

"I always sleep good up here. Can you wash my back since you're in here?" Linda lathers up Danny's back and puts the soap in the soap holder. She rubs the lather up his back, massaging it into his shoulders and the back of his neck. As she swirls the soap with her hands, he can feel her breasts pressing into his back. Her hands move down his back, around his hips and glide down to encourage his arousal.

"Hey – that's not my back," Danny says.

"It doesn't feel like you're too disappointed," Linda said, continuing to glide her soapy hand.

"What's gotten into you?" Danny said, turning around as the shower washes the soap down his back. Linda throws her hands around his neck and pulls herself up, wrapping her legs around his waist. Danny grasps her buttocks and lowers her down until he is fully inside her, and she kisses him passionately. He thrusts and rocks her wet body in the steam-filled air, surprised and excited at the same time, as he has never experienced this before. Backing her against the shower wall, they melded together as the climax shuddered through them. Linda slid down his body, kissed his chest and rinsed off, stepping out of the shower. The water was becoming tepid as Danny quickly finished washing up and getting out to towel himself dry. He was confused and quite surprised by the change in Linda's normally conservative behaviour and wasn't even quite sure that he was comfortable with it. He shrugged it off as just a spontaneous moment of passion inspired by their anniversary weekend getaway.

Linda brought Danny a coffee as he sat down at the kitchen table.

"You were a seductress and a fireball last night and again this morning in the shower; that really took me by surprise."

"Didn't the spontaneity of it make it extra exciting?" Linda said, putting her arm on his shoulder and pulling at his earlobe.

"I guess so; I mean, the sex was good, I'm just not used to seeing you being so aggressive."

"Well, hurry up and finish drinking your coffee. I've got plans for this kitchen table if you're up for it." Danny furrows his brow and looks up at Linda like she has lost her mind.

"My God, woman, what's gotten into you since yesterday?"

"You should see the look on your face," Linda said, bursting out laughing.

"Okay, we're even for that mouse thing I did; you really had me going there for a minute," Danny said with a sigh of relief.

"Maybe I was kidding, maybe I wasn't," Linda said, walking over to the sink with the empty mugs.

Danny scooped up the ashes, cleaning out the woodstove, and dumped the bucket in the firepit outside. They finished up the lasagne for lunch and packed up the car for the drive home.

"That was one glorious weekend," Danny said, turning onto the gravel road from the laneway.

"Thank you again for the beautiful pendant," Linda said as the sun coming in the car window sparkled the diamonds.

"Thank you for the great pocketknife; I'll think of you every time I use it."

"Maybe you should pull over to the side of the road and we can climb in the back seat," Linda said, rubbing the top of Danny's leg.

"Just stop it, you're starting to make me nervous."

"I'm just having some fun with you," Linda said, laughing at his boyish apprehension.

"I don't know what's gotten into you lately."

"Maybe I've been thinking about bringing a little Danny junior into the world." The words clanged through his head like a swinging church bell. Now her intentions made sense; now he understood her actions.

"I'm ready if you are. Maybe even a little Danielle junior will come along." Danny smiled at the possibility and was still smiling as he pulled up in front of the garage. Linda took their bag upstairs while he emptied the contents of the cooler into the fridge. Now that she had put the bug into his ear, he couldn't stop thinking about having an innocent, cute face smiling up at him, a little pair of hands eagerly pulling the contents from the cooler and helping him return them to the fridge. He imagined tiny footsteps racing across the floor and outstretched arms reaching out to embrace him as he scooped the overflow of love up to his chest and poured it into his heart.

Linda came halfway down the stairs, just far enough to be visible from the kitchen. Sunlight streamed through the landing window, highlighting the silky flow of her auburn hair as she slid her hand down the wall rail. The seductive shadow of the nightie veiled her body as the untied laces of the top bow dangled down freely.

"Are you almost finished in the kitchen?" Linda said.

Danny looked over to the staircase as Linda pulled the center bow loose and turned to go upstairs. He closed the fridge and walked towards the stairs, unbuttoning his shirt. He knew she wasn't kidding this time.

CHAPTER TWENTY-NINE

It was the last class of the day as Luker walked through the boys' changing room, checking the shower for stragglers. The remaining students scattered from the room quietly aware of the reputation that preceded him. Walking to the gymnasium, he opened the door to the vacant weight room and then closed it again with disappointment. It was well into the school term, and the boys who were at his mercy during class had learned not to avail themselves to him after school.

Stuffing some notes into his briefcase, he locked up his office and walked down the empty hallway to go home. He had routinely walked these hallways for more years than he could remember, and he was counting the years left before his retirement would bring this familiar passage to an end. As he left the teachers' parking lot, he thought of himself as being fortunate for having gotten away with the indiscretions that would have otherwise brought an early end to his career. He hadn't been so fortunate years ago when his wife had come home unexpectedly one day and had found him in an unforgivable situation with one of his male students. What she witnessed was reprehensible and drove a final ugly spike into an already troubled marriage. He now faced the consequences of having to come home every day to an empty house, but still, it didn't change him. He didn't give a second thought to the emotional carnage he left behind in the wake of satisfying the voracious appetite of his abusive perversion. In his mind, there were no victims here, only victories.

Setting his briefcase down in the hallway, he changed into his sweatpants and sweatshirt. The subtle aroma of the small pot roast drifted through the air and caused his stomach to growl its approval. He lifted the lid and stirred the carrots around in the slow cooker, an appliance he had learned to make good use of in the absence of having someone to cook for him. The steam billowed up from the frying pan as he poured water over the quick-fry beef flavoured rice. The water bubbled and spit as he turned down the heat and covered the pan for its twenty-minute duration. Luker sat at the kitchen table shuffling through his mail, tossing the bills aside in search of anything that would be more interesting than the daily barrage of flyers screaming out their last chance offers.

Sliding the pan of rice off the burner, he sliced up the pot roast and made himself a plate to take into the living room. There was absolutely nothing on at this time of day, so he put the six o'clock news on, which barely held his interest, but served its purpose; it was noise. Scraping a slight bit of fat into the garbage, he washed up the dishes and puts the leftovers into the fridge. It was quite a mess for one person to make, but he wouldn't have to cook tomorrow; it would just be a case of nuke and serve. Wiping off the stove, he looked at his watch, and it was almost time. Seven o'clock was his usual time to lace up his running shoes and go out for his nightly jog. Alternating between running and walking, it would take him one hour to jog the three blocks down the street, through the park and along the lakeshore and make his way up through the back streets to his house. He had perfected the route to be neither too long nor too short, and he liked the variation of scenery it offered him along the way. Within three blocks, he was off the busy city street and running through the tranquillity of the shaded park. The pathway along the lakeshore offered him the refreshing breezes off the water, and the final leg through the quiet backstreets allowed him to push himself as hard as the energy he had left would allow.

Luker walked up his driveway huffing and puffing with perspiration beading off his brow. Spinning the top off a water bottle, he tipped it back and had it drained before he had reached the bathroom doorway. He pulled off his clinging sweat clothes and circled in the shower, feeling the relief of the water spraying the sweaty heat from his pores. Drying off, he pulled on the fresh sweatpants he had placed on the counter and walked into the bedroom with the towel around his neck. Just as he pulled the towel up over his head to dry his hair, he felt a sharp poke spiking into him and an arm firmly around his neck. Trying to free the towel from his head, he stumbled forward, knocking the nightstand over, and then violently charged backwards, blindly crashing his assailant and himself into the dresser, breaking the mirror and sending the lamp smashing to the floor. Danny hung on tight, feeling the struggle peter out of Luker, and dropped him on the bed.

Luker groggily woke up laying on his stomach with his chin pushing into his mattress. As his head clears, he remembers struggling and tries to bolt up from the bed. His arms hang over the mattress, and the ropes around his wrists tie him soundly to the bed frame. He can feel the rope rubbing into his ankles, holding them tight to the mattress as it winds around the other side of the bed frame. Duct tape wraps around his legs above his knees, and he can't move — he is laid out like a lobster. Danny puts a chair beside the bed and sits down, leaning forward with his elbows on his knees and his fingers locked together.

"You certainly made quite a mess of your room, Mr. Luker. That would call for a detention, but I see you are all tied up at the moment."

"Fuck you. What do you think you're doing here?"

"I'm here to start you on a special program. You know what those are all about, don't you?"

"I'm not playing guessing games with you."

"You know what I'm talking about, or maybe you've been getting away with your sexual abuse for so long, you're oblivious to the damage you've done."

"I don't know who you are, but you've got nothing on me."

"Oh, I've got something on you, alright, you sick bastard; I had something on you years ago when you were molesting me and other students in your class. I was too intimidated to come forward, but you were counting on that, weren't you? You've been counting on that all your career. I've had to live with that decision hanging over my head."

"You had nothing."

"Nothing? You call Tom Becker taking his own life because of what you did to him nothing, you heartless bastard?" Danny said, pulling Luker's head up by his hair and kneeing him in the face. "It meant something to me." Danny pushed Luker's head back down as blood ran out of his nose and down the side of the bed.

"I know who you are now, Rosen. It's unfortunate that Tom took his life," Luker mumbled through swollen lips.

"You took his life from him, Luker; you're the one to blame. He put an end to his suffering; he couldn't see any other way out.

"Believe me, I never thought he would do something like that."

"And if you did, would you have stopped? Don't fucking kid me. You're a Goddamn predator. If it had of been me in that weight room, I swear to God I would have caved your head in with a fucking barbell."

"So, what now? I can't bring him back; you can't bring him back."

"No, I can't bring him back, but I can sure as hell bring some solace back into my life by righting a huge injustice. You see, Luker, I've been haunted and tormented almost all my life by monsters like you, both in the flesh and in my nightmares. There's been almost no relief until I've been able to slay these dragons one by one, purge them from my life and my nightmares. I've been getting tired of the running, the hunting, and the slaying, but I can see the end; I'm almost done now. My mind will finally be free, and I can sleep peacefully knowing that justice has been served, not only for me, but for all the other victims that have suffered through their lives. Tom's death will be avenged, but, more importantly, your reign of terror on vulnerable lives will end. It should have ended a long time ago."

"You're going to kill me?"

"I'm going to see that the punishment fits the crime; if it seems severe, it is only representative of the pain and suffering you've caused over the years," Danny said as he duck taped Luker's mouth. Danny goes out to the garage and returns to the bedroom a few minutes later.

"Let me up," Luker tries to scream in panic through the duct tape.

"This is a little system I use that works quite well. I plug the timer into the wall, and it gives the person such as yourself time to think about why you made me kill you. It gives you time to experience the same terror you inflicted on your victims. It gives me time to remove myself from the unpleasant ending. I take no pleasure in witnessing the punishment, I have already experienced and seen enough suffering. I plug the extension cord into the timer and the other end into my device of choice that suits the punishment. In your case, it's your electric drill. I've attached a one-inch spade bit to the drill, and I think you know where that's going."

Luker struggles against the ropes around his wrists as his muffled screams deaden against the duct tape. Danny takes the pocketknife from his jeans and cuts a slit in the back of Luker's sweatpants. Setting the knife beside him on the bed, he tapes the drill trigger in the *on* position and slowly wiggles the spade bit through the slit pants. A high-pitched wail reverberated up Luker's throat as the cold steel travelled up his rectum. Danny sets the handle of the drill tightly between Luker's legs and then crawls backwards off the bed.

"You have about fifteen minutes before the timer activates the drill. Think about Tom and all the other young boys you violated before and since. Think about how they were screaming, even if you couldn't hear them. Think about all the ones who will be screaming themselves awake in the dead of the night from their nightmares for the rest of their lives. I'll be one of the lucky ones now. You'll be one less monster chasing me in the night, one less ghost from the past haunting my memory," Danny said as he left the room.

CHAPTER THIRTY

Kent looks at her watch and sits down in the chair at the front of Casey's desk. She opens the case file on Brooks and bites away at the inside of her lip as she relives the details of the case. She skips past the graphic photographs, as the images from the murder scene are still fresh in her mind, clicking through her memory like a horrendous slideshow.

"Sorry I'm late; the coffee shop was jammed," Casey said as he pulled her cup from the cardboard tray.

"Thank you," she said, taking the coffee. "It's okay; I've only been here a few minutes." Kent parts the brown paper bag and has a look inside. "Chocolate glazed, chocolate-dipped and chocolate fudge; I see your sweet tooth is in full working order this morning."

"I ate the double chocolate on the way over."

"Why am I not surprised."

"I almost forgot I got you a blueberry muffin," Casey said, pulling another bag out of his coat pocket.

"How thoughtful; thank you again."

"Don't mention it. Anything new turn up in the Brooks investigation that I don't know about?"

"You know all the details of the autopsy; the same drug was in his system as in the other victims, and of course he bled to death – we saw that for ourselves."

"It's his past I was hoping would shed some light on the case. I found out he had a stepdaughter: Gloria. I tracked her down and found out she has been estranged from him since she was in high school. When I informed her of Brook's tragic death, she said he was already dead to her – no love lost there. I tried to question her on her relationship with him, but she simply said she had put that part of her life behind her. I asked her if anyone would have reason to kill her stepfather, and she just shook her head and closed the door."

"She would be about the same age as our killer," Kent said.

"I think she is hiding something, holding something back."

"If her relationship was bad with her stepfather, she has closed that chapter of her life. If she does know something, she is reluctant to talk about it, afraid it will open old wounds. She is probably more concerned about protecting herself than protecting any suspects."

"She may know our killer and not even realize it," Casey said in frustration.

"I located his ex-wife," Kent said. "Pretty much the same reaction, but not as dramatic. She has remarried and just said the past was in the past and was reluctant to discuss anything about Brooks. Maybe she was protecting her daughter."

"Well, it looks like Brooks had a toxic relationship with his family in the past, and it seems like some of that past has spilled over onto our killer."

"Maybe if I tried to talk to Gloria woman-to-woman, I could get a little further with her."

"Excuse me while I take this call," Casey said. Almost finished her muffin, Kent felt her stomach roll and suddenly lost her appetite. Thoughts of another gruesome murder scene loomed in her mind and were confirmed by the expression on Casey's face. She watched as his eyebrows flinched up and down and his fingers tapped on the desk as if sending out a Morse code message of nervous energy. Until he put that phone down, the optimist in her was holding out for a slight glimmer of hope that her fears were unfounded. Her woman's intuition told her she was going on a car ride and to save her optimism for another day.

"God damn, I can't believe it he's done it again," Casey said, pounding his fist on the desk.

"I'm going to assume that call wasn't good news."

"Bloody well right, it wasn't. Fourteen — fourteen murders this guy has pulled, and we haven't been able to catch up with him yet. This is bad; this is really making us look bad. We look like we are sitting around with our thumbs up our asses while this guy runs around the city like the exterminator."

"We're close, Casey; we're really close this time. I'll go talk to Gloria. I'm sure I can get some leads out of her."

"We got nothing concrete; unless she talks, we don't have shit."

"We're close to solving these cases, I can feel it. Something has to break soon."

"I hope you're right; we better get going. If the last murder scene bothered you, you're not going to like this one much better just a heads-up."

"The last one was bad, but they've all bothered me, and I know they are getting to you as well – we're only human."

"Let's just keep our wits about us and we'll be fine; sorry I got a little worked up."

"Where are we headed – into the killer's old neighbourhood again?"

"No, not even close, but it's another teacher again, a high school gymnastics teacher this time, by the name of John Luker."

"Murdered in his home?"

"Yes. Last night, they just found him; forensics isn't even there yet."

"Who found him? Talk to me, Casey, I feel like I'm conducting an interrogation here."

"Sorry, this has got me a bit rattled. Luker was a jogger. Apparently, he went out every evening after dinner, and, last night, the killer was waiting for him when he got back. He had a jogging buddy who ran with him every morning and who found him and called 911."

"A Wednesday-night murder; that's a change of pattern for our weekend killer."

"Yes, most of the murders have happened around weekend events – believe me, I've kept track of that. In Luker's case, the opportunity was there every night for the killer to lie in wait for him while he was gone. He chose the opportunity when it suited him."

"Doesn't seem like there would be any connection between Adams and Luker. They taught at different grade levels, years apart, at different schools, so I would say right off the bat that these are two isolated cases," Kent said.

"Luker was also still teaching; looks like I might have to go back to school to get some answers," Casey said, pulling into Luker's driveway.

"You still haven't told me how he was murdered."

"Let's just say our killer must have had a real big problem with Brooks and Luker. Best prepare yourself; it isn't going to be pretty," Casey said, getting out of the car. Kent braced herself for a grisly scene, going into the house. She knew if Casey was shaken by what he had learned, it would be an unsettling sight for her to witness. She could feel the thump of her heart against her Kevlar vest as Casey conferred briefly with the responding officers he had spoken to on the phone. She sallies her courage and walks down the hallway with Casey behind her to Luker's bedroom.

"Oh my God," Kent said, seeing the drill lodged in Luker's blood-soaked sweatpants. "I can't believe what I'm seeing."

"It's like a déjà vu moment with the timer and the blood-soaked bed, but with a drill this time; I'm sorry you had to see something like this again."

"I'll be alright, Casey. After seeing Brooks, I'm not surprised at what we are going to find anymore."

"The killer has gotten his message through loud and clear to Brooks and Luker. He's avenging his own abuse or someone else's from the past to resort to this type of horrific punishment."

"Like he did to Brooks with the saw, he left Luker alive waiting for that drill to go off. I can't even imagine the terror he must have felt," Kent said. Casey pictures the spinning drill tearing and twisting through his bowels and shudders.

"Hopefully, it was quick, and he went into shock. It wouldn't have taken long before he bled to death." Casey walks around the bed and doesn't mention to Kent the sight of the pool of blood Luker had vomited down the side of the bed through his nose.

"Assuming our killer was one of Luker's students that he sexually assaulted, that was decades ago, and obviously it wasn't reported, or if it were, it was covered up; otherwise, Luker wouldn't still have been teaching there. I think going to the school and trying to dig up clues after all these years will just be a waste of your time. It will wind up being another dead end. I've got to get Brook's stepdaughter to open up. It's our only chance for a potential lead."

"I suppose you're right. The way it's been going, our killer soon will be running out of rope or out of victims, so we have to do something."

"It has to stop. We have to make it stop. I don't want to have to come into another horrendous murder scene like this again."

"Something's gone awry this time," Casey said, looking around the room at the smashed lamp, broken mirror, and overturned side table. "There's been a struggle here; things didn't go quite as smoothly for our killer this time. It looks like Luker tried to put up a bit of a fight."

"He was in better shape than the other victims; the sedative must have taken longer to knock him out," Kent said.

Casey moves closer to the side of the bed to take a close-up picture of the drill positioned between Luker's legs. As he steps forward, he can feel a hard object under the tip of his shoe. He takes the picture and then bends down to look under the bed. There lying on the carpet was the impossible, so impossible that he stared at it for a moment, convincing himself it was real. Reaching into his pocket, he pulled out his white handkerchief and delicately picked the object up.

"Look at this," Casey said, tilting the engraved pocketknife in the tremble of his fingers.

"I don't believe what I'm seeing for the second time today. I knew we had to get a break eventually," Kent said excitedly as the forensics officers entered the bedroom.

"Handle this like your life depends on it," Casey said, placing the knife in the evidence bag. "If we are lucky enough to get a fingerprint match, I'm going to frame it to hang on the wall in my office."

"I'm pinching myself to make sure I'm not dreaming at the sudden turn of events," Kent said, giddy with excitement. The optimist in her was hoping the newfound evidence would bring this rollercoaster of an investigation to its conclusion. Her intuition was in total agreement this time around.

CHAPTER THIRTY-ONE

Danny opened the trunk of his car and placed in the bags containing the items he had so efficiently used — the heating element, a timer and extension cord, rope, duct tape, syringes. Closing the trunk, he watched as his new next-door neighbour brought her garbage bag to the curb.

"Hello, Danny Rosen; don't know if you've met my wife, Linda, yet, welcome," he said, extending his hand.

"No, I haven't had the pleasure; thank you. I'm Barbara Kent," she said, shaking Danny's hand.

"Saw a police car a few times in your driveway; figured either you were on the force, or my new neighbour was in trouble already."

"No, that was me," Kent said, laughing. "Been on the force for fifteen years now."

"I feel a bit safer now in these crazy times having an officer live next door."

"I don't know how much safer you'll be; some days, it's hard to keep up with it all."

"I know what you mean. I'm with the conservation authority, and some days enforcement is a bitch," Danny said, checking his watch.

"I look forward to meeting your wife," Kent said.

"Yes. I'm sure she's anxious to meet you; it's been a pleasure," Danny said, getting into his car.

*   *   *   *   *   *   *

Vince made a point of doing his grocery shopping on Fridays right after supper before the weekend shoppers crowded in and everything got picked over. The shoppers stopping in on their way home after work were long gone as Vince blocked the aisle beside a cardboard display with his cart. A lady with a small child waited patiently to pass through as he searched for his items on the shelf.

"Go around," Vince snapped at her as she backed her cart up and spun it around in the aisle.

The physical bullying days of his youth were behind him now; the one charge of assault on his record had been enough to deter him in his later years. He had to be happy with verbally intimidating people now.

"Have a nice evening, sir," the cashier cheerfully said.

Vince just ignored her as he pushed his cart through the checkout lane and loaded his car to head home. Looping the bag handles on both hands, he plodded up the two flights of stairs, determined to carry everything up to his unit in one trip. Setting the bags on the floor, he turned the key in the apartment door and then bent over to gather them up. A sudden pain was sharp and straightened him up; then, he felt the weight of the bags drawing his arms down to the hallway floor, his body instantly following. Danny dragged Vince's limp body into the apartment and closed the door.

Vince blinked his eyes into focus as he laid on his couch. He remembered last standing in the hallway and swung his feet to the floor, sitting up on the couch and looking around the room, confused. He noticed ballpoint ink on his hands and looked down at his palms. Printed on the left palm were the words "Our youth was a living hell." The right palm read "Payback is a bitch."

"What the fuck," Vince said, jumping to his feet. He reached into his pocket for his knife, but it wasn't there. Picking up a carving knife, he slowly enters his bedroom, finding it empty. Opening the apartment door, he looks up and down the hallway and then turns to see his grocery bags on the kitchen counter. Vince scrubbed his hands, watching the white soap turn blue as it rinsed down the drain.

"I made lots of kids' lives a living hell, who gives a shit," Vince said as he rubbed the words from his hands.

After washing his hands, he checks the apartment one more time for an intruder and his other pants for his pocketknife. He finds himself at a loss to make sense of what just happened.

* * * * * * *

Danny hangs his coat up in the closet while humming a tune to himself.

"You seem to be in a good mood today," Linda said, giving him a hug.

"I am I think I've gotten a lot of things off my mind lately, and it's made a big difference in my daily mood."

"Well, that's good. You seem to be pretty chipper since our little conversation on the way back from the cabin."

"Yeah, that has a lot to do with it too."

"I met our police lady neighbour this morning; she seems very nice."

"Yes, she is. I met her last week, actually. She seems to be a very busy lady."

"She's a sergeant and is working with a detective as a lead investigator on these red rope murder investigations."

"She appears to be very capable. I'm sure they will be able to solve them soon," Danny said, unrolling a sheet on the table.

"What do you have there?" Linda said, sliding her hands to his chest from his shoulders.

"Some plans for a jungle gym I was thinking of building in the backyard."

"Wow – you are pretty excited about our little conversation. Talk about putting the pressure on me."

"No pressure; nothing wrong with planning ahead."

"You're planning way ahead. You'll have little him or her mountain climbing before they can walk."

"Well, yeah; that's a given."

"It's nice see you looking so forward to being a father," Linda said, kissing his cheek.

Danny was looking forward to being a dad. He was going to make sure his little one would never experience the childhood traumas that he had had to endure growing up. He would do his darndest to keep the monsters out of his children's life. He never wanted to hear them screaming in the middle of the night because of real-life monsters that came after them in the day. He never wanted to see them become dragon slayers to clear the torments from their minds like he had been forced to do, but he was done now. The last monster had been purged from his nightmares. The last dragon had finally been slayed; justice had been served. After everything he had done, Vince was indeed going to be sorry for the rest of his life.

* * * * * * *

Vince pushed his grocery cart up the aisle, looking at the crumpled shopping list in his hand. Taking a box of crackers, he knocked two other boxes to the floor and thought *not my problem* as he walked away. Further down the aisle, an elderly woman asked if he could reach something off a higher shelf.

"Do I look like I work here?" he said to her, continuing down the aisle.

As he placed a carton of eggs in his cart, he didn't know who sergeant Kent was or that she was excitedly telling inspector Casey they had gotten the lucky break they had been patiently waiting for. Pushing his cart towards the checkout lane, he wasn't aware that the fingerprints on the knife found earlier in the week at a murder scene were a positive match to ones in the database. Putting his grocery bags on the seat of his car, he couldn't know Casey and Kent were on the way to his apartment building. Pulling into his underground parking spot, he didn't notice the two unmarked cruisers sitting in the parking lot. Vince unlocked the door to his apartment, watching his back this time, wary of his unsettling experience from the previous Friday. Entering his apartment, he dropped his grocery bags on the floor as he faced two guns and two badges pointed at him. As he looked over his shoulder, two more officers grabbed each of his arms and put him in handcuffs.

"Vince Lowe, you are under arrest for first degree murder," Casey said.

"What are you talking about? I never killed anyone." Vince watches as Kent walks over to the pulled-out drawers of his desk and puts a dried, blood-spattered pink carnation and a partial sheet of frog stickers into evidence bags.

"That's not my stuff! I don't know where that came from."

"We found rope, duct tape, syringes, all kinds of evidence under the spare tire cover in his trunk," Kent said to Casey.

"Someone was here last week and planted all that stuff; I've been framed."

"We found your knife at a murder scene with your initials and fingerprints all over it."

"Someone set me up, I didn't kill anyone."

"Tell your story to the judge; I'm sure he'll understand. Show him your rap sheet – I'm sure he'll be impressed with that as well," Casey said as they took Vince out of the apartment.

Kent comes into Casey's office and sets the two coffees down on the desk.

"You look extra happy this morning," Casey said.

"I don't think I've stopped smiling all week," Kent said, putting the cardboard container in front of Casey.

"What is this?" Casey said, opening the container. "Two chocolate éclairs. Are you sure you're feeling, okay?"

"Just this one time; I thought it called for a celebration."

"I couldn't agree with you more. What a relief to finally close this difficult investigation. I was beginning to have my doubts."

"Vince Lowe is going away for a very long time. Everything has fallen into place. Besides having a ton of evidence in his possession, he lived in the neighbourhood growing up and had Adams and Luker for teachers."

"He's been in trouble since he was a teenager; I doubt he will even get parole in twenty years."

"He is still claiming innocence," Kent said.

"I think I would be as well if I were on the hook for fourteen murders."

"I just wanted to say thanks for your support, Casey; there were some pretty tough days there to get through."

"No, thank you for sticking by me. I never doubted your resolve for one second."

"I'm glad the killer has been apprehended, but I'm going to miss our morning meetings."

"My door is always open; don't be a stranger."

"Let's eat these damn things before I change my mind," Kent said.

* * * * * * *

Danny got more than he bargained for, and he couldn't be hap-pier. He scooped up two armfuls of love and poured it all into his heart at once. When he unloaded the cooler after a trip back from the cabin, he had two pair of hands eagerly helping him return items to the fridge. The twins often kept him and Linda running in two directions at once, and the frequent visits from Aunt Connie to help out when they were babies were always more than welcome. Danny was already working on plans to add a bedroom onto the cabin.

"We can make do with adding bunkbeds in the bedroom for now," Linda said.

"They won't be wanting to share a room forever, you know."

"They are only four years old, for crying out loud."

"It doesn't hurt to plan ahead," Danny said. "Besides, we could use the extra room for company. What about when Connie wants to come up?"

"You're right. Maybe you should be considering a fourth bedroom."

"You know…" Danny said, tapping his pencil on the table.

"I was just joking," Linda said.

"It's actually not a bad idea; it wouldn't be that much more work. Think about it: the kids will want to have their friends up when they get older. Connie will have another boyfriend, maybe get married and have kids to bring along."

"Well, what was I thinking? We should be considering three extra bedrooms."

"Now you're being facetious," Danny said.

"I am. I will keep my eye open for bunkbeds, and you can work on your plans for an addition."

"I've got it," Danny said. "I'll convert the storage building into a guest cabin for sleeping. It's perfect, already insulated; all I have to do is put a window in and some flooring."

"You love that storage space."

"I won't miss it now. I can build a smaller shed for the tools and the wood."

"I like that idea better, then, and there's no rush to do it until we need it."

"Perfect. I'll take the kids out to play in their jungle gym while I cut the lawn and give you a break."

Danny junior and Danielle climbed on their jungle gym as Danny cut the grass. Barbara Kent sat on her back deck watching them as they played and marvelled at how much they had grown. The twins spotted her from the lookout deck and happily waved as she smiled and waved back at them. There was something familiar about the red-flecked rope hanging down that was tied to the seats of the swing set. She pondered the thought for a moment and then discarded it into the abyss of images she had managed to unstick from her mind. She preferred to enjoy the memories she had made getting to know the happy Rosen family that lived next door.

* * *

AcuteByDesign, Publisher

Printed in the United States of America

AcuteByDesign
the little book company that could
A Michael Marion Sharpe Company

Michele Thomas
Executive Publisher

Printed in Great Britain
by Amazon